Taken Away

Patricia Yager Delagrange

TAKEN AWAY Copyright © Patricia Yager Delagrange 2015

Cover Copyright © 2015 Griffith Designs

Layout by www.formatting4U.com

Names, characters and incidents depicted in this book are products of the author's imagination, or are used fictitiously. Any resemblance to actual events, locales, organizations, or persons, living or dead, is entirely coincidental and beyond the intent of the author or the publisher.

All rights reserved. No part of this book may be reproduced or transmitted in any form or by any means whatsoever, including photocopying, recording or by any information storage and retrieval system, without written permission from the publisher and/or author.
Printed in the U.S.A.

ALAMEDA, CALIFORNIA

Digital ISBN: 9781954395039
Print ISBN: 9781954395022

To all the animals who I have shared my life with as well as those who are still alive. To Jackson Montgomery, Mocha, Java, and Annabella Rosa who have already gone over the Rainbow Bridge and to Annabella's son Jack, as well as UJE and Remy who sit with me while I write. And to my huge black Friesian horse, Maximus, who takes me on long walks through the forest where I get most of the ideas for my books.

CHAPTER ONE

"Hey, Bradford, aren't you goin' to class today? It's too early in the semester to go skippin' out, bro."

My friend Brian was a joker and never left well enough alone. Every word out of his mouth blared loud enough for anyone walking through the quad in the middle of campus to hear.

I stopped dead in my Jordans and took a deep breath. My head was killing me, and Brian knew how to push my buttons. Why did he always act like my freaking mother?

"I'm cutting class today, Brian. Is that okay with you?"

"Another all-nighter, Bradford?" He cackled like the Wicked Witch of the West, and my head throbbed.

"Could you just take notes for me, and I'll get 'em later?" I hated English Lit, and Brian had taken notes for me before. I figured it was no big deal this time, either.

"Dude! No can do. I've gotta leave class early to see my advisor about changing my schedule around for soccer practice. You'll have to take your own notes." He paused, grabbed my shoulder. "You okay, bro? Your face is all red. Better get outta the sun."

Curling my lip in a sneer, I shrugged off his hand, did a one-eighty, and headed for class. Guess it wouldn't kill me to spend the next fifty minutes trying not to fall asleep at the back of the classroom.

The lecture hall, a huge domed room that held up to four hundred students, had a stage at the front and a podium equipped with a microphone, so those of us in the nose-bleed section could still hear the professor. It was my favorite spot-less chance I'd be called on to answer any question the teacher might have about the book I was supposed to be reading.

I'd just slumped down in my seat when someone whispered near my right shoulder. "Do you have a pen or pencil I can borrow?"

I turned and gazed straight into the biggest, bluest eyes I'd ever seen outside of those television commercials for dry-eye problems. Long, blonde hair draped over several books perched on her lap. Sun-bleached bangs hovered above eyebrows a shade darker than her hair. Her mouth curved into a smile and I held my breath, captivated by the gleam of her straight teeth.

She leaned closer. "I said, do you have an extra—"

"Yeah, sure." I grabbed one of the pens I kept tucked in my shirt pocket and handed it to her.

"Thanks. I don't know what happens to all the pens I buy every semester. They disappear into the netherworld or something." She smiled again. "I'll return it to you at the end of class."

My heart hip-hopped, flipped, and dive-bombed into my stomach. She resembled the winning model I'd just seen on the front of that month's Sports Illustrated magazine, captioned "The Top Ten Beach Beauties of California".

"I'm Jessee Bradford. Nice to meet you." Lame intro, but at least she'd know my name. My mouth clamped shut, and my throat felt sort of scratchy. I swear, it was as if I'd forgotten how to speak English.

"I'm Serena. I usually sit down in front, but I was so running late. I got totally stuck at the beach, painting the waves."

A long, transparent purple skirt flowed over her knees where it met with tanned bare feet. She wore a toe ring, something I hadn't seen since high school. It suited her somehow. Kinda went with the rest of her outfit, which wasn't much. A sleeveless ribbed top exposed full breasts, dark perky nipples protruding beneath the thin cotton. I detected the faint scent of lavender and instinctively inhaled deeply. Intoxicating.

The professor began his lecture so I kept my mouth shut. He had a habit of calling on students who, in his words, thought of the classroom as a "social interactive venue".

Serena took notes, scribbling away furiously. She looked up every few minutes, brows furrowed in intense concentration.

Me? I couldn't think straight, couldn't get her face out of my head. That smile. The way her expression changed when she said she'd been at the beach, painting the waves. She struck me as a free spirit, carefree, sort of a hippie.

The next forty-five minutes I spent staring at the professor like a zombie, trying my best to appear engrossed in whatever he was saying. But I nodded off every few minutes. Each time my head drooped toward my chest I'd pop back up to soldier-straight position and take a quick peek at Serena, just to make sure she hadn't been an illusion.

My eyes fluttered open again when my notebook shifted. A hand splayed across the empty page.

"Hell-lo?" Serena dipped her head in front of my face. "Class is over. Not that you'd notice."

I glanced around the room. Students clogged the exit doors. A hot blush crept up my neck and face. Great. I just made a super impression on this girl with my engaging conversation, coupled with my avid interest in our English Lit class.

"Sorry. I must have been thinking about something else," I mumbled and headed toward the nearest exit. I felt a tug on the back of my shirt. Turning around, I came face-to-face with Serena's enormous blue eyes.

A pen dangled from her fingertips in front of my chest. "Do you want to come to the beach with me? It's another gorgeous Santa Barbara day."

I took the pen from her slender fingers. I didn't need to think twice about my answer. "Sure. I'm through for the day anyway."

That was a bald-faced lie. Equine Physiology class started in ten minutes, but Brian took excellent notes. I didn't need to worry.

We meandered across campus. She walked on the grass, feet mincing through the greenery like a wood nymph from a child's storybook about fairies and princesses.

"So, Jessee Bradford, what do you do for fun?" She flitted around me like a dragonfly, her skirt billowing in the mild breeze.

I reached out and grasped her hand. "I loan pens to female students who don't come prepared for class."

She didn't let go of my hand, and my heart thrummed.

My cheeks burned and I dipped my head.

"You get embarrassed too easily, Jessee Bradford. But it just makes you more handsome. Are you shy?"

Her smile showed teeth so white they sparkled. I felt beyond embarrassed, but at the same time, I was mesmerized. My tongue morphed into a piece of sandpaper, scraping the insides of my mouth. I swallowed and looked up at the cirrus clouds edging toward the dormitory buildings on this side of campus, giving myself a few seconds to cool down.

"I do volunteer work in my spare time. Don't have much opportunity for fun. I'm majoring in Veterinary Medicine."

The breeze blew one long piece of perfectly straight blonde hair across her face. I reached out and tucked it behind her ear.

She slowed to a standstill and my fingers slipped through the end of the strand then rested on the curve of her waist.

"Volunteer work?" She laid her forearm on top of mine and squinted up at me, shadowing her eyes with her other hand.

"At the Santa Barbara Animal Shelter. They host a free spay and neuter clinic every other weekend."

She twisted away and ran toward Skye beach. I followed her to the bottom of the cliff's stairs and stopped to watch her skip to the edge of the water where the seaweed floated in and out with the swiftly encroaching tide. Skidding to a halt, she slipped when a wave splashed the bottom half of her skirt, and she reached out to grab my hand.

I took hold of her outstretched fingers and pulled her toward me to break her fall. She turned in my direction. Her full breasts grazed my cotton shirt, and she looked up and smiled.

I don't know what I was thinking, but I lowered my mouth to hers in an extra slow, searching kiss. My God, I wanted this to last forever.

The way she pressed her body closer to mine indicated I hadn't offended her, and I savored every second of our lingering kiss. Once again, I detected the faint scent of lavender and my head reeled.

When I kiss a girl I keep my eyes open. Serena pulled back, her eyes remained closed for several seconds, and I hoped that meant she enjoyed it.

"What about you, Serena? What do you do when you're not painting the waves at the beach?"

She leaned into a backbend in my arms, her hands stretched far out above her head like a ballerina, as if reaching to the ground. My hands tightened around her waist so she wouldn't fall.

After bringing her body upright, she grinned and placed a finger on my lips, rubbing it slowly from side to side, her mouth set in a serious line.

"I'm an art major but I knew how to paint before I came here." Her bottom lip stuck out in a pout.

"Then why'd you enroll at U.C.?"

She continued to trace my lips with her finger, and I found it hard to concentrate. I just wanted to kiss her again.

"My father said he wouldn't-" she made air quotes with her fingers "-gift me my inheritance early, if I didn't get my degree. This is my last year."

"So when June rolls around you'll receive enough money to live independent of your parents?"

She dropped her finger from my lips and turned her head toward the waves. A crisp, light breeze blew off the water and her nipples stood erect under her stretchy top.

"Daddy said he'd give me the majority of my inheritance now instead of waiting until, you know, he dies. Yeah, that was the deal."

All of a sudden her body language changed drastically.

She turned and faced the ocean, her folded arms tucked under her breasts, brows furrowed, mouth set in a straight line. Gone was the happy-go-lucky expression I'd seen since we left class together.

I moved to her side, put my arm around her shoulders and gave her a squeeze. "Let's get outta here."

She glanced up at me, eyes glassy. Her lips quirked up in a half-smile. "Okay." Stretching up on her toes, she gave me a quick kiss on the cheek. "Where are you taking me?"

I turned my wrist to check my watch. "It's almost eleven o'clock." I lifted my eyebrows. "Do you like pizza?"

She grabbed my hand and ran toward the stairs leading up from the beach, laughing, dragging me behind her. Her mood was infectious. We raced to the top of the stairs where I playfully tackled her from behind. We fell on the grass, out of breath from scrambling up forty feet of steps.

Her breasts moved up and down as she lay on her back, staring at the sky, her breathing labored. "Vegetarian," she managed to puff out. "Hold... the... pineapple and anchovies."

I leaned over her, blocking out the sunlight, and our eyes met in a concentrated stare. "You're beautiful, Serena."

She raked her hand through my hair and pulled my face closer to hers. Her lips were warm and soft, her tongue hot and moist. My left thigh inched its way over, until I lay on top of her. The sound of her sigh was all I needed to push me over the edge.

She managed several words between kisses. "We should go."

I slid off her and slumped onto my back on the grass. "Wow."

"You're going to fall in love with me, Jessee Bradford."

My head spun. Had she just said what I think she said? I sat up and looked over at her. "Why's that?"

Her hair splayed out over the grass like a Japanese fan, tiny daisies peeking through the blonde strands. Every inch of her perfectly oval face was tanned and a light sprinkling of freckles spread across the apples of her cheeks and nose.

"Because you can't help yourself, Jessee Bradford."

I had trouble remembering what I'd asked her and shook my head. Had she said I was going to fall in love with her?

"You know we almost look like twins." She touched the side of my jaw with her fingers and smiled. "Both of us blond and blue-eyed. But I'm missing the dimple on the right side of my mouth. And the cleft in my chin."

I stood up and stretched out my hand. She grabbed it and pulled herself up.

"Let's go, Serena...?"

"Middleton."

My mouth fell half-open and I peered at her. "As in Middleton Veterinary Hospital?"

"The same." She walked toward the center of campus, her sheet of hair swaying side to side.

As soon as her words coalesced in my brain, I ran to catch up with her. "Your father's the philanthropist? That David Middleton?"

"The third," she answered, her tone haughty yet playful.

"And you still want to eat pizza with me?"

She whipped around so fast I almost smacked into her. "I don't give a crap what my parents think about the men I go out with," she cried, eyes flashing.

I stepped back, stretched my arms in front of me, palms facing outward. "Whoa. I was just teasing. I didn't mean anything by it."

She closed her eyes, angled her head downward, and sighed.

"Sorry. I didn't mean to yell at you." She grinned as if she was hiding something. "I already told you. You're going to fall in love with me, Mr. Bradford. Now let's go to Bertolucci's. I'm starved."

O-kay. She overreacted about being a Middleton and going out with someone like me. Perhaps she was one of those roller coaster types; up and down with their emotions. I had no clue. I didn't know her.

Yet.

We walked the rest of the way in silence. She grabbed my hand and swung it back and forth, skipping past the Student Union building and dormitories. I jogged beside her on our way to the parking lot.

She appeared to have gotten past her anger or whatever it was. And if she wasn't pulling my leg, this meal would be very enlightening.

My future girlfriend was the heir to a family fortune.

CHAPTER TWO

Two and A Half Years Later

"Dr. Bradford, you have a call on line one."

I'd turned the Nextel phone hooked to my belt on low and asked the front desk receptionist not to put through any calls unless it was an emergency. I didn't want to be interrupted when I was with a patient—in this case a pregnant Golden Retriever whose temperature had shot above one hundred and five degrees.

After scanning the radiograph, it looked as if she had a dead fetus in her uterus, and it was poisoning her. She needed surgery to extract it along with what appeared to be five additional premature pups, or she'd die from septicemia. My two assistants used a blanket sling to carry the lifeless-looking dog to the O.R. for emergency surgery.

I reached around and pressed the button for line one, irritated at the interruption. "Jessee Bradford."

"Jess, it's me."

I'd worked for Middleton Veterinary Hospital since graduation from the university. For the last two years Serena had never phoned me when I was at work. I knew right away it must be important.

"Hey, babe, what's wrong?"

Several beats of silence ensued. "Could you come home?"

I stood up and the stool rolled away, slamming against the side of the examination table. "Now?"

"Yes," she whispered. "I need to talk to you. Now." It sounded as if she had a cold, and I knew she must have been crying.

"I'm on my way to surgery. A pregnant Golden Retriever who'll die if I don't get into the operating room in the next few minutes."

The sound of a dial tone roared in my ear, telling me exactly what Serena thought of my answer. But I had an ethical responsibility to provide essential services for animals when necessary, to save their lives and relieve suffering. I was determined to operate on this dog. Throwing aside my stethoscope and white jacket, I rushed into the room adjacent to the O.R., scrubbed thoroughly, then grabbed the nearest gown and surgical mask.

Dr. Anazzio was already prepping the dog for surgery. She swabbed the dog's belly with Betadine while I pulled on a pair of surgical gloves.

"Thanks, Francesca." I stared down at the dog's distended belly, then turned to the surgical nurse, who suddenly and efficiently appeared at my side. "Do me a favor, would you, Maryanne?"

"Anything for you, Dr. Bradford," she answered with a twinkle in her eyes.

I could almost see her smile hidden behind her mask, and I grinned beneath mine.

The surgical team at Middleton Veterinary Hospital was the best I'd ever worked with. I spent the majority of my surgical rotation right here. The other hospitals I worked for couldn't compare to the efficient and caring group of individuals at Middleton. We were close friends, and joking with each other alleviated the stress and strain inherent in our jobs.

"Would you please call Serena and tell her I'll be home as soon as I finish up here? I'd appreciate it."

Her eyes flicked in Dr. Anazzio's direction and back at me. "Sure thing." She rushed through the glistening steel double doors leading out of the operating room.

Forty-five minutes later I peeled out of the parking lot in the cherry-apple red '68 Mustang I bought as a present to myself after receiving my Doctorate. I drove forty miles an hour through the designated twenty-five m.p.h. streets of Santa Barbara until I reached our house overlooking Sandpiper Beach.

Serena's shiny black convertible BMW stood in the driveway. I screeched to a halt next to it and bolted for the front door, grasped the brass knob and gave it a turn. Crime in this small city was almost nonexistent and we never locked our front or back doors, especially during the daytime.

My gaze shot toward the deck overlooking the beach. Serena

stood at the railing with her back facing me. Her hair hung to the middle of her back, and she wore one of her signature purple blouses. It dipped low over her left shoulder, showing silky smooth, tanned skin.

My heartbeat slowed, and I matched it with my footsteps. "Serena, I'm home," I called out, relieved she was still in the house and hadn't disappeared as she'd done twice before when we had an argument.

She angled her head in my direction, and I noted her tear-streaked face, mascara running from her lower lashes to the bottom of her chin.

"It's about time," she answered, turning back to face the beach.

Coming up behind her, I surrounded her slender body with my arms, bringing my hands together across her belly, nuzzling my face in her neck. "You okay?" She smelled of lavender, and I closed my eyes, drinking in her captivating scent.

Her head shook left to right. Whenever she was mad at me her temper manifested itself in yelling and the occasional thrown book or two. Her silence and tears were unusual.

"Come inside, babe. We can talk." I tried to turn her around in my arms but she stiffened and grasped the railing with white-knuckled fingers. "Or we can talk out here. The sun will be setting soon. We can watch it go down together."

"I'm pregnant."

Whoa! This was a surprise. Serena had been taking birth control pills since the day I met her, two-and-a-half years ago, several months before we both graduated.

I moved my hands from her waist, covered her tinier hands holding the railing and slowly peeled them away from the redwood. She turned toward me and buried her face in my chest.

I laid my chin on the top of her head and gave her a hug. "You're not happy?"

She pulled back, looked up and gave me a stony expression.

Personally, I was over the moon that she was having my baby. I didn't want another woman in my life. I'd been in love with Serena since the day we met.

Apparently, it was different for her.

"I don't want it." She pushed past me into the front room. I followed her and sat down on the couch, elbows on my knees, my head bent in my hands. I didn't want to pressure her but it was only fair that I explain my feelings.

She turned her back to me, physically distancing herself, standing like a statue in front of the windows. "I want an abortion."

Shaking my head, I stared at the floor, shocked at the decisiveness in her voice. "This is our baby." I looked up. "Not just yours, Serena. It's mine too."

"But it's my body." She turned. "I've already made the appointment."

I stood but didn't step toward her, my hands clenched at my sides. "And I'm supposed to agree with you because you're the one carrying the child? Just because I can't physically get pregnant my feelings don't matter?" I let out a slow breath. "Well, I'm not okay with it. The idea makes me sick."

Theoretically, I was all for freedom of choice, but when it came right down to it, and it was my own kid, it was a different story altogether. I already felt proprietary about the baby growing inside her.

I'd never gotten a girl pregnant before. Back in my early college days I'd been meticulously careful about making sure my girlfriends were on the pill or I'd use the best brand of condoms available along with spermicide to be extra cautious.

I didn't want to be a father before now. I was determined to get my degree, and during those six long years at U.C. Santa Barbara, there hadn't been a problem.

But now I didn't consider "it" a problem.

She refused to look me in the eye. Her silence irritated me.

"Look. You have the money from your father. You could use some of it to hire a nanny. That way when you want to go to the beach to paint, someone can take care of the baby. And when our child is old enough to be in daycare or pre-school or whatever, you won't need a nanny any more, right? You'll have almost as much free time as you do now." I paused, thinking of the best way to convince her and prove that I understood her hesitation. "I know you have a dream, honey. You're an artist. I get that."

She looked more pissed off now than I'd ever seen her. And I didn't understand why. She was already shaking her head before I even finished talking.

"No, Jess. I'm not changing my mind."

We had various options we could pursue if we had the baby, but she wouldn't consider any of them?

"Serena, be reasonable. For God's sake, you're talking about a human being here. Our baby. Don't you care about that? What the hell's wrong with you?" I paused, anger bubbling to the surface. "Look at you." I gestured at her with my hand and raised my voice. "You won't listen to a damn word I'm saying. You've made up your mind? What the hell does that mean? I don't have a say in this? I'm the father, aren't I?"

The moment the words escaped my lips, I knew I shouldn't have said them. I took a deep breath and walked over to where she stood, glaring at me. "I'm sorry. I shouldn't have said that. I'm just upset. Why can't we talk about this like a couple, not you making the decision for both of us? We're in this together, and you're not willing to budge one inch about something I should have a say in as well."

She slumped down onto the couch, grabbed my hand, and pulled me down next to her. "I never wanted to be pregnant. I want to paint. I don't want to burp a baby, feed it bottles, change dirty diapers. Shit! You know that."

I draped my arm around her shoulders and pulled her closer to my side. "Yeah, I know that. But check this out. What about we get married, have our baby, convert one of the bedrooms into a studio and you can paint at home? Come on, honey, that doesn't sound so awful, does it? We can make this work."

It looked as if she was coming around a bit. She stopped screaming at me and she also stopped crying. She leaned back on the couch pillows, arms folded under her breasts, looking toward the beach. Maybe she was seriously thinking about what I said.

She nodded, not a glint of "happy" showing on her lips. "I know you want this baby, and it's not like I hate kids. But my work means everything to me. I need my head to be in the right space so I can paint, otherwise I'd... I'd just die." I kissed her cheek then nuzzled her neck. "I know, babe. I've always known. But having a baby doesn't mean that has to stop. Don't you see?"

She stood up again and faced the window, gazing out at the Pacific Ocean. "Oh, God! I'm so confused. I never pictured myself married. To anyone. And having a baby? I don't want to be tied down. What if I freak out? What'll I do then?" She turned around to face me, hands on her hips. "What if I can't do this?"

I got to my feet and wrapped my arms around her. "Like I said, we can hire someone so when you need to get away you can just leave, ya know? And I'll try to be here in the evenings as much as I can too. You know I'll help out. We're in this together. We always have been. Just because we never set a date to get married or talked about when to have children doesn't mean I haven't thought about it. We talked about marriage before."

She pulled back and looked up at me. "We put it out there hypothetically, but we weren't all that serious about the whole thing, and you know it."

I looked in her eyes, alarmed by her interpretation of our past conversations. "Well, I was serious. It wasn't hypothetical to me. I want to marry you. Now is as good a time as any, especially since you're carrying our baby. Don't you wanna marry me?"

She sighed. "Yes, I'll marry you." She shrugged. "I guess that's what people do if you're gonna have a baby."

This was the first time she mentioned going through with the pregnancy, and I held my breath, hoping she wouldn't change her mind.

I dipped my head and gave her a chaste kiss. "You love me, don't you?" I paused. "I love you more than anyone on this Earth. I thought you felt the same about me."

"Of course I love you."

"Then let's get married. Whenever you want. I mean, in the next nine months or so." I grinned.

She plopped down on the couch, looking a little exhausted and a lot dejected. "Okay, I'll marry you. I don't care when. Pick the date and I'll be there, maternity dress and all." The sides of her lips quirked up a tiny bit.

I released a huge breath.

Wow. She'd finally come around.

CHAPTER THREE

Eighteen Months Later

"Serena, honey, where are you?" I clutched the dozen pink roses in my right hand, the box of See's chocolates in the other, and shoved the front door shut with my foot. I'd come home early to spend some quality time with my wife. I found it almost impossible to take extra hours off from work so I pleaded a headache and rushed home.

Taking the stairs two at a time, I reached the second floor landing. Four bedroom doors lined the long hallway, two on each side. The first one on the right was Sofia's. The door stood half-open, but when I pushed it a few inches to catch a glimpse of the crib, I discovered it empty.

Two o'clock and Sofia should have been taking a nap. The door to the left stood wide open—Serena's studio.

At this time of day she'd be painting, deep in concentration, dabbing at the canvas with a brush dipped in one of her favorite pastel oil colors. The windows facing the ocean were open and the sound of the waves roared so loud, it was like standing right next to the shoreline.

But Serena wasn't sitting on the paint-spattered stool as I hoped. The palette lay on top of the stool's seat where she always placed it after she finished for the day, and her brushes were meticulously lined up like skinny soldiers on a dry towel.

At the end of the hallway to the left was our bedroom, and to the right the spare room we used whenever guests stayed the night. All the beds were made, comforters neatly folded in big squares at the bottom. Both rooms had their own baths, but they, too, were unoccupied.

I rushed downstairs to the kitchen and left the roses and candy on the countertop then ran back out to the deck though I would have seen her there when I walked in the front door. No Serena.

Retracing my steps, I walked back to our bedroom and Sofia's room and looked, I mean really looked around. Nothing appeared out of place. Everything looked normal. Clothes lay inside the dryer at the end of the hall upstairs. I stuck my hand inside and grabbed a towel. It was still warm, probably from Serena's usual morning load of wash.

I ran back to the kitchen to look next to the toaster where Serena always laid her purse. It still lie there, car keys in the side pocket. I rushed to the foyer. Sofia's stroller sat next to the front door.

What the hell was going on? This didn't make sense. I didn't know what to do. Should I call the police? It was too soon to panic, wasn't it? Serena hadn't expected me to come home early. I usually walked in around six.

But I couldn't imagine where she'd go. And without the stroller, she'd have to carry Sofia. But at this time of day Sofia always took a nap.

I sat down at the kitchen table, telling myself I'd seriously contemplate for five minutes where they might have gone. Then I'd make a decision. I didn't want to act rashly. But if nothing sounded plausible, I'd call the police.

Then again, if memory served me right, a person had to be missing for twenty-four hours before she or he was considered missing, right? Hell, I had no idea. Maybe that only applied to children and not adults. I'd heard of an "Amber Alert," but that happened when someone kidnapped a child, right?

But hey, this was Serena we were talking about. She breastfed Sofia for several months. I read about the bond that formed between a mother and her child during the nursing phase. And Serena had been caring for Sofia every day since giving birth. Sofia had turned nine months old the day before yesterday.

Serena wouldn't need to kidnap her own daughter, unless... Hadn't she seemed distant for the last few months? I chalked it up to postpartum depression, raging hormones, body changes, breastfeeding. Could her behavior have nothing to do with giving birth and everything to do with me?

I never gave the idea any space in my head. And certainly nowhere in my heart. Serena loved me as much as I loved her. She meant everything to me. And Sofia was my daughter. They were my world. Every day I looked forward to coming home from work and seeing them, Serena standing in front of a canvas, brush in hand, stroking with bright colors.

Sofia would be lying in her crib. I'd tip-toe into her bedroom and lean over the side rail to stare at her. Invariably she'd be sucking her thumb, tiny butt in the air, little legs tucked under, milk drool dripping out the side of her perfectly formed ruby-red lips.

I always envisioned Serena and me as husband and wife. I'd thought about that for months before it actually happened. But having a child? My happiness at knowing Serena was pregnant and having my child couldn't compare to the stark reality of Sofia's birth—her head cresting in the delivery room, the sight of her forehead, then her nose, then her mouth. When the rest of her little body slid out into the world, I remember thinking, "What have we done?" Sofia was ours. We created her out of our love for each other. She was magnificent. A miracle.

Where were they?

CHAPTER FOUR

The rest of that day and night passed in a blur, a never-ending parade of police, FBI, detectives. A constant stream of people traipsing through our home. An Amber Alert had been issued and the house transformed into a whirlwind of activity.

I told my story at least fifty times. The details never changed. I didn't need to worry about what I said the last time I was asked. The story remained the same every time I told it, to whomever I told it.

The day they went missing remained engraved on my brain as if written on a slab of concrete. When someone said, "Tell me exactly what happened when you found Serena and your daughter Sofia missing," I spewed out the identical tale.

At around eleven o'clock that evening I stood on our deck, staring out at the waves breaking along the shoreline. A full moon graced the cloudless sky, and a path of light glowed from the edge of the horizon to the back of the house. I pictured Serena with Sofia in her arms, walking toward me.

"We'd like to talk to you again, Dr. Bradford," Agent Caruso from the Los Angeles County FBI office interrupted my thoughts, startling me.

I turned around, nodded, then followed him into the front room and sat on the couch.

Detective Rodriquez from the local Santa Barbara police was already seated opposite me, facing the deck. The agent joined him and they took out their notepads and stared at me.

"Could you tell us about the other," Agent Caruso looked down at his notes and flipped back several pages, "two times you told us your wife left. Where did you say she went?"

I looked from the agent to the detective and tried to rein in my frustration. We'd been over this numerous times, but I knew they had to put together all the pieces, so I repeated my story. Again.

"A few months after we were married."

"When was this?" Agent Caruso said.

"About a year and a half ago. It was a warm day, so it must have been during the summer. Probably on a Saturday or Sunday. I remember I wasn't working weekends at the time." I paused, reliving the scene. "Serena was a few months pregnant and I knew she wasn't feeling good." I shook my head. "Maybe I should have been more understanding.

"Anyway, she'd been complaining about feeling sick every morning. She said if she wasn't pregnant she'd be able to paint. She lost her concentration, her center, her..." I stumbled, trying to explain the inexplicable. "Painting was her life. Bottom line, she resented not being able to paint."

They both looked at me with expressionless faces. Did they even have a clue what I was talking about? But that didn't matter. I was telling the truth which was all that mattered.

"I yelled at her—something I rarely did. When I look back on it, I should have been more empathetic. I couldn't relate to how she must have been feeling. I said something like, why didn't she stop it with the negative attitude and be happy that in a few months we'd have a beautiful baby to love for the rest of our lives. Something like that." I shrugged. "She walked out of the house and was gone overnight."

"Did you try to follow her, go look for her?" The agent glared at me with unblinking eyes.

"Like I told you before, Serena didn't, doesn't, have many friends. Painting is a solitary endeavor, and she doesn't have any sisters or brothers, just her parents. I figured she went over to her parents' house, and I couldn't phone over there."

I paused, shook my head. The Middleton's rejection still stung after several years. Probably always would. Their haughty attitude rubbed me the wrong way. "Like I told you, Serena's parents don't like me." I held up a hand to interrupt myself. "I should say, they've never even met me because they believe their daughter married beneath her. A career as a veterinarian wasn't shee-shee enough for them."

"Did you drive over there, see if her car was at her parents' house?" The detective stared straight into my eyes, unmoving, even though he already knew the answer.

I let out a big sigh. "Ye-es," I drew out the word. "I drove by but, like I told you, their house is surrounded by a ten foot high concrete wall. I couldn't have seen if she was there or not. So I waited until the next morning and she showed up around breakfast time."

"Did she tell you where she'd been?" Agent Caruso tapped his pencil on the top page of his notebook.

"She said she'd been with her mom and dad, and I believed her. Said she was sorry, and I forgave her. I apologized for what I said the night before." I shrugged again. "That was it. No big deal."

"And the second time? When did that happen?" the detective chimed in.

"A couple of months ago. She took Sofia with her. We had an argument and—"

"What did you argue about that time?" the agent asked. His tone sounded accusatory. It was obvious he had the impression Serena and I had a volatile relationship, and that just wasn't true.

"We rarely argued, Agent Caruso, and you're implying we did."

"I'm not implying anything, Dr. Bradford. It must have been quite a fight for her to take your daughter and desert you."

"She didn't desert me." I pinched the bridge of my nose with my thumb and forefinger and breathed in a deep, cleansing breath, trying to reduce my stress level before I answered. "She left for the rest of the afternoon and she wouldn't answer her cell phone. I was worried about them."

"Why were you so worried? Did you think she would harm herself or the baby?" His eyes bored into mine like a drill.

I shook my head. "No. I mean, not exactly." I leaned forward and grasped my hands together between my knees. "Serena is, uh, delicate."

"You mean unstable?" The agent's face looked as though he'd be happy if he found out Serena was a raving lunatic. Then they could begin looking for some madwoman roaming the streets, screaming obscenities at passersby.

"I didn't say that." I didn't try to hide my irritation at his insinuating Serena was crazy. "She was... she's an artist. She feels things differently than you and I do and—"

"What was the fight about?" Agent Caruso interrupted.

"She told me I worked too much. I spent more time at the clinic than at home. She was lonely staying here all the time by herself. I didn't pay enough attention to her and Sofia. That type of thing."

"Is that true?"

"That I didn't pay enough attention to her? Well, I understood where she was coming from. She stayed home all day. I was at the clinic for ten, sometimes twelve hours a day. I promised her when she got pregnant I'd be here to help out with the baby after work. But emergencies happen that are out of my control. It's a twenty-four hour animal hospital." I stopped, recalling that particular day. "I told her I'd try to spend more time at home, cut back my hours, organize more outings together on the weekends if I wasn't working."

"And did you do that?" The detective leaned back and fiddled with his pen, his eyes never leaving mine.

"I tried. But it didn't always work. People bring in their pets at all hours, and sometimes the dogs or cats are so sick you have to operate immediately. Hours pass. Suddenly it's the middle of the night and you're just leaving the O.R." I paused and tried to think over our last year together. "I noticed a certain distance on her part, as if she was pulling away a little, but maybe I imagined it. I don't know." I raked my hand through my hair and tucked myself into the cushions of the couch.

"What do you mean by her pulling away, this distant feeling?" The agent leaned back.

Four eyes watched every one of my facial nuances. Unnerving to say the least.

"She seemed a little more quiet, less happy. The only time I saw her smile was when she was in her studio, painting. Otherwise..."

"Otherwise?" the agent asked, one eyebrow tweaked upward. "Any change in your sex life?"

I stood up and knocked my leg into the table separating the three of us, pushing it several inches toward them. "That's none of your business," I said between gritted teeth.

Agent Caruso's expression remained unchanged, and he looked up at me. "Sit down, Dr. Bradford. Just answer the question. Everything about you and your wife is our business right now. If we're going to have any chance of finding her and your daughter, we need to know everything about your relationship. So we can know where to look. We need all the clues to be able to piece things together."

I sat down on the edge of the couch and fiddled with my wedding ring. "We haven't made love in about two months, alright? She complained about being tired, not feeling herself." I shrugged. "I thought she might be pregnant again, but she said she wasn't. I didn't want to pressure her or make a big deal out of it. I was busy. She stayed up almost every night painting til all hours. Time slipped by. I don't know. I thought things would get better."

"Did you seek sexual satisfaction outside your marriage?" The agent sounded almost bored, his words spoken in a monotone.

They could probably hear my teeth grinding. I looked to the side, inhaled deeply through my nose once then again, trying to contain my temper. "No, I did not have sex with anyone outside my marriage. I love my wife, Agent Caruso."

They looked at each other and Caruso closed his notebook and Rodriquez did the same. They both stood at the same time—the dynamic duo.

Caruso stuck the notebook in his breast pocket. "That's all for now." They walked out of the room.

I felt as though I'd done something wrong. They wanted to paint a picture of me as the neglectful husband. And that just wasn't true. Marriage wasn't always birds and bells and happy faces. I believed Serena and I basically had a good marriage.

A pebble of doubt edged its way into my heart. Had Serena left me?

And taken my child with her?

CHAPTER FIVE

Detective Rodriquez asked me for the names and phone numbers of Serena's father and mother. I guessed it was only a matter of time before they entered the picture. Serena was an only child, and she came from a wealthy family. Her parents refused to come to our wedding, and they wouldn't spend one nickel on a wedding gift. I'd never even met them.

For two years I'd been working at Middleton Veterinary Hospital and David Middleton didn't even know. Then again, MVH was just one of many buildings in Santa Barbara stamped with his name on it—one of the perks of being a philanthropist. He could shelter his millions from the IRS under the guise of charitable contributions. "Old money," Serena called it, and since she kept her maiden name, the name Bradford meant nothing to David and Barbara Middleton.

The staff at Middleton knew the tale of Serena Middleton and Jessee Bradford. We were a tight-knit group and I'd counted on their discretion since the day we'd gone out to dinner for my first staff meeting. After numerous beers to go along with the pizza, I explained how Serena and I met, which segued into her getting pregnant and our subsequent "unapproved-by-her-wealthy-parents" marriage. At the end of the evening, when I asked the staff to forget what I just told them, they looked at me and said, "Told us what?"

Serena had pointed out the house where she grew up. I had insisted on seeing where it was located, wanting to get a sense of her background, a glimpse into the environment behind her childhood. We took a drive to the top of the hills and she handed me a set of binoculars. That was as close a look as I ever got of where she lived her younger years.

Santa Barbara is a wealthy community. Before I was accepted

into U.C. Santa Barbara's six-year veterinary medicine program I visited there from my home in the Lakeside area in Southern California. Most of the houses were surrounded by ten-foot walls and iron gates. I wouldn't have been surprised if I'd seen a moat encircling some of them.

And one of those mansions was Serena's home. At least it had been her home before she enrolled at U.C. and insisted on living in the dorms. Since she and I had gotten together, the 1106 Montecito Way address was a place she visited alone. After graduation her father lived up to his word and gifted her the majority of her inheritance.

That's when she purchased the house we lived in together.

Serena didn't see her parents often. It took many hours of discussion, arguments if I wanted to be honest about it, before Serena agreed not to bring Sofia to her parents' house. I believed it was disrespectful to me as well as our marriage to allow David and Barbara Middleton the privilege of meeting their granddaughter while they continued to ignore my existence. If and when they were able to accept Serena's husband, they could meet Sofia.

"I'll have to find their phone numbers," I told the detective.

Rodriquez looked at me, his brows dipped in a vee. "I've never met them, Detective."

His stare made me feel distinctly uncomfortable, like a bug under a microscope. But I should have seen this coming and knew I'd eventually have to explain.

"They didn't approve of my marrying their daughter." I pursed my lips, trying to come up with a succinct way of telling the story. "Look. I didn't come from money. They wanted their daughter to marry somebody else."

"Do you know for a fact they never came to visit your wife? While you were at work, maybe?"

I shook my head. "Serena would have told me."

Rodriquez cocked one eyebrow. The side of his mouth edged up into an "almost" smile. "Or not."

I shrugged and walked into the kitchen to find Serena's address book. He stood to the side while I thumbed through the pages.

"Here it is." I pointed to the page.

He took the address book and sat down at the table. I assumed

I'd been dismissed and returned to the front room, too exhausted to care what he thought about my marriage. I just wanted my wife and child back.

Several moments later, Detective Rodriquez informed me Serena's parents were coming to our house to look around, see if anything looked odd or out-of-place.

I nodded, keeping my thoughts to myself. I could tell he wasn't interested in hearing them anyway. How would her parents know if something was out of place? They'd never been to our home. Now they were going to stroll through our house, looking in our closets, touching Sofia's things?

I was livid but refused to show it. Even though this was a complete waste of time, I'd be polite and courteous. I didn't want to do anything to slow the progress of the investigation into my wife and child's whereabouts.

Serena and Sofia had been missing for almost twenty-four hours. Or more. I arrived home the day before at two o'clock, and it was now noon the following day. Who knew how long they'd been gone before I arrived home.

While I stood in the kitchen, about to pour my third cup of coffee, the doorbell rang. I looked outside the kitchen window and saw a black limo parked at the curb, taking up space enough for three cars.

My steps tentative, I walked into the front room and looked toward the foyer. Detective Rodriquez, Agent Caruso, four or five policemen and a few others I hadn't met turned their heads toward the front of the house. I knew it had to be Serena's parents and braced myself for our first meeting.

Agent Caruso and Detective Rodriquez stood up and walked to the foyer as a policeman pulled open the front door. Caruso and Rodriquez identified themselves and they all shook hands.

David Middleton was a tall man, about six feet four inches, with a full head of steel-grey hair, a thick white mustache, and blue eyes. I guessed Serena got her gorgeous eyes from him. He wore a dark gray suit with a maroon tie and super-shiny loafers. Distinguished would be the word to describe him. Women might call him handsome.

Barbara Middleton looked much younger than her husband, maybe in her early fifties with shoulder-length, strawberry-blonde hair streaked with blonde highlights, deep-set brown eyes, slim figured and big-busted. She wore a white ribbed top that showed off her tanned arms and neck, along with a pair of navy-blue slacks and white strappy heels. Men would call her strikingly beautiful.

"Please join us." Detective Rodriquez gestured toward the front room.

The Middletons stepped down into the front room and sat next to each other on the couch facing the deck.

They'd never met me so I surmised they didn't know who the guy was, standing off to the side, leaning against the piano, staring in their direction.

I didn't want our first encounter to exacerbate their already negative estimation of me, so I tentatively walked toward them and stuck out my hand.

"I'm your daughter's husband. Thanks for coming."

Not expecting any sort of positive reception, it still surprised me when David Middleton suddenly stood, towering above my six-foot one-inch frame, and pressed his face inches from mine.

"What have you done with our daughter and granddaughter?" he spit out, his face flushed in anger, eyes blazing.

I held his unwavering gaze, second for second. I was not backing down any more than he. "I would never do anything to hurt them. I love Serena and Sofia. Which is more than I can say for you," I ground out between clenched teeth.

I expected an unfriendly introduction but never the slam of my father-in-law's fist into the side of my face. Next thing I knew I was laying flat on my back on the front room carpet.

"Oh, my God. David, what have you done?" Barbara Middleton raced over to me. I lay on my back and rubbed my jaw.

Rodriquez and Caruso grabbed Mr. Middleton, one on each side, and pushed him down onto the couch. His face had turned purple as he continued to glare at me while his wife laid her bejeweled hand on my forearm and gently patted it.

I took a seat on the couch across from them and tucked myself into the corner, massaging my jaw. Two policemen hovered over me, watching my every move. A third pressed a bag of frozen peas in my hand. I thanked him and placed it against the underside of my jaw.

The silence echoed off the walls of the front room until Agent

Caruso walked between the two couches and stood in front of the fireplace, facing us. "Mr. Middleton, I'm going to ignore what just happened because I know you're upset, but I'm trusting you'll keep your fists to yourself. Understood?"

David Middleton jerked his head up and down once, and the agent continued. "Our idea..." He gave a nod in the detective's direction. "...is to have you look through your daughter's possessions—bedroom, clothes, personal articles—and tell us if you notice anything different, not normal, out of place, surprising. Anything at all that catches your eye, triggers an uncomfortable feeling."

He paused and tapped a cigarette out of his pack of Marlboros, holding it between his fingers, unlit. "We're looking for any clues as to why she might have left. At this point it doesn't appear she and your granddaughter have been kidnapped. There's no evidence of a scuffle, the doors were locked, her purse and keys are still here. It looks as if the two of them disappeared into thin air." He glanced at Mrs. Middleton. "You might recognize something your husband misses. Were you close to your daughter?"

Barbara Middleton pulled at the bottom of her shirt, straightening it over her abundant bosom. She looked nervous. I equated that with her being in different surroundings as well as a situation over which she had no control. The Middletons were wealthy and I assumed their experience with the law was limited, if not non-existent.

"We were close, up until a few years ago." She glanced over at her husband. "We didn't see her much after she graduated from the university and moved in with..." She gave me a quick half-smile, looking sheepish.

I smiled. "Jessee Bradford. Nice to meet you."

"It's a pleasure to meet you, too," she answered. "And Sofia is such a lovely child." She shifted her gaze to her lap and fiddled with the material of her slacks.

It took a few seconds for her words to register and I slowly eased myself to a standing position. The frozen bag of peas hit the floor. At the same time, I noticed the look on her husband's face as he turned in her direction and frowned.

"You've met Sofia?" I whispered.

Both of them glanced up at me. Neither of them said a word. A firm hand grasped my shoulder, pushing me back down onto the couch. I glimpsed to the side as one of the officers parked himself directly behind where I was sitting, his hand glued to my shoulder.

My mind whirled. Serena had lied to me. She'd taken Sofia to see her parents? I wanted to puke.

Agent Caruso pinched the bridge of his nose and shook his head. When he looked up, the whites of his eyes were crisscrossed with tiny red veins. "Look. We're all here to figure out how we can find Serena and Sofia. That's the most important issue right now. I'd appreciate if we could all try to get along for the minimal amount of time we'll be together."

He turned from me to the Middletons and back. The Middletons nodded in agreement. I did my best to keep my mouth shut before I said anything that would fuel the acrid fire burning in my gut that David and Barbara Middleton had set aflame.

I was incensed the two of them had had any interaction whatsoever with my daughter. But if I was honest with myself, I blamed Serena for this. She hadn't been truthful with me. And I thought we held no secrets from each other. A dirty speck of doubt niggled in the corner of my mind.

"So, let's get on with this," Caruso continued. "Each minute they're missing is another minute we're further away from finding them."

They followed him up the stairs into Sofia's bedroom. My heart ambled its way up into my throat. I hated the thought of the Middletons touching my daughter's things. But bottom line, if either of them could help me find my wife and child, I'd be grateful.

CHAPTER SIX

I was glad I couldn't hear what they were saying as they went through every room in our house, looking for whatever clues the agent and detective hoped to find. After thirty minutes they returned to the front room.

David had his arm around Barbara's shoulders, and she dabbed at her eyes with a tissue. His demeanor hadn't changed. He remained stiff, brows furrowed, silent.

"Find anything?" I asked, looking from Agent Caruso to Detective Rodriquez.

They both shook their heads.

Detective Rodriquez excused himself for a moment. Agent Caruso cleared his throat and shot a quick glance my way before he turned toward the Middletons as they sat on the couch. "When was the last time you spoke with your daughter?"

Mr. Middleton slapped his hand on the armrest and shook his head. "You've asked us the same question several times, Agent Caruso. Our stories are not going to change. We haven't heard from her in almost two weeks. It was a Tuesday."

Agent Caruso seemed like the type of guy who kept his cool no matter what. I hadn't once seen him agitated since I'd met him. If a firecracker went off next to him I doubted he'd even flinch. "And how is it you know the exact day?"

David Middleton took a deep exaggerated breath and closed his eyes. After he opened them his voice was low, a steady monotone. "My wife and I were celebrating our thirtieth anniversary. Serena stopped by to wish us well."

"Did she say anything, do anything that would make you think she was unhappy, that she was being hurt in any way?" Caruso gestured in my direction. "Had she had a fight with her husband?" He paused when he noticed the Middletons shaking their heads in unison. "Anything?" he urged.

"No. Unfortunately not," David Middleton answered.

Barbara Middleton's faced drooped like a melting candle. "I'm sorry, no."

The agent looked over at me and shrugged. Caruso stood up and the Middletons stood as well. I followed the three of them to the front door.

The agent stuck his hand out toward David Middleton. Between his fingers was one of his business cards. "If you think of anything…"

"We know," David Middleton interrupted, grabbing the card out of the agent's hand. "We'll call if we hear from her."

"Thank you for your time," the agent said.

I made eye contact with Barbara Middleton and nodded. She smiled, but it looked more like a grimace. David Middleton ignored my existence. Same-o, same-o.

The agent shut the door behind them then turned around and looked at me, his face inches from mine. "We set up a wiretap on your phone. If someone calls, wait two rings before you answer. Understood?"

I nodded and trudged to my bedroom. The only room unoccupied by a member of law enforcement. I left the door ajar and laid on top of the comforter. I hadn't slept since I arrived home yesterday afternoon and I fell into a disturbing slumber.

Beethoven's Fur d'Elyse ringtone jangled my brain awake. I turned to look at the clock. Five p.m. I counted one ring, two rings then picked up the receiver, my stomach lodged in my throat.

"Hello," I croaked then cleared my throat. "Hello?"

"Jessee, it's Francesca." For the first time since joining the staff at Middleton, I was disappointed to hear Dr. Anazzio's voice. I had hoped it would be Serena.

"Hold on a sec." Detective Rodriquez had pushed open my bedroom door, his eyebrows raised in question. "It's Dr. Anazzio. I work with her." His face returned to its usual grim expression, then he turned and left the door wide open.

I wasn't sure whether everyone was listening to my conversation but, frankly, I didn't care. My world had already turned into an open book. There wasn't much they didn't know about my private life at this point, and anything they didn't know they'd come to find out soon enough.

"What's going on, Jessee? You left feeling ill yesterday and didn't show up this morning. Are you okay?"

I hesitated. Agent Caruso explained they wouldn't be able to keep this a secret much longer. Not if it involved the daughter of a wealthy Santa Barbara couple whose philanthropic endeavors helped keep the city in the shape it was today. News stations would soon begin broadcasting Serena and Sofia's disappearance. But maybe that was a good thing. Then perhaps others would be on the lookout for them.

"Serena and Sofia are missing." I choked on the last word.

I heard her intake of breath, and my vision blurred with oncoming tears.

"My God. Were they kidnapped?"

I started to sob. Up until then, while talking with agents and detectives and police officers I'd been able to keep an emotional wall between them and me: a concrete moat. Just like the one around the Middleton's mansion.

"Nobody knows." My words spewed out between tearful exhalations. "The FBI and detectives and local police have been here since yesterday afternoon."

"God. I don't know what to say." She paused. "Do you want me to come over? Can I do something?"

"No, but thanks for asking. I've gotta go. Can you tell the staff what's happened? I don't know when I'll be back at work but..." My voice quivered.

"Jessee, stop. Don't worry about work. I'll take care of everything here. We have some great veterinary assistants working for us. We've got it covered." A few beats of silence ensued. "If there's anything..."

"Thanks. I'll call when I can." I replaced the receiver on the handset and suddenly remembered I hadn't phoned my grandparents. What in the hell was wrong with me?

Growing up, my mom and dad and I visited Nana and Grampa in Iowa almost every summer and sometimes at Thanksgiving or Christmas. I loved staying at their farm. They always had a slew of animals: chickens, goats, dogs, cats. Grampa had engendered in me the love of animals I had today, and the empathy he always showed toward them touched my soul.

When my parents died, Nana and Grampa had been my rock when I needed consolation before, during, and after the funeral. And right now that's exactly what I needed.

I recalled the time after Serena got pregnant and we decided to get married, I had the opportunity to take over my grampa's veterinary practice in Iowa. Serena wouldn't even talk about it. She couldn't imagine not living near the ocean. She also had a negative view of people in the Midwest. She never mentioned having visited anywhere but sophisticated cities in Europe and the East Coast. Her snooty upbringing hadn't done anything in the way of expanding her narrow-minded view of our own country.

Back then it wasn't a deal breaker for me so I let it go. Who could dislike living in Santa Barbara? It was a city people described as "for the newly-wed or nearly dead." Since Serena and I had been about to become the former, I acquiesced and we stayed in this house in Santa Barbara.

Nana and Grampa never met Serena, but I had planned on visiting them in the near future to introduce them to my wife and child. I sent pictures when Sofia was born but I'd been so busy at the clinic since getting married that our phone conversations had dwindled to birthday and Christmas greetings.

I noticed my iPhone lying on the bedside table, grabbed it and scrolled through my contacts. Within moments Nana's cheerful voice answered.

"Nana, it's Jessee."

I heard an intake of breath. "Jessee! My goodness, how are you?" she cried. "Just a minute, dear. Harper! It's Jessee. Pick up the other phone."

I heard a click then the deep rumble of Grampa's voice. "How're you doin', son? Is it Christmas already?" he asked, chuckling.

I closed my eyes and prayed I'd get through this conversation without blubbering. "I'm sorry for not calling more often, it's just—"

"No need to apologize. I know how busy it can be workin' at a clinic. I did my rotation in Des Moines at the emergency—"

"Harper," Nana interrupted him on the other line, "will you let the boy speak, for heaven's sake? You've told him that story a thousand times."

Silence edged its way through the speaker of my cell phone. "I.. I'm..." I stuttered. "I wanted to tell you that... Serena and Sofia are missing and the FBI and police are looking for them." There. I said it. The tightness in my chest loosened and I took a deep breath.

"Oh, my good Lord," Nana whispered.

"When did this happen?" Grampa said.

"Yesterday when I got home from work they weren't here. The FBI doesn't think they were kidnapped, but it can't be ruled out completely. Serena might have taken Sofia and left on her own. Her purse, her keys, her car, all their clothes, Sofia's stroller— everything's still in the house."

Once again my eyes welled up and I blinked back the tears. "I don't believe Serena would leave me and take my only child with her. But I hope to God they weren't kidnapped because..." My voice shook with more than twenty-four hours of pent-up emotion and I coughed, swallowed. "I wanted to call you..."

"Is there anythin' we can do?" Nana asked, her voice filled with sympathy and understanding.

"The FBI might contact you even though I told them you never met Serena and she'd never call you. I gave them your phone number, so if they call..." My voice trailed off.

"I wish there was somethin' we could do." Grampa's voice sounded strained, like a loud whisper.

"Thanks, Grampa. I love you both."

Nana's worried voice spoke volumes. "Will you call us and tell us what happens?"

"Of course." I pressed the End button on my cell phone before I totally lost it. I stood and quietly shut the bedroom door then curled up in a fetal position on my bed. I put a pillow in front of my face and let out all the fear and sadness I'd held in since coming home yesterday. Where the hell were they? I'd do anything to have them back.

I closed my eyes. "Please let them be safe," I whispered. "Please come home, Serena. I love you, Sofia."

I thought sleep would be impossible, but when I next looked at the clock I'd dozed off for an hour. I took a long, hot shower then dressed in clean clothes. I didn't remember eating anything since yesterday at lunchtime and knew I better have breakfast or lunch or whatever meal I should eat right now.

After taking a deep breath I opened my bedroom door and walked to the kitchen. My feet stopped when I reached the doorway. I counted eight men and women interspersed amongst a slew of unidentifiable electronic paraphernalia. Open briefcases lay on the kitchen counter. Telephone lines zig-zagged along the baseboard and up to the kitchen table, connected to larger-than-life telephones with antennae. Everyone was mumbling, their words indecipherable. It reminded me of the scene in the movie Ransom with Mel Gibson when his son is kidnapped by a member of the police force.

Agent Caruso caught my eye and lifted his brows. "Problem?"

I shook my head. "Just hungry." I gestured toward the refrigerator. "May I?"

He nodded and continued typing on his laptop and talking on the Bluetooth hooked to his ear.

My stomach growled but I didn't feel like eating. My heart ached so bad, I knew I would burst out in tears again, and once I started it wouldn't be easy to stop. I bit my lip and the taste of blood burst on my tongue, salty and tangy at the same time.

I kept picturing some man with a nylon sock pulled over his head grabbing Serena around the neck, pushing her into Sofia's bedroom, forcing her to pick up the baby then demanding she walk out the front door and into his car.

A twist in my gut made me glad I hadn't eaten yet. My hand dropped off the handle of the refrigerator door. Maybe I'd eat something later.

I walked out to the deck. Orange and pink strands of light settled across the horizon. Sunset in Santa Barbara. The tide was out, the waves had subsided, the only sound the tinkling of the wind chimes. Serena purchased them at the arts and crafts fair held on the beach boardwalk every Sunday. Their metallic song could be heard here and in our bedroom, which faced the ocean.

Serena loved the water: the sound, smell, feel. She always said the ocean was part of her soul and her reason for not moving out of the area. When Grampa had made the offer for me to take over his practice, I knew immediately she'd never move to Earlham, Iowa.

Now I wondered if she'd ever come back here, or if she'd ever see the ocean again.

* * * *

The next day

A special nationwide news broadcast was scheduled to announce Serena and Sofia's disappearance. Mr. Middleton was offering a five hundred thousand dollar reward for any tip leading to their being found.

Forty-eight hours after my wife and child went missing I stood in front of too many television cameras to count. After listening to Barbara Middleton's heartfelt plea for their daughter and granddaughter's release, all lenses pointed in my direction. I stepped to the small dais erected on our front lawn.

My eyes panned the crowd of people standing in front of me on the lawn and sidewalk. "My name is Jessee Bradford. I'm Serena Middleton's husband and Sofia's father." My eyes teared up, and I cleared my throat, glanced from left to right at the various cameras. "Serena, if you're listening to me, honey, I love you. And I love our baby." I paused and stood up straight, needing to appear in control. "To whoever has taken you, I want you to know, I promise we're going to find you. And if you're listening to this I want you to know something else." I pointed my finger toward the cameras. "A five hundred thousand dollar reward is more money than you're worth. Someone will go to the police just to get that reward money. So turn yourself in. Or call me. The number is at the bottom of the screen." I looked straight into the lens of the nearest camera. "I'm waiting."

I stepped down off the dais and walked through the front door into the house.

Voices yelled out.

"Mr. Middleton, what do you think happened to your daughter and granddaughter?"

"Mrs. Middleton, is it true you and your daughter were estranged because she married against your wishes?"

At this point I felt sick to my stomach. Then I remembered I hadn't eaten since finding out my wife and child were missing. I took a few moments alone on the deck to clear my head then headed for the kitchen where I found Agent Caruso and his staff, all still attached to their equipment.

He turned in my direction. "Need something?"

"What if she kidnapped my daughter? Isn't there something I can do? Legally, that is."

He leaned back in his chair and blew out a puff of air. "Here's the thing. The majority of child abductions are committed by a mother, father, or other relative. By virtue of the marriage, a husband and wife both have custody of their children. But, if she thinks just because she's the mother that she can take her child away from you, she's wrong. Parental kidnapping or child abduction, even by a family member, is a punishable felony. She's depriving you of your legal right to custody by illegally taking the child out of the jurisdiction which is outlawed by the federal Parental Kidnapping Prevention Act. Plus, each state must abide by custody decisions made by another state's courts."

I nodded.

"But what you gotta do is obtain a custody order. You don't have to obtain a custody order to report the abduction to the police as a crime, but at least filing the custody order in Family Court can lead to other resources to assist you in locating your child. You follow me?"

"I understand."

"If the judge gives you an order of temporary custody, the police can legally serve her with a copy of the order and she'll have to give the child back to you. Then there'll be a hearing and the judge will decide what to do next."

I nodded again, my lips pursed, thinking.

"Get yourself an attorney," he mumbled then turned back to his computer and began typing.

Forty-eight hours turned into seven-two hours, which slipped into one week then two weeks then a month. One day no one came by the house.

Then I was truly alone.

CHAPTER SEVEN

July

So, I hired an attorney, got a temporary order of custody, and went back to work. And waited for David Middleton to read all about me in the newspaper, put two and two together, come to the realization his low-life son-in-law worked for Middleton Veterinary Clinic, and make sure I was fired. But they'd been missing for almost six months and so far that hadn't happened. I guess I should consider myself lucky to still have a job.

I found out from Detective Rodriquez that Serena's father hired a private detective to search for his daughter the day after she went missing. Six months and they'd come up with zip.

Agent Caruso told me his gut opinion. He said Serena just got up and left with the intention of disappearing without a trace. He'd worked numerous cases involving kidnapped victims as well as people who had intentionally disappeared. He explained the best way not to be found would be to take nothing—no car, no stroller, no clothes, nothing. Just walk out. In his experience, that appeared to be exactly what Serena had done. So why hadn't David Middleton's P.I. found her after all these months? Just shows money can't buy everything.

I didn't know which hurt more, the idea they'd been kidnapped and murdered or that my wife had deserted me and taken my only child with her. I couldn't fight the facts. The FBI had no evidence pointing to a kidnapping. And with each passing month they weren't found, I finally resigned myself to the devastating fact they were never coming back.

I phoned my grandparents several times at home to tell them there hadn't been any news. But today I called the Bradford

Veterinary Clinic directly. It had been more than two years since Grampa made me the offer to take over his practice and I declined. He understood my position and told me he would be scouting other prospects to take his place. So far he hadn't found anyone and at eighty-one years old he was more than ready to retire.

"Bradford Veterinary Clinic, Kathy speaking. May I help you?"

"I'd like to speak with Harper, please. This is his grandson, Jessee."

Her voice rose several octaves. "Jessee! It's so nice to hear from you. Just a moment and I'll get him on the line."

She placed me on hold and within seconds I heard my grampa's baritone voice. "Any news?"

"Nope." I paused. "Remember when you offered me the chance to take over your practice?"

"Ye-es," he drew out the word nice and slow.

"I was wondering if the offer's still open." I held my breath.

"You're seriously thinkin' about leavin' California?"

"I've gotta get out of here. It's been six months and I don't think they're coming back." My brain stalled on the last words and I inhaled deeply. "If you're still planning on retiring, I'd like to take you up on your offer."

"Still haven't interviewed anyone I'd like to hire. So yes. Be my pleasure to have you." I could see him in my mind's eye, leaning back in his old leather office chair, feet propped up on the scarred wooden desk. "When you expectin' to arrive? Rose will wanna get your room ready."

I shook my head and smiled for the first time in days. I was already looking forward to seeing them. "I'll just be staying with you until I find my own place. You don't need to go to any trouble."

"No trouble a'tall, son."

"Well, I have to give my two-week notice, get the house squared away then I could be on the road. That okay with you?"

"Don't matter. As long as you're comin', we'll be here waitin' for ya'."

We said goodbye and I lay back on the bed pillows and thought about our conversation. I needed to move away from this city, this house, where Serena and Sofia and I had lived together. The hole in my heart felt almost palpable.

At times, in the middle of the night, I'd press my hand over my chest and rub, searching for the indentation. I was sure a part of my heart had cracked off and been absorbed by my body. Perhaps missing that part of my heart explained the times I'd find myself out of breath, unable to inhale completely.

When that happened I'd excuse myself at work and run to the bathroom, lock the door behind me and stand with my arms stretched over my head, struggling to take a full breath. I'd lean over the basin and splash cold water on my face then rub with a paper towel until it hurt. I'd turn on the fan, the noise so loud I hoped it would drown out the sound of my sobs. Pressing my back against the wall, I'd stuff my shirt over my mouth to quiet the cries emanating from my heaving belly.

These emotional episodes lasted for several minutes, but I never experienced more than one a day. Sometimes several days would pass before another hit me, always unexpected and frightening in its intensity. If it occurred at home, I'd go to our bedroom and lie down or just flop on the couch and wait for it to pass.

Outside of work and home, I'd sometimes find myself looking for the nearest place to be alone, whether a changing room in the department store or the nearest restroom. One time I pulled off to the side of the road, the tears and the pain in my chest forcing me to stop the car.

I had to get the hell out of Santa Barbara and the memories it held. There was no escaping the occasional phone call from Agent Caruso informing me the police still hadn't found Serena or Sofia. That would continue no matter where I lived. Nevertheless, I hoped a change of environment and my grandparent's loving company would help me heal.

I'd lost my grasp on the thin string of hope that Serena and Sofia would be found, and the situation was intolerable enough for me to move away. As time marched on, the statistics stacked higher and higher against their being located. I yearned for their return but either their bodies would be found or they'd be discovered leading a new life somewhere else. Either way, Serena and I would never be together again.

Suddenly I faced a dilemma. If I were to move out of California, should I sell our house? What about Serena's BMW? Immediately following our marriage, we'd gone to see an attorney to have our will drawn up. The money Serena received from her father made her a millionaire several times over. After we married she insisted we combine all our assets, much to the horror of her father. But Serena had always been rather stubborn and had refused her father's advice that I sign a pre-nup. However, I just couldn't bring myself to relinquish our home and Serena's car. It just felt so... final.

I had to abandon the city and home where she and I had met, conceived our child, and Sofia had been born, but I'd leave the details of selling the house and her BMW for later. It was just too much for me to handle right now.

Once I had that plan in mind, the prospect of confronting my co-workers at the clinic loomed before me. I didn't look forward to explaining myself, especially given my precarious emotional state. If they asked me the expected questions, I'd surely break down in front of them—something I dreaded. Would they try to talk me out of it? Tell me I was running away, that I should stay and face life "head on"?

As the senior vet at Middleton Veterinary Hospital, I called a staff meeting each week. So when I asked everyone to meet in the conference room at six o'clock that afternoon, it wasn't unusual.

Sitting at the head of the conference table at 5:50, I watched the staff trickle into the room, in various stages of exhaustion. Dr. Francesca Anazzio had just ended a twelve-hour shift. Maryanne, the surgical nurse, had begun her day at noon, so she still looked bright and awake.

Thomas and Patti, our veterinary assistants from U.C., were the most animated of the bunch, having worked four-hour shifts. We all stressed ourselves to the breaking point every day, performing unscheduled surgeries which sometimes ended in our patients' deaths.

Dogs being hit by cars constituted the trauma "du jour" in a twenty-four-hour vet hospital. We were open dawn 'til dawn and had built a reputation for rapid-fire evaluation, diagnosis, and treatment, along with the requisite high costs to the owners to go with it.

When everyone was seated I leaned forward in my chair, hands flat on the table, and took a cleansing breath. "Hi." I flipped my hand upward in a half-wave, inept as usual heading up a staff meeting. My forté had never been public speaking, and though these were my friends and I worked with them daily in the trenches, I still felt inadequate when speaking in front of them, watching them watching me.

"Um, I called you here for this meeting because I have something important to tell you." I looked from face to face, down one side of the table to the other, each of them glued to my every word. They probably thought I'd tell them news about Serena and Sofia, and I wished I didn't have to disappoint them. I was afraid they might be angry about the bomb I was about to drop on them.

Just say it and get it over with. I couldn't sugarcoat the fact I was leaving them stranded, with no one equally as experienced to take the helm. "I'm resigning and moving to Iowa." There, I'd said it. A whoosh of air escaped my lungs.

Francesca's brows shot up into her dark bangs. "What the hell?"

"You're not serious." Maryanne shook her head and looked as if she was about to cry.

The two interns, Thomas and Patti, didn't know me as well as the others and sat silent, watching while members of the team stated their negative opinions of my departure.

I held up my hand to forestall any additional comments. "Listen, everybody." Heads were still shaking, but I had their attention and the room became quiet.

"I've always thought of this clinic as home." I looked from one face to the next, meeting each person's eyes as I continued. "I love you guys. It's been a tremendous learning experience working with you, getting to know you, partying with you after work sometimes." I smiled and noticed I was the only one doing so. "Look." I glanced down, fiddling with the pencil I was holding. "This thing, uh, with Serena and Sofia..."

I shook my head, trying to think how to say what was in my heart. "Ever since they went missing... it's messed me up. Living in that house, all the memories—it's like their ghosts are still there with me." My eyes blurred with imminent tears, and I inhaled deeply, then continued in a rush of words. "I have to move away, so I'm going to Iowa to take over my grampa's vet practice. I've gotta do this for my sanity, and I'm sorry if you think I'm deserting you. That's not my intention."

Francesca eyed the others sitting around the table and gave me a mini-smile. "I think I speak for the rest of us when I say we understand, Jessee. I can't imagine what you've gone through, what you're still going through: the not knowing, the constant wondering if they'll be found. And it must be impossibly difficult being in the same house where you all lived together."

She paused and swiped at an errant tear that had escaped down her cheek. "I wish you well in your new practice in Iowa." She glanced at Maryanne and nodded.

Maryanne's lips quirked upward in a smile. "Ditto for me, Jessee. You know how much we all love you, and we'll miss you, too. But I know you'll do a fantastic job in..." Her brows furrowed. "Did you say Iowa?"

I chuckled and everyone laughed along with me. "I know, I know. Iowa isn't exactly California. And it certainly isn't Santa Barbara."

Thomas put in his two cents. "Uh, duh."

"Yeah, right," Patti added.

"Where in Iowa? I mean, what city?" Francesca looked completely confused.

"Earlham," I responded. "E-A-R-L-H-A-M," I spelled out. The blank looks on their faces told me I'd better elaborate. "Marion Robert Morrison lived there as a boy and attended school in the Earlham Academy building that's now the School House Museum. At least that's what Grampa told me."

Patti frowned. "Earl... ham? Sounds like a type of sandwich."

I laughed and gave her a withering look. "You don't pronounce it "Earl" then "ham". It's pronounced 'earl-um'."

"Who's Marion Robert Morrison?" This from Thomas, the other intern.

I could see Francesca trying not to giggle. "Give it up, Francesca. I can tell you know what I'm talking about."

She leaned back in her chair and looked around the table. "They're too young, Jess. Marion Robert Morrison was John Wayne, guys." She paused. "Duh."

Maryanne rolled her eyes at Francesca. "So when do you have to leave?"

"I have to put all my furniture in storage, lease the house, pack up my car." I paused. "Consider this my two-week notice."

"I'd suggest a going-away party but I don't want you to leave." Francesca blinked her watery eyes over and over, and I knew she was trying not to cry. "Is there any chance you'll change your mind?"

She and I were close friends, and my moving away would be hard on both of us. I shook my head and looked at her, tears edging their way toward my eyelids. "Sorry, but I have to leave. I just can't stay here."

I stood up, signaling the end to the meeting. Everyone closed in around me, and each of them gave me a hug. I'd miss them but I needed to do this for my peace of mind. What I had left, that is. The panic attacks were as frequent as ever. I was going crazy living here.

CHAPTER EIGHT

The farthest east I'd driven on my own was a short trip over the California border to North Lake Tahoe into Nevada one summer when I was a teenager. All other trips were with my parents to visit Nana and Grampa. Traveling had always been a distant dream for me, something I thought Serena and I would do someday when Sofia was a little older.

My parents died in a car accident in my second year of college. Being the only son, I'd looked forward to introducing them to the woman I'd marry. My mom and dad always wanted to be grandparents. Their deaths were unexpected and unnecessary. A drunken sixteen-year-old plowed into their car going sixty-five miles an hour through a stoplight. "They never knew what hit 'em," one officer told me. What a cliché. I missed my parents every day of my life since then.

To my surprise, Francesca and her husband wanted to lease the house. She and Mark had gotten married a year ago and they'd been searching for a house to buy with no luck. Our home was the perfect size for the children they hoped to have, and she tactfully mentioned they were interested in buying it if that became an option in the future.

Packing up Serena's and Sofia's clothes and other personal belongings was a challenge. Wrapping Serena's paintings in special paper along with boxing up her favorite skirts and tops was like a knife to my gut. I had to take a break in the middle of folding Sofia's tiny garments.

Another piece of my heart cracked off, and Fate kicked it into the corner. An internal clock was ticking, urging me to be done with packing my former life as quickly as possible. I gave myself three days in which to complete it. If I put it off or took too many breaks for crying jags, it would never get done. So I put my nose to the grindstone and finished in two days.

Now it was time to say goodbye to my home and Santa Barbara. I grabbed a bite to eat at our favorite Mexican restaurant on State Street, El Caballo, then got in my car and sped down US-101, destination Earlham, Iowa. I wanted to get there as soon as possible and start my new life.

I felt so alone. This wasn't a scenic trip for me. The last thing I wanted to do was visit tourist spots along the way with no one to share them with. The need to plant myself in a new environment and settle down remained my sole focus. I calculated I could reach Earlham in about two to three days if I drove twelve to fourteen hours a day, seventeen hundred and forty-five miles total.

I drove through the night on the first leg of the trip— six hundred and eighty-five miles of long, drawn-out strips of highway, to the border of Utah. By then it was mid-morning the following day, the air already hot and dry. Shimmering heat danced across the hood of the car.

I pulled into a rest stop, parked in the farthest corner under a shady tree, and slept for a few hours in the car. I awoke sweaty and disoriented, but after taking a short stroll around the grassy area, I bought an ice-cold Coke and a bag of peanuts and got back in the car.

July was baking and the A/C in the Mustang stopped working around noon. I felt as if I was inside a crematorium, sitting on the black leather seat with my hands on the ebony steering wheel. But by eight o'clock that evening it had cooled down considerably. I made a quick call to tell my grandparents of my impending arrival, picked up dinner at the drive-thru at McDonald's and got back on the interstate. I had four hundred and fifty-five miles to go before I arrived in Winterset County where the small town of Earlham was located.

I'd never driven so far in such a short amount of time. It was uncomfortable sleeping in my car at rest stops and next to impossible given my height and the size of the Mustang. I'd tilt the driver's seat back and stretch out my legs but I'd wake up every hour to turn over on my side, only to discover that was a futile endeavor.

All my hopes for mental freedom when I backed out of the driveway in Santa Barbara trickled away as the miles on the odometer increased. Remembrances of my wife and daughter clung to my heart like sticky cobwebs, unshakeable in every nook and cranny of my mind. I needed that connection with family and was anxious to see my grandparents.

When I turned right at the mailbox marked 234 Chestnut Avenue, I was more than ready for a home-cooked meal and a soft bed at my grandparents' farm.

Nana was pulling clothespins off a pair of coveralls flapping in the warm evening breeze. I could barely see through the bug-spattered window of the Mustang. But when she turned in my direction, the clothes basket nestled against the apron tied to her generous waistline, and she smiled, impending tears blurred my vision.

Memories of summer visits with my mom and dad flooded my mind. How many times had this scene been repeated: the three of us pulling up to the farm after days of driving, Grandma standing just as she was now at the clothes line or kneeling in the garden pulling weeds. For the first time since Serena and Sofia went missing, I felt I'd come home.

I parked the car next to their bright yellow two-story house. Off to the left stood the red barn where I'd spent countless hours playing knight in shining armor with a pitchfork. A mustard-colored tractor was parked next to the open barn doors.

Caught up in remembrances of times past, I didn't notice Nana standing outside the passenger door until she tapped on the dirty window with her knuckles.

"Jessee, come on outta the car, honey. Supper's ready. We've been waitin' for ya'."

Wisps of gray hair framed her round face, glasses perched half-way down her nose, and her red lipstick appeared to be recently applied. Yes, she'd been waiting for me. It made my heart sing to realize someone was happy to see me.

I dragged myself out of the car and stretched my arms above my head. The cramps in my legs loosened as I walked around the front of the car to give her a big hug. She smelled of Fabergé cologne and my eyes misted at the scent. After twirling her around in my arms, I set her down and she fussed with the bun at the nape of her neck. "I'm too old for that kind of nonsense. I might have a heart attack, for cryin' out loud."

She'd used the same expression for maybe thirty years now, and it touched my heart. "I've missed you, Nana."

She stretched out her arms and grasped onto my shoulders, looking me straight in the eyes. "How're you doin'?"

I looked at her closely, every wrinkle in her face a testimony to a life lived with kindness and caring. "I've been living on the edge. But now I feel like I'm home again."

She brought me in for a hug and patted my back as she would a baby. I needed nurturing at this moment and felt so lucky to have Nana's shoulder to cry on.

I sniffed back the tears and smiled. "What's for dinner?"

She gave me a playful slap on the arm. "Go in and wash up for supper. I'll go find your grampa."

The screen door still creaked as it always had, and I grinned when it slammed into my back side after I crossed the threshold. Some things now rubbed me the right way although back then I complained every day about them.

I followed my nose to the kitchen, the rich scent of fried chicken wafting through the house. Picking up the lid on the frying pan, I breathed in the savory aroma of spices and bacon. One of Nana's secret recipes. Suddenly fingers tweaked the hair at the nape of my neck, and I knew it had to be Nana. I guess it was better than pulling on my ears. I remembered her doing the same thing when I was eight years old.

"Jessee Bradford, put that down right now! Didja wash your face and hands yet?" She gave me a fake withering look, and I grinned back at her.

"I'm going, I'm going." I ran out of the room and took the stairs two at a time up to the second floor.

CHAPTER NINE

The door to my old bedroom was ajar. I stood outside for a few seconds then pressed my palm against the polished dark wood and pushed it open. It looked the same as the last time we'd visited. A single bed sat in the far left corner, three casement windows lined the wall facing the side yard, an antique oak armoire to the right, two posters above the bed, one of Kathy Ireland, the other Cindy Crawford. My grandparents had one grandson, and they'd always made me feel special. They considered this "my" room and it had remained so ever since.

I stood in the middle of the room, my heart in my throat, reliving the old days with my mom and dad here at the farm. Nana's voice shot through my reverie.

"Jessee, supper's on the table," she announced.

I scurried into the bathroom across the hall and washed my hands, scrubbed my face with a wash cloth then ran down the stairs.

"Hey, where's my grandson?" Grampa called out from the kitchen.

I turned the corner as he was drying off his hands at the sink. He hadn't changed much. A little heavier around the waistline, but otherwise he was a sturdy, well-built man, six feet two inches tall, a hundred and ninety pounds. His face looked clean-shaven and his full head of gray hair was streaked with more white than last time I'd seen him. His smile lit up the kitchen, which had grown darker since it was nearing seven o'clock.

Dusk was settling in, and the sounds of crickets could be heard through the open windows. This was exactly how it had been so many times before and I sighed with relief at the sight of both of them standing in the kitchen waiting for me.

"Grampa, you look great." He wrapped me in a big bear hug and I patted him on the back. "Hope I didn't make you wait too long for dinner. You usually eat earlier than this."

He shook his head and put his arm around my shoulders, guiding me to the table. "We woulda waited dinner for you no matter what time you rolled into town. I've been lookin' forward to this day ever since you phoned."

We scooted our chairs in, and I looked around at the feast Nana had prepared: fried chicken, mashed potatoes, fresh green beans from her garden, biscuits from scratch and homemade iced tea. My stomach growled the moment my butt hit the seat, and I stuck my hand out toward the plate of chicken.

"You don't say Grace any more, Jessee?" my grandmother asked, looking at me with one eyebrow crooked upward.

"Sorry, Nana." I folded my hands in front of me in prayer, and waited for Grampa to say Grace.

"Heavenly Father," he began, eyes closed, head bowed toward his empty plate. "Bless this meal Rose has prepared for us today with the bounty from our garden. And bless our grandson, Jessee. Let his time here in Earlham be happy and filled with Your love. Amen."

Nana opened her eyes, grabbed the serving spoon, and filled my plate with more food than I'd ever be able to eat. I could feel a smile unconsciously forming on my lips. How blessed I was to have the two of them in my life, especially now.

"I'm lookin' forward to showin' you around," Grampa managed between bites. "Around the clinic, I mean. Do you wanna relax for a few days, get used to bein' back in Iowa?"

I glanced up from my full plate of food and watched him chew. I grabbed a biscuit and buttered it. "I need to get back to work. The sooner the better. Tomorrow would be great." I paused, both of them studying me. "I'll be okay."

They both remained silent, nodding, though I got the impression they didn't believe me.

"Really," I said.

Nana laid her hand on my forearm and gave it a squeeze. "We know ya' will," she whispered.

Once again my eyes teared up. "I leased the house in Santa Barbara to some friends of mine and put everything else in storage. I'm here to stay." My voice sounded a little shaky and I cleared my throat. "I had to get away from there."

Nana stood up and opened her arms as she came toward me. I

turned toward her and she curled her arms around my shoulders, cradling my head against her waist. "We're so sorry this happened. I don't know what to say 'cept you're welcome to stay here for as long as you want. You can live here in this house if that suits your fancy." She returned to her chair, and I swiped the tears that escaped down my cheeks.

Grampa gave a little cough and straightened his posture. "I'm sure they're doin' everything they can to find 'em."

"I'm sure they are. It's just so frustrating, not knowing where they are or... why she left."

He nodded. "Stay with us, son. We'd love to have you. What you've gone through—" He shook his head and stared out the window into the night. "I can't imagine..."

I stuffed my mouth with a forkful of green beans while trying to get my emotions under control, chewed then swallowed. "Thank you both for welcoming me into your home."

"There will always be a place for you here," Nana said. "We love you."

"Well, eventually I plan to buy a place of my own, but..." I glanced from one to the other, "but right now I need to be with you. You're my family."

"That's settled then," Grampa said. "You're a big boy, used to bein' on your own." He caught Nana's eye and grinned. "We were young once, weren't we Rose?"

She gave him a playful slap on the wrist and stood up to pour us more iced tea. "Don't hardly remember, Harper, and I bet you don't either," she added. She refreshed my glass with tea. "Homemade apple pie and coffee, Jess?"

I leaned back and patted my already too-full stomach. "You know I could never pass up your apple pie, Nana. Sure," I nodded, "bring it on." She furrowed her brows. "I mean, yes, I'd love a piece."

It had been a long day and tomorrow promised to be even longer if I was to accompany Grampa to the clinic. I climbed into bed soon after we finished eating, the cool cotton sheets and soft bed like a soothing balm to my soul. I was looking forward to my new life here in Earlham. And I owed it to my grandparents for making the transition easier than I expected.

CHAPTER TEN

I set the alarm for six a.m. but awoke before it buzzed. The scent of vanilla and frying butter wafted through my half-open bedroom door and I breathed in the aroma in one deep inhalation: Nana's famous French toast! I showered and shaved then dressed in a crisp, white, button-down shirt and khaki slacks along with my black-and-white Vans, strapped my watch to my left wrist and ambled downstairs.

Nana was just turning over one of four pieces of bread in a huge black skillet. When she saw me enter the kitchen she beamed. "Good mornin', hon. Ready for breakfast?"

I kissed her on the cheek and got out three plates and silverware. She'd already placed three mugs for coffee on the kitchen table along with cloth napkins. It was then I realized how much I'd miss this if I moved into my own place.

After I sat down, I glanced out the window that overlooked the front yard. The lawn flowed like a green carpet from below the kitchen window all the way to Chestnut Avenue. Homes in Iowa came with way more land than those in California. You didn't feel as if you were living on top of your next-door neighbor.

Grampa strode in a few minutes later wearing pressed blue jeans and a checkered shirt and well-worn cowboy boots. He kissed Nana on the cheek and sat down across from me. "Mornin', Jessee." He tucked the napkin into the vee at the top of his shirt.

Grasping the handle of the coffee pot in the middle of the table, I poured him a cup. The scent told me this was no Folger's brand from the local grocery store. It rivaled any aroma curling through the air at the Starbuck's back in Santa Barbara. After pouring a cup for Nana and myself, I leaned back and waited for her to place the plate of French toast on the table. When she was seated Grampa said Grace and we all dug in.

"Mmmm," I moaned. "This is delicious." Nana nodded her thanks. "I'm kind of nervous, Grampa." I wiped my mouth with the cloth napkin.

He took a sip of his coffee and sat back in the chair. "You were always diligent and carin' when you were around animals here on the farm. You'll do just fine, son."

When we finished eating, Grampa and I jumped in his white four-wheel drive GMC Sierra truck and headed for the clinic.

Butterflies flitted in my too-full stomach, and I took several deep breaths to calm my nerves. "Think I can handle this? I'm not used to being the only doctor."

"Yup." He didn't elaborate.

His confidence in me was unwarranted since he'd never seen me at work, but I tamped down my jangling nerves and settled in for the short ride. The truck was only a few years old, the drive comfortable and relaxed. After five minutes we reached the center of Earlham proper.

The town's population hovered around fifteen hundred people. A small Chamber of Commerce was located on the left side of Main Street. Next door was Tilly's Five and Dime, then Pauline's Antiques, Shafer's Lights, and at the end of the street, an auto repair shop.

On my side of the street sat Billy's Diner, a barber shop, a pharmacy, and a used clothing store. A sign at the corner pointing to the right read Dr. Harper Bradford, DVM. He turned the truck in that direction. Early twentieth-century, two-story homes lined both sides of the street, all with meticulously groomed lawns edged with flower beds. At the end of the cul-de-sac stood a Victorian house: my new place of employment.

He pulled up, parked at the side of the house, and got out of the truck. I stepped out and looked up at the clinic.

The house's exterior siding was painted dark green with maroon around the double-hung windows and oak front door. The trim along the edges of the roof and porch was off-white, a contrast that made the house stand out against the background of blue summer sky and wispy cirrus clouds.

I would surmise the animals, along with their owners, were more comfortable passing through this clinic's doorway as opposed to the typical sterile veterinary establishments of a big city. It would surely allay the inevitable fear of bringing one's animal friends to visit, no matter the reason.

We stepped through the door into a cozy foyer where an attractive dark-haired woman in her mid-forties sat behind an old-fashioned desk. Her hair fell to her shoulders, pulled up on the sides with tortoise-shell barrettes.

"Kathy Powers, this is Dr. Jessee Bradford, my grandson. I told you he'd be comin' to take over the practice."

Kathy's green eyes lit up, her smile wide and welcoming. She stood and grasped my hand in a firm shake. "Nice to meet you, Dr. Bradford. I've heard all about you from your grandfather. I look forward to working with you."

I flushed at the possibility of Grampa telling her stories of the crazy things I'd done when I was in my teens on visits during the summer. But she appeared so enthusiastic about meeting me that I put my worries aside and grinned back at her.

"Nice to meet you too, Kathy. You'll be a tremendous help. You can guide me through the maze of running this show all by ourselves."

"Don't worry," Grampa interjected. "I'll be just down the road. I'm not goin' anywhere but fishin' and sittin' on my front porch with a good book." He patted me on the back, and I followed him through the swinging door past three examination rooms.

Each room was decorated in country fashion with lace curtains, antique wooden chairs, and oak cupboards where the medical supplies were kept. At the end of the hall was another room that held the patients' files, x-ray machine, and a desk. To the left was the operating room furnished with all the necessary up-to-date medical equipment. I was impressed. This was no backwoods facility. The well-appointed interior of the house exuded a calm, non-hospital atmosphere. I knew right away I'd enjoy working here.

Grampa's office was located on the other side of the O.R. I sat across the desk from him and Kathy brought each of us a cup of coffee. The same rich aroma of the coffee Nana brewed for breakfast wafted through the room.

"This is the only small animal clinic for forty miles. People come here from all 'round Madison County, even though they could drive a little further into Des Moines." He looked at me and squinted.

"I've worked all my life to make this practice what it is today, and I believe I couldn't leave it in better hands."

Reaching across the desk, I stuck out my hand. "I won't disappoint you." He grasped my hand and gave it a firm shake. "You can count on me to uphold the standards of practice your clients deserve. That's how I work, no matter where I'm employed. But I understand this is your life's work, Grampa. And if I have any questions, I'll come running to you."

He nodded and stood. "Agreed. Now, let's get down to business. My first patient's here." He pointed to a green light on the bottom of the phone. "That indicates there's someone waitin' in an exam room. Kathy flips it on right after she finishes with the intake evaluation. You'll know what room the patient's in cause she places the file in the see-through holder located on the outside of the exam room door and tags the file with a number. The number one patient you see first and so on. You get the drill. Pretty basic, but it works."

"Got it."

We walked down the hall to see Patient Number One.

CHAPTER ELEVEN

The clock on the wall chimed six times. I couldn't believe the workday was almost over. It had passed in a blur of ten cats, seven dogs, one King snake, and a hamster. Grampa accompanied me to examine each animal and introduced me to the owner as well as the patient.

Most of them were surprised that Dr. Bradford, Senior, planned to leave the practice in the hands of someone so young. I didn't interject I'd been through vet school and practiced for almost three years at one of the most prestigious vet clinics in Santa Barbara, or that I was going to be twenty-nine years old.

Next to Grampa, who was over eighty, I guess I did look rather youthful. The elderly men and women who expected Grampa to examine their pets needed time to get to know me. For some of them, Grampa had been their vet for decades and change didn't come easily.

Even for our last client of the day.

I opened the door to the examination room. An uproar of deep barking and scrabbling nails on the slick linoleum floor greeted me. Before I knew it, I was lying flat on my back, looking up into the chocolate brown face of the largest Labrador Retriever I'd ever met.

His front paws straddled each side of my upper body and his back legs were spread on each side of my lower torso. Not a dangerous situation, since he was intent on licking my face with a tongue that must have been twelve inches long.

"Brewster, off," a female voice yelled.

I couldn't see anything besides Brewster's gold eyes and deep brown underbelly, noting that he'd been fixed. Labradors weren't known for their aggressive behavior, and Brewster's pushy affection was harmless.

The dog retreated, and I guessed someone had pulled him off my chest. My grampa reached down to give me a hand up, chuckling the entire time. I gave him a dirty look, stood up, and brushed off the front of my pants. That completed, I straightened, rubbed my hands together and looked up to see Brewster's owner standing on the other side of the room.

And our eyes met.

"I am so sorry, doctor." She tried to rein in her pet, whose leash had become wrapped around the bottom of the stool I should be sitting on while conducting my examination.

Grampa patted me on the back. "I'd like to introduce my grandson, Dr. Jessee Bradford. This is Brewster's mom, Laura Driscoll."

Laura was about my age, or maybe a little younger, about five feet seven inches tall, with long black hair that flowed just below her shoulders in a straight glossy sheet. Her eyes locked onto mine and she smiled.

And it seemed as if someone had turned on an extra light in the room.

"It's a pleasure to meet you, Mrs. Driscoll." I reached over the leash to grasp her outstretched hand.

Her pale skin blushed a deep pink as she gave my hand a firm shake. "Just call me Laura." She glanced at my grampa, her lips set in a tight line.

My turn to be embarrassed. I must have committed some sort of social faux pas. When I looked over at my grampa, he shrugged. It was obvious he wasn't going to help me out of this.

I turned my eyes in Brewster's direction. He chewed on the middle of his leash like it was a meat bone. "What brings you here, boy?"

"He's been acting kind of strange, Dr. Bradford." She glanced from me to Grampa then back to me again.

I unhooked the leash from his collar and held the big dog's head between my hands and looked into his eyes. "What do you mean by strange?"

"Well, he's not eating as much as he used to and—" "How long has he been off his food?"

"Um, I'd say a couple of weeks."

I grabbed the stethoscope hanging around my neck and stuck the buds in my ears. "Let's see what we can hear." I knelt down on the floor.

While listening to his heart and lungs my eyes roamed the room. Laura's hair was parted on the side and covered half her face, which had lost its smile. I assumed she was worried about her pet.

She stared at Brewster, who was standing in front of me, his tongue lolling out the side of his mouth. Laura's jet-black eyebrows drew downward, meeting above a straight nose that ended in a modest point above plump lips covered in pink gloss.

"Lungs and heart sound fine."

Grampa stood off to the side to allow me space enough to examine the dog, and I noticed him nodding. I glided my hands up and down the sides of the dog's belly, along his back, down all four legs and paws. Scanning the chart, I noted Kathy had already taken his temperature, which was normal. His shots were up-to-date and he'd been healthy for the first five years of his life.

I stood up and looked over at Laura. "I'd like to draw some blood. Run a few tests. Just to make sure we don't miss anything."

Her face looked paler than when I'd first come in the room, her eyes glassy. "Do whatever you need to, Doctor." She glanced down at Brewster, who by now was licking my hands and sniffing around my feet. Laura frowned.

"I'll get Kathy and have her take Brewster to the back room so she can get a blood sample. You can wait in the lobby. She'll bring him out when she's finished," I told her.

She gave a quick nod then walked out.

Kathy took Brewster to the back room, and I turned to my grampa. "What was that all about?"

Grampa gestured toward his office and I followed him. After shutting the door behind me, he sat at his massive wooden desk in his weathered leather chair and leaned back. "Laura's husband was killed two years ago in Iraq. Brewster was his dog. He's her last real tie with him, if you know what I mean."

I stared out the window overlooking the back lot that abutted an apple orchard owned by the mayor of Earlham, Patrick Morrison, a distant relative of Michael Morrison, a.k.a. John Wayne.

"What a drag. How was he killed?"

He edged forward in his chair and explained in a low voice. "I heard he was with another soldier. It was night time. He stepped on one of those bombs hidden in the ground. His partner made it but..." He ran his hand through his hair and took a deep breath. "Someone told me all they found of Jeff were his identification tags. By the time they were able to sift through the debris the next mornin' they didn't find much else."

I sat back and thought about the horrors of war, the thousands of people killed and maimed while fighting for whatever cause they believed in. "Well, I'm sure Brewster will be fine. I'm running the blood test just to make sure. To get a baseline. He hasn't had one since he was a pup. I'd rather err on the side of caution."

Grampa looked at me over his frameless spectacles. "Hope so. The lab picks up specimens every mornin' at six o'clock if we call them by seven this evening."

I pushed myself out of the chair. "I'll make sure Kathy's phoned them." He shook his head and smirked. "What?"

"Believe me, she's already phoned the lab. No need to worry about Kathy. She's as efficient as the day is long."

"All right. Then I'll tell Laura I'll call her with the results."

He gave me another smug smile. "What did I do this time?"

He shook his head. "It's Monday, so tell her we'll have the results the day after tomorrow." He gestured me out of the room.

When I met Kathy at the front desk, no one was in the waiting room. "Where's Laura Driscoll?"

She gestured with her head toward the front door. "She told me to tell you it was nice to meet you and she'll wait for your call. I explained we'll have the results of the blood test on Wednesday so you'd speak with her then." She paused and chuckled. "She said she had to hurry home and feed Brewster his dinner. He eats promptly at seven."

I glanced out the window toward the front of the house, noticed there were no cars parked outside and wished I'd had the chance to tell her goodbye.

CHAPTER TWELVE

On Wednesday I received the lab results for Brewster, which showed an elevated level of white blood cells. Somewhere in his body he was fighting an infection. But where?

I buzzed Kathy at the front desk, and she picked up right away. "Yes, Dr. Bradford."

I sighed. "Kathy, do you think you could call me Jessee? You don't like being called Mrs. Powers, do you?"

"I don't think of myself as Mrs. Powers. I'm just Kathy."

"And I'm just Jessee. We don't have to be so formal." I paused, knowing she'd never acquiesce to my request to be called by my first name. She was a gem, kind and empathetic and superb with the animals and their owners. But she acted as if a hierarchy existed, and Grampa and I were above her in some way because we held degrees in veterinary medicine. Oh, well. I guess I'd have to get used to her addressing me in the formal manner.

"Anyway, Kathy, could you get Laura Driscoll on the line? I'd like to talk with her about Brewster's lab results."

"Sure, Dr. Brad... uh, I mean, Jessee."

I smiled, shaking my head. In moments she buzzed me and I picked up the line. "Jessee Bradford speaking."

"Hello, Dr. Bradford. This is Laura Driscoll. Kathy told me you have Brewster's lab results."

Her voice wobbled, and I hoped I'd be able to allay some of her fears right away.

"I'm looking at them now. We can rule out cancer and kidney and liver problems, which are the biggies, so don't worry about those."

She let out a big breath. "I'm so glad. Then what's wrong with him?"

"Well, his white cell count is elevated so he's fighting off some kind of infection, but I just don't know what it is. I'd like you to bring him in again so I can look him over, perhaps take an x-ray."

"When could I come in?"

"I'll transfer you back to Kathy, and she can schedule an appointment, okay?"

We said goodbye and I continued with my day. I had a full schedule, and Grampa had left me alone for the first time. He reminded me he lived around the corner and if I needed him for anything he'd be here at a moment's notice.

In truth, I already felt comfortable. Though some people acted a bit leery of the new, younger version of Dr. Bradford, by the end of an appointment, I sensed they took me seriously and could see I knew how to help their pet.

Right after lunch break I pulled the patient folder marked with the number one off the door with a yellow Post-It stuck on the front. It read, "Laura Driscoll has an appointment at 3 p.m. today." Six patients later, I snagged the next folder and noted Brewster's name on the chart.

I gave a little rap on the door and opened it cautiously, peering around the corner. I didn't want a repeat performance of my last entrance. Laura had a tight hold on Brewster's leash while she sat snugly in a chair.

"Hi, Laura," I chirped then bent down to pat Brewster on the head. "How's he doing today?"

"He only ate half his breakfast. What do you think's wrong with him?" The look on her face spelled intense worry, and I instantly wanted to say something to lessen her concern.

I straightened up and opened Brewster's file. "Let me tell you what I'm thinking." Bending down, I opened Brewster's jaws and pointed my pen light into his mouth. I sniffed near his lips. "Is his breath usually this bad?"

She blinked several times and stared at me. "Geez, I don't know. Now that you mention it, when he licks me in the face I've noticed it smells like..."

"Rancid eggs?" I quirked up my brow.

She grinned then covered her lips with her hand. "That's funny. Yeah, it smells pretty bad. Why?"

I took a seat in the chair next to hers. "I'd like to take an x-ray of his skull."

She dropped her hand from her mouth and her lips set in a tight line.

I raised my hand to stall anything she might have said. "He may have an abscessed tooth, which is causing the bad breath and the lack of appetite."

Her shoulders sagged and she sighed. "That doesn't sound too scary." She looked at me with raised eyebrows.

"If my diagnosis is correct, no, it isn't scary. I'd have to sedate him and pull the tooth then put him on antibiotics and he should be just fine in a few days."

Her smile went from one side of her face to the other, and I hoped to God I was right about her dog. I didn't want anyone's pet to be sick, but I didn't want Brewster to have any serious illness after what Grampa told me about Laura's past.

"Why don't you wait in the lobby and we'll take the x-ray. If I'm correct, I'll know right away. Then we can schedule the surgery, okay?"

She handed the leash to me then walked out the door and down the hall to the waiting room. I buzzed Kathy, and she met me in the x-ray room and helped me lift the hundred-pound dog onto the table, holding him steady while I took the x-ray.

"Would you take Brewster while I read the radiograph, Kathy?"

Kathy grabbed the leash, and Brewster dragged her out of the room and down the hall. I clipped the developed film on the board and turned on the backlight. Staring at the black and white image on the screen, I grinned. An abscess was clearly discernible under the left side of his jaw.

"Gotcha," I mumbled under my breath. This would make Brewster's mom very happy.

I buzzed Kathy and told her to have Laura Driscoll come into my office. I'd just taken a seat behind my Grampa's desk when she reached the door.

"Come in. I've got something to show you."

She sat down in the chair in front of my desk, and I pointed at the x-ray with a pencil. "Here's a picture of Brewster's jaw. Here's the lower left side. There's the abscess." I turned toward her. "It's an easy enough surgery to perform, and Brewster should be back to his normal eating habits in no time at all."

I noticed her bottom lip quiver, then a tear dripped off the edge of her jaw. "Thank you so much."

I sat behind my desk and leaned toward her. "I haven't done anything yet, but I'm glad this story will have a happy ending." I pushed the tissue box her way.

She took one and dabbed at her nose. "You must think I'm crazy, crying like this over a... a dog."

I shook my head and sat back in my chair. "I became a vet because I love animals. If anyone can empathize with how you feel about your pet, I hope it's me. I've seen many pets die from unnecessary accidents, cancer, preventable illnesses, you name it. It never gets easier watching their humans have to let them go."

She was still crying. And I was trying to make her feel better? "But Brewster isn't dying, Laura. He'll be good as new as soon as I pull out that tooth and drain the abscess."

Tears flowed down her cheeks and I came around to the other side of the desk and sat in the chair next to her. She looked at me and swiped her cheeks with her hand.

"Brewster has a lot of good years ahead of him," I said.

She nodded and the corners of her mouth turned up a tiny bit, but she still looked sad. "Thank you. It's just... he was my husband's dog and..."

I patted the top of her hand. "My Grampa told me about your husband. I can see why your furry friend means a lot to you."

She turned her palm up and clutched my hand. I was so surprised I glanced down to see whether I'd imagined feeling her grasp. Her nails were painted a subtle shade of pink, and a tiny strip of lighter-colored skin wove around the finger where her wedding band used to be. It had been two years since her husband's death so I surmised she must not have removed the ring until recently.

I squeezed her hand, and our eyes locked. My insides melted at the same time that my heart skipped a beat or two. Just when I noticed I was having a difficult time getting a full breath, she let go of my hand and stood up.

"Thank you again, Dr. Bradford. I'll talk to Kathy and set up an appointment for the surgery."

I pushed back my chair and stood in one quick movement. "I'll see you then," I answered then watched as she turned and headed toward the front of the office, leaving me wondering what had just happened between us.

CHAPTER THIRTEEN

On Friday at three p.m. I sat at my desk eating a sandwich Kathy brought me from Billy's diner down the street: turkey breast with tomato and lettuce on whole wheat bread. The buzzer suddenly made its quirky sound like a dying bee.

"Dr. Bradford, an Agent Caruso is on line two."

My mind did a mental backflip to the past and I tried to swallow the bite I'd just taken out of my sandwich. There were days when I didn't think about Serena and Sofia at all, though I could count them on one hand.

I forced my arm to stretch out, watched my fingers curl around the phone, dreading what I might be told and hoping this might be my first taste of good news.

"Hello, Agent Caruso."

"Dr. Bradford. Two bodies were found In Los Angeles County."

"Oh, my God." Panic coiled like a snake deep in my gut. I had hoped he'd be telling me Serena and Sofia had been found alive.

"There's been some decomposition, but one body is that of a female matching your wife's height with long blonde hair. The other is that of an infant perhaps one year of age though we're not as sure about that. We'd like you to identify the bodies."

"Jesus," I whispered under my breath. "I thought people only did that sort of thing in the movies."

"You're correct. The L.A. County Coroner typically shows only digital photos in order to identify bodies."

"Then why is this situation any different?"

"Well, initially we tried to contact Mr. and Mrs. Middleton since they live in this area but he and his wife are on a yacht in the Caribbean. It would have saved a lot of time and money if we could have shown them a picture."

"Can't you just send me a photograph then?" It suddenly hit me. "Why wasn't I the first person notified?"

A long pause ensued, then the agent cleared his throat. "If we were strictly following normal protocol I would have contacted you first, Dr. Bradford. But in this case, uh..."

"What's going on, Agent Caruso?"

"Let's just say that when pressure is applied at a certain level of bureaucracy, protocol changes to accommodate the family members of the dead person."

I let out a totally fake laugh. "You mean Serena's parents pressured the higher-ups to notify them first?"

"That, yes. And also, uh, they want the bodies identified upfront and personal. No digital photos, if you get my drift."

"Oh, so that's where I come in to play, right? Otherwise Serena's parents would have been the ones to identify the bodies. But because they're out of the country you were allowed to contact me." I shook my head. "Well, that is rich, Agent Caruso. Unbelievable."

"We've booked you on the red-eye tonight from Des Moines to Los Angeles. You could return tomorrow, be back at work the next day."

It took me a few seconds to switch my world to a new schedule, but I had to do this. I wanted to do it. "E-mail me the information, would you?"

"Certainly. And I'll be there to pick you up at LAX."

I hung up the phone and reached across the desk to touch the picture of Serena and Sofia with my fingertips. Not knowing what had happened to them was worse than knowing, no matter how awful the truth, so I tried to prepare myself for what was ahead of me.

After buzzing Kathy, I waited for her to come to my office. She sat down across from me, notepad and pen in hand, waiting for my instructions.

"I just talked to Agent Caruso, the FBI agent heading up the investigation into my wife and daughter's disappearance."

She nodded. "I remember you told me the story your first day here with your grandfather. Any news?"

"I'm flying out tonight to L.A. I'll be back tomorrow around five p.m. I'll ask Grampa to cover for me, but I wanted to tell you what was going on." I paused and tried to control my voice as I told her about the two bodies that had been found and the possibility they were my wife and daughter as well as the need to personally identify the bodies.

Kathy covered her mouth with her hand and her eyes glistened. "Oh, my goodness," she whispered.

I closed my eyes for a few seconds and took a deep breath. When I opened them she leaned over and patted my hand. "I'm sure this waiting has been hell for you, Doctor, but I hope it's not them. For your sake as well as your wife and daughter's. Your grandfather and I will take care of your patients. That's the least of your worries."

"Thanks, Kathy. I appreciate your help." I stood up and pushed back my chair. "I better get out of here and talk to my grampa. I think we're done for the day anyway."

She looked at her copy of the daily schedule. "Yes, you're finished. Mrs. Kempster cancelled her four o'clock appointment."

"Could you print out the itinerary Agent Caruso e-mailed to me?"

Moments later, print-out in hand, I walked to my car and sat inside for several minutes, perusing the flight plan. It would take me thirty minutes to get to the Des Moines International Airport and my flight left at eight p.m. I had plenty of time to eat dinner and pack.

When I pulled my car up to the side of house at the farm I suddenly felt mentally exhausted, dreading what I might have to do: identify two dead bodies. I mean, what kind of whacko would want to harm a woman and her child? The possibility they might be Serena and Sofia made me sick to my stomach.

I'd never been to a morgue and, though accustomed to seeing disease, injury, and even death of animals, I'd never seen a decomposing human body, and certainly not people I loved in such a state. What if the coroner pulled aside the sheet as they do on the television, and I had to look down into the rotting face of my little girl?

I dragged myself through the front door and found Nana and Grampa in the kitchen preparing dinner. Nana peeled the potatoes, and Grampa was snapping the ends off a pile of green beans. The tasty scent of chicken roasting in the oven would normally make my stomach growl. Though Nana was fixing another of my favorite dinners, I honestly didn't think I could eat a bite.

"What're you doin' home so early?" she asked.

I gave her a quick peck on the cheek and sat across from Grampa at the kitchen table. "I have to fly to L.A. tonight."

They turned toward me, two sets of eyebrows raised in question.

"I got a call from the FBI agent in charge of the investigation into Serena and Sofia's disappearance. I have to identify two bodies found in the L.A. area."

Grampa stopped snapping green beans in mid-air. Nana blinked several times, her mouth hung half-open. She came over and sat next to me, putting her arm around my shoulders.

"You don't have to do this alone." She looked pointedly at Grampa. "Harper? You could go with him."

He nodded. "You bet. If you need me, I'll fly with you to Los Angeles."

Tears came to my eyes. They were the best grandparents anyone could have. I shook my head.

"Thank you but no. I'd appreciate your covering for me at the clinic, though. I should be back by tomorrow night." I paused, working through my thoughts about this ordeal. "I can do this by myself."

"Are you sure?" Nana asked. "You're just tryin' to be brave. And you don't have to prove anything to us. How many people would do somethin' like this all alone, honey?" She paused and looked at Grampa then at me. "Can't they just send you a picture, Jess?"

I explained the story about Mr. and Mrs. Middleton's influence in a few quick sentences then pushed my chair back. " So there ya' go." I stood up. "I'll be fine. Really. But thanks for offering to go with me, Grampa. But what I really need is to know my patients will be taken care of while I'm away. That would mean a lot to me. Now, I've gotta pack. I have time to grab a small bite before I leave though."

Nana walked over to the sink. "Be at the table in twenty minutes. Gotta keep your strength up. Travelin' at all hours of the night can be stressful on your immune system."

I walked up the stairs to put a change of clothes in a carryall. Fifteen minutes later I was back in the kitchen saying Grace with two of the most unselfish, loving people I'd ever had the fortune to know.

CHAPTER FOURTEEN

The flight to L.A. took five hours with a layover in Denver and because of the time change, my flight arrived at 11:15 p.m. Pacific time. Agent Caruso paced outside the terminal, a cigarette dangling from his lips.

"Dr. Bradford." He thrust out his hand toward me.

I grasped it and gave him a solid handshake. "Call me Jessee." He nodded. "You sure work some late hours."

He shook his head. "I'm not officially on the job at the moment. Buy you a drink?"

I shook my head.

"Tee-totaler?" he asked.

"No, just tired. Alcohol puts me to sleep, and I want a clear head."

"I can drive you to the morgue right now and get it over with."

It sounded to me like more of a suggestion than a question but I agreed with him. "I assumed we'd go early tomorrow morning, but yeah. I'd like to have this over and done with as soon as possible. I won't be able to sleep either way."

"Ah." His eyebrows slowly raised. "Never seen a dead body before?"

"Human? No. And as much as I want closure, I hope to God it's not them." Fear reeled me in like a fish on a line, and I wished I could be back in Iowa, safe and sound in my bed on the farm.

He dropped the cigarette to the ground and stubbed it out with his shoe. "Ready?"

We hurried across the street, dodging the heavy traffic of travelers in shiny new SUVs, old beaters and more than a few limousines, and ducked inside one of the many parking garages. His recent model Crown Victoria was comfortable and air-conditioned. In August, Los Angeles weather could be hot even at this late hour.

We passed through block after block of hotels, strip malls and office buildings before the scenery changed to run-down houses. Twenty-five minutes later, we pulled into an underground parking facility at Los Angeles County Morgue.

My sweaty hand slipped off the door handle when I tried to get out, and I wiped my palm on the side of my pants and tried again. I heaved myself out of the passenger side. I was so afraid my small family would be gone forever. The dread in my gut churned like something alive.

"Sorry you have to go through this." He patted me once on the back.

I nodded and trudged along beside him. He pressed the elevator button. The doors opened with a ping. We stepped inside, and the light flickered on the ceiling, matching the quickened beat of my heart.

He pressed "B" for Basement. Within moments the doors opened again. The dimly lit hallway stretched for several hundred feet. We stopped at a set of double metal doors at the end of the hall marked "Employees Only" in red letters plastered across their shiny silver exterior.

Caruso turned to me and nodded, pushed the right door with his hand and let me enter ahead of him. The smell accosted me right away, my nose filling with a nauseating odor of Pine Sol mixed with what smelled like bleach with an extra dash of something unidentifiably revolting.

I covered the bottom half of my face with my hand and took a breath through my mouth while I followed him through another set of double doors into a room the size of half a football field. It was freezing, and I already wanted to step back outside into the muggy night air.

Out of the corner of my eye I noticed someone stepped through a door to our right. Caruso stopped and turned toward him. "Dr. Carson," the agent said.

They shook hands.

Caruso turned toward me. "This is Dr. Bradford, the gentleman I talked to you about this morning."

The doctor was dressed in blue hospital scrubs, a white mask dangling from his neck. We shook hands and he hurried off toward the left side of the room, lined with square metal doors that looked like mini-refrigerators, each with a silver handle. He stopped half-way down the length of the wall and turned toward me.

I pursed my lips together as tightly as I could and nodded. Dr. Carson pulled the handle toward him, and the door clicked open. As he slid the heavy-duty gleaming tray out of the dark hole, I stared at the opposite wall, just wanting this over as quickly as possible.

His voice was almost a whisper. "Dr. Bradford?"

I squeezed my eyes shut then reopened them and looked down. Even though the skin covering the woman's face was partially gone in places, it was obvious this wasn't Serena. I let out a whoosh of breath and shook my head. "It's not her," I croaked.

He slid the body back into the gaping hole in the wall and I followed him a few feet further down to the next door.

In my heart I already knew this body wouldn't be Sofia. Weren't the chances of my daughter being found with a stranger remote? I was ready this time. When I glanced down at the tiny figure lying on the silver slab I shook my head again, turned away and walked out the double doors, through to the next double doors and waited for the FBI agent to join me.

Within seconds Caruso pushed the door open, and we retraced our steps to the elevators. I didn't speak. Neither did he. I hoped never to repeat this experience, though I knew I might have to, no matter how wretched it made me feel.

We returned to the parking lot. He backed out of the space and stopped the car for a second. "I booked you in the Motel 6 by the airport. I'll pick you up tomorrow morning at nine so you can make your flight." He pulled forward and zipped up the lot's sharp incline.

I nodded though he couldn't have seen me. My throat had squeezed shut. I wasn't sure what my voice would sound like if I spoke. I heard him, but couldn't answer.

"I hope you don't have to experience this kind of thing again, but I can't promise you won't have to." He took a quick look in my direction. "You all right?"

I cleared my throat and opened my mouth, shut it, then opened it again. "I'll be fine," I answered, not sure whether I was telling the truth.

I just wanted to get back on the plane and return home, knowing

I wouldn't be able to sleep that night. Or the next one. Wondering where my wife and child were had become a constant in my life, a niggling, hurtful twitch in my soul that ached to be put to rest.

The only thing I could do would be to put distance between me and California and my memories of Serena and Sofia. They still haunted me, though mostly at night in my dreams. A part of me wished that, if they were dead, they'd be found soon. Another part of me yearned to be told they were still alive.

CHAPTER FIFTEEN

I dozed off several times while lying on the lumpy mattress watching television, glancing at the bedside clock every few minutes, waiting for the bright green digital numbers to reach 8:00 a.m.

I showered, dressed in clean clothes, and watched the news until Agent Caruso arrived. The trip to the airport took only a few minutes. We shook hands and I thanked him for everything he'd done and was still doing for the investigation.

I fell asleep on the return flight and awakened just as we touched down in Des Moines a little after 5:00 p.m. At six o'clock I turned into the driveway leading to the farm. Ravenous from having only eaten the small breakfast served on the flight, I couldn't wait to taste whatever Nana was serving for dinner.

She was in her usual place at this time of day—standing at the kitchen counter. This time she was peeling sweet potatoes. She turned when she heard my shoes on the hardwood floor.

"Oh, Jessee." She sounded as if she might cry, dropped the peeler and rushed over to hug me, then pulled back to look in my face, her eyebrows lifted.

I shook my head and gave her a half-smile. "It wasn't them."

She hugged me again and I breathed in the light scent of the Fabergé perfume that was so Nana. She gestured toward the kitchen table. "Sit down. Supper will be ready soon." She pulled a pitcher of iced tea out of the fridge, poured me a glass and set a napkin next to it.

I let out a deep breath. "I'm so glad it wasn't Serena and Sofia. I hope I never have to do that again."

She pulled out a chair and sat across from me, hands folded on top of the table. "What do you really think happened to them?"

I looked into the bottom of my glass of tea and thought for a few seconds. "From the beginning Agent Caruso said it looked like Serena just up and left. Simply walked out. Her purse was sitting right on the counter with money, her credit cards and cell phone. She could have hitchhiked to God knows where, changed her name, be working for cash." I took a deep breath and met Nana's gaze. "I left Santa Barbara because I believe she deserted me. And that hurt me, bad. I was so devastated and missed them so much, I was having panic attacks all the time and felt sick every single day."

I shook my head back and forth. That old expression, "The truth hurts", glared at me like a neon sign inside my head. "She makes me so furious. I feel so cheated and devastated, angry, frustrated. Sometimes I want to just punch a hole in the wall with my fist."

"But why would she do that? If she didn't want to be married, she could have gotten a divorce."

"I know, right? But then her father would have been royally ticked off. We got married after Serena received most of her inheritance early, before her father died, and she insisted we commingle our assets. She felt that was what married couples were supposed to do. Her father was furious. He wanted me to sign a pre-nup and Serena refused. California's a fifty-fifty state and she's worth millions. But I didn't marry her for her money." I shook my head, trying to figure out a logical reason behind Serena's actions. "Even though I believe she left me, if they're never found I might have to continue identifying dead bodies for the rest of my life." I noticed I'd raised my voice. "I'm sorry. I'm just venting."

She patted my forearm, and the look on her face showed how much she empathized with me.

Leaning back in my chair, I gazed out the window at the front yard. The end of August, and the grass turned browner every day. Nana turned on the sprinklers every night, but the temperature in late summer could reach over one hundred degrees, and keeping it green was near impossible.

"Jessee?"

I looked at her. "Sorry. My mind's all muddled today. I didn't sleep much last night."

She stood up and laid a hand on my shoulder. "Why don't you go freshen up? Take a little nap if you want. Supper won't be ready for another thirty minutes."

I grabbed my glass of iced tea and dragged my body up the stairs. More mind weary than physically tired, a nice cool shower sounded perfect. Seeing dead bodies could do that to a person. After languishing in the shower for a half hour, I felt awake and refreshed.

When I entered the kitchen, Grampa was already seated at his place across from mine. Nana always sat at the head of the table for easy access to the stove and refrigerator.

"Rose told me about your trip. I'm happy it wasn't your wife and child."

I pulled out my chair and sat down. "Me, too. How'd it go at the clinic today?"

"No problems. I enjoyed being back."

"Oh, Harper," Nana scolded him. "You've been retired for almost what, a month now? And you're already complainin' that you miss your work."

He chuckled under his breath. "Won't deny it. I love bein' around the animals. And the people, too." He gave the table a small tap with his hand. "I almost forgot. Kathy wanted me to tell you Brewster's surgery's scheduled for Monday of next week."

"Laura's dog?" Nana asked me.

"He has an abscess under one of his lower teeth," I explained. "I'll have to extract it. He hadn't been eating much so she brought him in to see me. Or, I should say, Grampa. She didn't know Grampa was retiring."

"Isn't she the sweetest thing?" Nana scooped more carrots out of the dish and onto her plate.

"Well, I don't know." I shrugged. "She seems like a nice enough young woman."

She served Grampa more sweet potatoes then handed him the plate of butter. "She has a great personality. And Brewster's a lovely dog."

I frowned. "Sounds to me like you're trying to hook the two of us up." I stared across the table at my grampa, who finally looked up from his avid knife and fork endeavors.

He shook his head. "No," he said, and continued chewing.

I looked at Nana then back at Grampa. "I'm still a married man."

"Of course you are." Nana glanced at me for a few seconds. "Oh, Jessee, I'm sorry, I didn't..." She set down her fork and knife and pinched the bridge of her nose with her fingers. "You spend all your free time with us, honey. On the weekends you help me with my chores and such. You never go out with any young people your age." She paused. "I just want you to have fun. Life isn't all about work. And you look so depressed sometimes." She paused again. "It might help take your mind off everything."

I stared at the sweet potatoes on my plate. They were the color of one of Serena's paintings of a Santa Barbara sunset. "I never imagined a future without Serena and Sofia."

"I know." She patted my arm. "But it would be good for you to have some fun with a friend whether that person is a boy or a girl."

"Rose," Grampa interrupted. "He's not a boy, for Heaven's sake."

Nana worked her mouth into a tight line. "Harper, you know darn well what I mean."

He nodded and ducked his head.

Nana continued. "You remember your old friend David Squire? He still lives in Earlham. You could give him a call sometime."

I moved my head up and down in agreement.

She frowned. "Is it because you're livin' here? I don't want you to feel you have to keep us company night and day."

This time I was the one intent on maneuvering a small pile of potatoes onto my fork. "Of course not. I like living here. It's just... it's complicated. I have to talk to an attorney. I've just been putting it off, I guess. I don't know what to do."

Nana cocked her head to the side and frowned. "Don't know what to do about what?"

"Well, if they can't prove Serena's dead, should I..." I inhaled deeply and plunged on. "I feel guilty even saying it, but should I divorce her? Am I even allowed to divorce her?" I chewed and tried to swallow past the lump in my throat. "They went missing January fifteenth. When is it okay for me to move on with my life?" I glanced at the calendar hanging on the wall. "Geez. It's almost September already. I guess I'll see an attorney to find out what my rights are." I shrugged. "I don't know. I'm not sure what to do."

Nana grasped my hand and held it tightly. "You'll figure it out. We just want you to be happy. Go out and have some fun. Just so you know, we won't feel like you're desertin' us if you go out once in a while, kick up your heels."

Grampa looked up from his dinner plate and his eyes twinkled. "You might consider callin' up a few of your old chums, perhaps make some new friends, go out to the movies or bowling or somethin'." He nodded at Nana. "Rose and I can get along just fine on our own, ya' know."

I took a deep breath and let it out nice and slow. "Maybe you're right." I pushed back my chair and looked at the two of them. "So... I won't have to ask your permission to go out after dark or anything like that, will I?" I said, trying to look serious.

Nana stared at me, eyes wide.

I tried not to smile but I could feel the edges of my mouth quirk up.

She slapped my arm. "Oh, go on now. You're pullin' my leg."

I chuckled. "I love living with you guys." I suppressed a yawn and stood up, my legs wobbly. "Would you excuse me? I'm really tired."

In truth, I needed to sleep away the memories of last night's ordeal, still clinging to my brain like flypaper. I shivered walking up the stairs to my bedroom. Silver handles on body drawers. Corpses covered in white sheets. The images kept popping up in my head. I dreaded ever hearing Agent Caruso's voice on the telephone again.

Serena and Sofia, where are you? How could you do this to me, Serena?

* * * *

I looked forward to returning to work on Monday morning. I had a full roster of patients to examine that day and missed being around my four-legged friends. When perusing the appointment book I realized I'd forgotten today was Brewster's surgery.

A little before two o'clock I took a short break at my desk and was sipping a cold Pepsi when Kathy buzzed me. "Laura Driscoll is here with Brewster, Dr. Bradford. Do you want her to wait in the lobby while you're in surgery?"

"Sure. I won't be long. Is everything set up?"

"Of course. I'll call the exchange and have them take our calls, then I'll bring Brewster back."

The surgery took thirty minutes. I was able to extract the tooth, clean out the abscess, and Brewster was awake and wiggling around within twenty minutes, though a bit wobbly on his feet. Kathy returned to the front desk and sent Laura back to the examination room where I was holding Brewster's leash with both hands.

When he saw her enter the room he leapt up and placed both paws on her stomach and licked her face, whining like a puppy. It was as if he'd been away for days.

"I think he loves you," I commented, laughing.

"Ya' think?" She took both his paws in her hands and set them on the floor. She knelt down and took Brewster's face in her hands and kissed him on each side of his jowls. "The feeling's mutual, believe me."

"The surgery was uneventful. I extracted the tooth, cleaned out the abscess. Make sure he finishes this bottle of antibiotics." I handed it to her. "The medicine will make sure a secondary infection doesn't occur after surgery." I held up the leash. "He's good to go. I'd like to do a recheck in a couple of weeks. You can make the appointment with Kathy."

Her smile was like a beam of light, her skin like that of a porcelain doll in striking contrast to her jet black hair, which shone like a sheet of polished marble under the fluorescent lights of the examination room. She'd highlighted her full lips with light pink lipstick. When she reached out her arm to take the leash out of my hand, the white blouse she wore stretched against the front of her chest, revealing full breasts hidden under a lacy bra. I blinked several times to get my mind back on track.

"Thank you again for taking such good care of Brewster. You don't know how much it means to me, Dr. Bradford."

I nodded, grasped the door knob, then turned toward her. "Do you think you could call me Jessee? Dr. Bradford sounds rather formal since we're about the same age."

She ducked her head, fiddling with Brewster's collar, then looked up at me. "I guess that would be only fair between peers."

I grinned and opened the door. "Remember to finish all the antibiotics," I said over my shoulder on the way out.

Even though I had a patient waiting, I returned to my office and sat down at my desk.

Laura Driscoll was a very attractive woman. I had to admit I wanted to get to know her better. My eyes wandered to the picture of Serena in a frame in the upper corner of my desk. I would always love Serena. But most of the time I felt so betrayed by her leaving, anger roiled in my gut like poison. But what if I was wrong and they'd been kidnapped? Should I remain alone for the rest of my life? And what if they were never found?

I gave myself an emotional shake. Grampa and Nana were right. I needed to have some fun, get out and live again.

Going out with Laura might be exactly what I needed to alleviate my depression.

CHAPTER SIXTEEN

Labor Day was a big event in Earlham. Residents hailed their parade as the biggest and best of all others in Madison County. Thousands of people showed up for the local marching bands and antique cars. Horses pulled carriages from one end of Main Street, down John Wayne Drive, past the tiny courthouse and local park, then back around and down Main Street again.

A band played music from the Beatles era as well as Country and Western. Everyone gathered around the central gazebo to hear the Mayor talk about what a safe place Earlham was to live. And the day always ended with a small fireworks display. People sat on the grass on blankets, some brought picnic baskets, others bought food and drinks at the various food stands located along the perimeter of the park.

Nana, Grampa and I were relaxing, sitting on the grass on one of Nana's handmade quilts, when I was assaulted by a wet nose pressing against my neck. I fell back onto the blanket and put my hands up in front of me to ward off any more of Brewster's doggie kisses.

"Brewster, get over here!" Laura lunged for his leash, missing it by inches. She stumbled and skidded to a halt on her knees in front of where we were sitting.

I grabbed Brewster's collar and forced him to lie down next to me, then looked over at her. "Having fun yet?"

The porcelain skin of her face and neck suffused with red, and I could tell she was embarrassed.

"I'm so sorry." She stood up and looked down at her white capri pants, now streaked with grass stains.

Nana smiled. "That's okay, Laura. Sit down and join us, dear."

Laura glanced at me then back at Nana.

"Yes," I agreed, moving over so she could sit down. "Brewster's already snagged his place. Why don't you join him?" I patted the blanket on the other side of her dog.

"Don't be shy. Sit down with us," Grampa urged.

Laura made an attempt to brush off the pieces of grass stuck to her pants, then sat down and grabbed Brewster's leash. "Thank you." She straightened her dog's collar in what looked like an attempt not to face the rest of us. Or was it just me?

"So, how's Brewster's appetite?" I asked, petting the dog on the head then letting him lick my hand.

Laura rubbed Brewster's back from his neck to his bottom and back with an affection I'd seen often in my career, and it made my heart clench.

"He's eating more than ever. But I don't want him to gain weight so I've cut back on the doggie treats, like bones and YipYaps. Now I'm giving him raw carrots and apples for a snack."

"Good idea." I glanced at my grandparents.

They looked like bookends, sitting next to each other with identical smiles on their faces.

"Why don't you two stroll over to the gazebo? They're playin' your type of music." Nana gestured toward us with her hands as if shooing us away. "Go enjoy yourself."

I glanced at Laura, and our eyes locked. I raised my eyebrows at her and she shrugged. I stood up and took hold of Brewster's leash while she pushed herself up off the blanket.

We headed toward the gazebo across the huge expanse of lawn, wending our way around various blankets and picnic baskets. Brewster tried to sniff every open basket he passed, and I kept him close to my side by holding his leash next to my thigh.

"I wasn't aware you knew my grandparents so well."

Laura waved at someone I didn't recognize before turning her attention to me. "Your grandfather knew my husband since he was a little boy. Jeff and I were high school sweethearts, so I've known Rose and Harper most of my life, too."

I shook my head and chuckled.

"What's so funny?" she asked, frowning.

"I'm not making fun of you. I'm just not used to living in a small town. People really do know each other around here. There's a real sense of community. I like that."

She smiled, and my heart sped up for a few seconds before reverting to its normal rhythm.

"Where did you live before coming here?" she asked.

"I'm surprised you don't already know." I raised an eyebrow and she slapped me lightly on the arm.

Brewster let out a loud bark, and I looked down at him. "What's wrong, boy?" I bent down and looked into his eyes.

"He hates it whenever there's any type of hitting or slapping or screaming. It's the oddest thing."

"How did you find that out?"

We reached the crowd in front of the gazebo where the band was playing. We stopped at the edge to watch as couples danced and swirled to the music. They were playing "A Hard Day's Night", one of my favorite songs.

"Jeff figured it out when Brewster was a pup. One day he was fooling around with one of his buddies. They fell on the floor, wrestling. Brewster went maniac, barking like a mad dog until they stopped. And whenever Jeff tickled me and I'd laugh and tell him to stop, Brewster would do the same thing."

I noticed her eyes glaze over and guessed she was reliving memories.

"I'm sorry about his death. That must have been awful."

She blinked several times as if she'd just woken up. "Yeah. He stepped on an IED."

"Improvised Explosive Device?"

"They told me he never knew what happened. He was killed instantly."

"War is a terrible thing," I murmured, shaking my head.

"It is. That's one of the few things Jeff and I disagreed on."

"You don't think we should be fighting a war in Iraq?"

"It goes deeper than that. I think people in the twenty-first century shouldn't have to resort to killing each other to have peace in the world."

"I agree with you. However, you're speaking as a person who has the privilege of living in the United States. The Iraqi people don't have it so good."

She turned her body to face me.

I could tell this was a subject close to her heart.

"So you believe our men and women in the armed forces should be over there, getting killed and maimed every day?" she said.

"War, politics, and religion are three subjects I never talk about on a first date."

"This isn't a date." She looked me straight in the eyes, unblinking. "So, answer the question."

"I wasn't referring to us exactly. But now that you mention it, could I take you out to dinner some evening?" The words flowed out of my mouth without my mind knowing it. But it felt right. I liked her.

"Are you asking me out on a date?"

I nodded.

"Okay, I'll go out with you. But given that we're not on a date right now, would you answer the question?"

I laughed out loud and she smiled.

"All right. I think war is horrible. Young men and women dying in Iraq is something I can't begin to relate to. But talking about peace often gets nowhere. Sometimes there's nothing left to do but strong-arm your way into these countries in order to accomplish what needs to happen."

"So the end justifies the means?"

I shrugged. "Sometimes. When it comes to human rights that need to be fought for, I believe it is. Talking about it didn't get anywhere."

"You sound like Jeff." She looked amused.

"Knowing how you felt about him, I think I would have liked him."

She turned back toward the gazebo, and we listened to the music. Brewster lay across our four feet, comfortable in his people-sitting job.

"He likes you."

She'd interrupted my thoughts, and I hadn't a clue who she was referring to. "Who likes me?"

She pointed down at the lab, his tongue lolling out the side of his mouth. "Brewster. It usually takes him a while to do this."

"Do you always listen to his opinion about the men you go out with?"

Her face sagged. Her smile disappeared. "I haven't been on a date since Jeff died."

I could have kicked myself in the butt. Talk about putting your foot in your mouth. "I'm sorry. I didn't mean—"

She raised her hand, palm outward. "Don't apologize. It was an innocent question."

"I'd be flattered if you'd go out with me then, Laura." Her name tripped off my tongue, and I got goose bumps when her eyes met mine.

She ducked her head, then looked up at me. "It never felt right before now."

"This feels right to me, too," I said, my gaze unwavering.

Time stood still, so cliché, but fitting in this instance. Our stare was broken when Brewster stood up and yelped.

"What is it, boy?" She bent down and took hold of his face.

I pointed to a couple of young kids wrestling on the ground near us. "That translates into violence in Brewster's world."

Laura grabbed his leash and held it with both hands.

"Can I walk you home, or were you going to stay for a while?" I said.

She shook her head. "I'm about ready to go. You?"

"I have to work tomorrow. I ate too much today. A walk will do me good."

We took our time wandering through the crowd. We walked side by side out of the park, down Main Street for two blocks then turned right on Oakhurst Lane. Half-way down the block she stopped in front of a pale green Craftsman-style house. A wooden sign with "Driscoll" carved on the front hung above the dark oak door.

"Are you free this Friday night?"

She bent down and stroked Brewster's back, looking up at me. "Where are we going?"

"Des Moines is only thirty minutes from Earlham. I thought maybe dinner?"

"Dinner would be nice." She straightened to her full height.

"Interested in doing anything afterward or would you like to play it by ear?"

The waning sunlight filtered through the trees overhead, and I noted once again how beautiful her skin looked, fair and translucent.

"Let's play it by ear. It feels weird to be doing this in the first place."

I put up both of my hands and backed up a few steps. "Absolutely. No pressure. I don't want to make you uncomfortable."

She turned toward her house. "See you Friday then."

"Around 6:30?"

She looked over her shoulder. "We'll be waiting."

Did she say "we"?

CHAPTER SEVENTEEN

I had several surgeries that week, which made the hours sweep by until Friday night. Grampa and Nana were understated in their response to my going out with Laura, but they both liked her and had known her since she was a young kid. They assured me I'd have a lovely time, then didn't say much more.

I didn't have a lot of experience dating women. There were only a few before Serena, and we'd been together a little over four years. Then they disappeared almost eight months ago, so I figured it would soon be five years since I'd been a single guy.

To join the ranks of the unattached felt weird. I planned to get out and have a good time, as my grandparents suggested. Truth be told, it was impossible to put a date on when it would be socially acceptable to begin dating after your wife had left or was taken. No Miss Manners book had been written to guide me through this. I was totally winging it, trying to do what was best for me given my life's circumstances.

Talking to an attorney was the only way to go forward if I wanted to begin divorce proceedings and sell the house in order to move ahead emotionally. It wasn't fair to Laura if I remained legally married to someone else, either. I didn't care what others might think, but I did care how it might make Laura feel.

But it seemed a bit premature, this talk of divorce proceedings. If my wife and child were taken, that is. But what if they hadn't been taken? My head spun.

Truth be told, Nana told me to listen to my heart and going out with Laura felt right. And I concurred with Agent Caruso and Detective Rodriquez. Serena most likely left me. No evidence pointed to the contrary.

But should I believe the FBI and the cops and my attorney?

My mind reeled with everything I'd heard from the authorities since the dreaded day they disappeared. However, the way I figured, it wouldn't do any harm to at least look into it. After gathering all the information, I'd make my decision then.

Friday turned out to be a whirlwind of emergencies. A dog had run in front of a car and been hit. The injuries weren't life threatening, mostly just cuts and bruises. But the episode interrupted the entire day's schedule and I missed lunch.

Then someone brought in their pregnant cat who delivered seven kittens in the early afternoon. Kathy volunteered to stay later than usual to make sure they were stable and planned to come back in the evening to check on them.

With the patient load I was carrying, it might be advisable to hire an assistant. The practice could afford the financial outlay for an additional salary, but I didn't relish advertising for the position and the requisite interviews.

I ran out of the office at six o'clock with just enough time to shower, shave, and dress before driving the few blocks to Laura's house. Not sure if it was considered good manners to bring a gift, I compromised and picked a bouquet of Nana's pink and yellow roses. After pulling up in front of Laura's house I grabbed them off the passenger seat.

I felt like a teenager as I walked up the path to her front door, carrying my bouquet of homegrown roses. My hair was still wet from the shower. I'd worn chinos and a blue button-down shirt with no tie and penny loafers. I hadn't selected a restaurant since I planned on looking them up on the internet that day, but I'd never found the time. The best laid plans and all that.

I raked my hands through my wet hair and cleared my throat before pressing the doorbell. Laura couldn't have been far from the foyer because she opened the door right away.

"Hi," she said, looking shy.

She wore a pink scoop-neck blouse with a short white skirt that reached the middle of her thighs. Her legs went on forever and, with her white high heels, she looked as if she were six feet tall.

"Hi." I thrust the flowers in her direction. She took them with both hands, pressed her face near the half-open buds and took a deep breath.

"These are my favorites. Did you ask Rose, I mean, your grandmother what flowers I liked?"

I shook my head. "No. The colors reminded me of you, so I picked them."

"Well, they're perfect. Come in." She gestured toward the front room. "I'll find a vase then we can be on our way."

She held the door open and I slipped past her and walked to the front room, which had been furnished in antiques. It reminded me of my grandparents' house, comfortable and homey, with a couch in front of the fireplace.

I sat down and waited, looking around. Framed photos graced the mantle, and I walked over to get a better look.

A wedding picture of Laura and Jeff took center stage— the perfect couple. She was smiling and gorgeous, her black hair in striking contrast to the white wedding gown. Jeff was a good-looking guy with dark hair and a mustache. He must have worked out with weights, the jacket of his suit straining against his chest muscles. I wondered what he'd done for a living before he went into the service.

"Ready to go?"

I jumped. She'd caught me off-guard, and I turned to see her placing the vase of flowers on the table behind the couch. I walked away from the fireplace and caught up with her in the foyer as she pet Brewster.

"The other night you said "we'll be waiting". Will Brewster be our chaperone for the evening?"

She laughed out loud and grabbed her purse off the side table near the door. "No, just a slip of the tongue." She bent down and kissed her dog on the top of his brown head. "Brewster's my best friend but I don't think I need a chaperone. I trust you. You come with an automatic stamp of approval from Rose and Harper."

We walked to the Mustang, and I opened the car door for her, then came around to my side and hopped in.

"I haven't seen such chivalry since... since ever."

I looked at her and tilted my head. "Maybe I'm a little old-school when it comes to how I treat women. I don't do it because I think you can't. It's more of a respect thing. My dad taught me by example."

"Where do your parents live?"

I started the engine and drove toward Main Street on my way to the freeway to Des Moines. "My parents died in a car accident in my second year at U.C."

"I'm so sorry."

"Yeah. I still miss them. Every day. What about you? Your parents live around here?"

"They moved to Des Moines a few years ago. I grew up in the house on Oakhurst. I wanted to stay in Earlham so they decided not to sell it. When Jeff and I got married it really helped that we didn't have to buy a home of our own."

I glanced at her. "Why'd they move to Des Moines?"

"Daddy's a banker. He was offered a vice-president position at the B of A. Mom wanted to make a go of her painting. They're in their fifties and neither of them is ready to retire."

I shot a look her way. "Your mom paints?" She nodded. "How would you describe her style? I mean, what kind of medium does she use?"

"She uses oil paints and she loves pastel colors. And she hates it when I tell her that her work is better than Monet's. Do you paint?"

A beat or two of silence passed before I answered. "Not exactly. I mean, no I don't paint. I…"

"Are you hiding something?" she teased. "Like you're a closet artist but haven't shown your work yet?" She laughed.

I wasn't ready to talk about my past, and I shook my head. "I don't have time for a hobby. My life is full enough with the clinic and helping out Nana and Grampa on the farm. What about you? Do you have a hobby?" I turned my head and found her staring out her side window.

"I ride," she said.

I laughed and she turned her head in my direction. Our eyes met. "You ride motorcycles, souped-up cars, what?" I asked and turned my gaze back to the road. The freeway to Des Moines was crowded on a Friday night and I had to concentrate on driving.

"Horses," she answered. "You probably didn't notice but my place is pretty big. There's a huge pasture out back with a stables and a covered arena."

"I took a semester in large animal physiology but decided to specialize in the smaller critters. What type of horse do you own?"

"A Friesian. He was a present from Jeff on our first anniversary."

When I glanced at her she was once again staring out her side window. Maybe she was feeling a little guilty about going out with me. I guessed we both had our particular reasons for feeling uncomfortable tonight.

I took the exit for downtown Des Moines and realized I didn't know where we were headed. "Oh, man." I slapped my forehead. "I forgot to ask if you had a favorite place where you'd like to eat. I meant to do a Google search today at work but it got so busy that I—"

"Don't worry about it. Do you like pizza, Mexican, or…"

"Italian. That is, if you'd like it too."

She pointed with her finger toward the front window. "Turn left on Fourth Street up here. There's a place called Gambino's. They serve the best vegetarian pizza in the world."

"So you don't eat meat?"

"Not since I was a teenager."

"And why's that?"

"I did a complete one-eighty when I was in high school. Living in a rural place like Earlham, in the state of Iowa, I had my fill of cows and pigs and chickens being slaughtered for their owners' dinners." She placed her hand on my forearm and continued. "Don't worry. I'm not going to get on a soap box about it or anything. It's just... I don't think it's necessary to kill animals in order for our species to survive. It's a totally personal choice."

I noticed when she removed her hand from my arm. It had felt so warm. I took a quick look in her direction. Her face had a serious mien and I was glad when I saw the glowing sign for Gambino's Ristorante.

Laura was such a solemn person but, once again, I surmised it involved the feelings about her husband's death only two short years ago. If I was her first date since he'd passed away, perhaps she was just now beginning to heal and would soon learn to smile and laugh again.

After parking down the street from the restaurant, we waited in the foyer for an available table. We didn't have to wait long. From the looks of the groups waiting in the lounge and outside on the front patio, larger parties were more typical here.

The hostess sat us at a table in the back in front of a window facing a huge backyard. Lace curtains were pulled back to reveal a tall fountain with cascading water and paths running in various directions through a large grassy area.

"Is that just for looks or could we actually take a walk after dinner?" I asked.

She stared out the window while she answered. "Mr. and Mrs. Gambino are friends of Daddy's. They love it when people take advantage of the grounds. Their children run the restaurant these days, but I still see Mr. and Mrs. Gambino sometimes when my parents and I come here to eat."

The waiter brought us menus and we perused them in comfortable silence. There were so many items listed, it was difficult to choose. "Any suggestions?" I asked after looking up and down the list of entrees for the third time.

She looked at me over the top of her menu and smiled. Her lip gloss glistened in the light of the candle at the side of our table. "I've been dreaming of their pizza. We could share a small one and you could order some Pasta di Gambino as a side dish. You'll love it."

I put my menu down and nodded. "Sounds good to me." The waiter strode up to our table the minute we put our menus aside. We ordered, and he brought two Cokes and a small plate of crusty bread with olive oil for dipping.

Laura pulled off a piece and tapped it in the oil then took a bite. "Mmmmm." She paused and chewed. "You dodged my question, you know. Back in the car."

I crooked up one eyebrow.

"When I asked if you painted, you said "not exactly". It was a pretty straightforward question, but you changed the subject and said you didn't have time for a hobby."

I leaned back in my chair and looked at her. She deserved to know the truth if she and I were planning to see each other more than once. And I had a gut feeling we'd go out again. I found her fascinating. She was a woman with an interesting past: a husband who'd been killed in Iraq, parents who lived nearby, she rode horses, she loved animals, she was intelligent, well-spoken, beautiful, sexy. My mind wandered.

"Jessee?"

I turned my attention back to her and realized I hadn't given her an answer. "I haven't told you everything about me. But could I ask you a question first?" She nodded. "Do you work? It never came up and I'm curious."

She grinned. "Yes, I work."

The waiter arrived with our meals, and we were temporarily interrupted while he set down a metal plate with steaming pizza slices arranged on it, dripping with cheese, then he laid a dish of Pasta di Gambino in front of me.

We busied ourselves for a few minutes arranging food on our plates. She took a bite of pizza and rolled her eyes. "This is heavenly," she crooned.

I took a forkful of pesto and swallowed. "Man, you were right. This tastes like... something I've never tasted before. Do they make their own pasta?"

She nodded and took another bite of pizza. "I teesh hawses." She tried to get the words out around the pizza in her mouth.

I laughed out loud. "Pardon me if I didn't catch that."

She wiped her lips with a napkin and chuckled, making a production of swallowing before she continued. "You asked me if I worked, remember? I said I teach horses. I'd say I break horses but that's not my style, though that's how people often refer to my work." She wiped off her fingers and looked at me. "I train horses that haven't been worked under saddle. They call them green horses. People bring me their colts, or their supposedly problem horses, and I teach them. The horses I mean. I teach them how to get along with humans... in a humane way."

My eyes widened, and I knew my mouth was hanging half-open. "But you look—"

"I know," she interjected. "I look so feminine." She made quotation marks with her fingers. "But I do have a shower and a bathtub, for goodness' sake. And I make my own schedule. Sometimes I don't have any horses at my barn. Then I have a lot of free time."

I must have been staring at her because she pulled back with a frown. "What is it? Did I say something wrong?"

"You are one of the most... I don't know how to say it." She tilted her head and our eyes locked. "You're the most interesting woman I've ever met."

She gave me a withering look and picked up her slice of pizza again. "No, I'm not."

"I won't argue with you about it, but I find you fascinating."

A deep shade of pink crept up her neck into her high cheekbones. She was so beautiful, it took my breath away. I watched as she dipped her head and the black curtain of her hair shaded her face.

"I'm sorry if I embarrassed you. That wasn't my intention." I paused. "You asked me why I diverted the conversation away from myself when we were talking about hobbies."

She looked at me and nodded up and down, very slowly, looking fearful, as if expecting me to reveal I was an ex-con or something.

"I was married. I mean, I am married."

Her eyes widened, and she put her palms on the table and was halfway out of her chair when I grasped her hand.

"No, it's not what you think," I pleaded. "Please let me explain."

She sat back down. "You have five minutes to explain. Then I'm out of here." She set her napkin on the table and sat back in her chair, arms folded over her chest.

"You asked me if I was a closet artist." She gave me a quick nod.

"My wife is the one who's an artist. Not me. She and my daughter went missing eight months ago. No one knows what happened to them or where they are."

She covered her mouth with both her hands. "Oh, my God. I'm so sorry."

"Me, too. I moved here to take over my grampa's practice because I had to get away from all the memories back home where we lived. In Santa Barbara."

"I had no idea. I thought you were going to tell me some story about—"

"About how I intended to ask my wife for a divorce as soon as I got home and gave her a call?" I teased, taking another bite of pasta.

"Uh, yeah, something like that."

"A gigolo I'm not, believe me. I'm a straight-up kinda guy. I'd never do that."

"But you are still married."

I swiped at my mouth with a napkin then laid it in my lap. "I have to find an attorney, see what my rights are, whether I can get a divorce or what. I just haven't done it yet." I shrugged. "I've been busy getting up to speed at the clinic."

"What a terrible ordeal to have to go through." She paused. "The Mayor is an attorney. He practices law on the side. Being mayor doesn't take up a whole lot of his time."

I nodded and brought another forkful of pasta to my mouth. "I'll have to call his office. Thank you for the referral."

She pushed her plate to the side. "I'm stuffed."

I patted my stomach and leaned back in the chair. "Me, too. Would you like to take that walk now?"

I paid for our dinners, and we went out into the backyard. It was a warm night, and we strolled along the pathway that weaved around the trees and flower beds dotting the grassy area. When we came back around we veered toward the front parking lot and I opened the car door for her before walking around to my side.

"I had a nice time tonight," she said after I pulled out into traffic.

I didn't want to push her so I didn't ask if she wanted to see a movie or anything. This was her first date since her husband had been killed. And my first date since Serena and Sofia went missing.

"Would you like to do it again?" I asked, the hope obvious in my tone. "I mean, go out on a date?"

She laid her hand on top of mine for a nanosecond. "I'd love to, Jessee Bradford."

My heart stopped for a second before it wiggled up my throat.

The first day I met Serena she'd called me by my first name as well.

CHAPTER EIGHTEEN

The following week Laura scheduled Brewster for a follow-up exam. When I pulled his chart off the door to the examination room, he cried and sniffed at the bottom of the door while I stood outside looking through the file.

I opened the door while perusing my notes. "Well, hello, one hundred pounds of hound." I grinned down at him.

Laura pulled on the leash dangling from Brewster's collar and reeled him in.

"Hi," she said while patting him on his smooth brown head.

His golden eyes watched my every step. I bent down to look in his mouth with my penlight. "How's he doing? Eating enough? Sleeping all day? What's his exercise level been? No lethargy? Does he come when you call him? Any behavioral change? Did you finish the course of antibiotics?"

I felt nervous and was talking too much. When I realized I wasn't giving her time to answer each question, I sat back on my heels and looked up at her.

Brows bent inward, she stared at me as if I were crazy.

"I'm sorry." I chuckled. "I guess I'm just nervous being around you now."

"Why?" She looked confused.

"I don't know." I shrugged. "Maybe because I've never dated a patient before."

She laughed and shook her head. "I'm not your patient. Brewster is. I just bring him in and pay the bills. Though I'm sure he'd love to go out with you if you asked him."

She grinned mischievously, which put me at ease. I stood up and leaned back against the door, giving myself some space so I could think straight. "I really like you. And I want to go out with you again.

It's sort of awkward because you'll be coming in here with Brewster and if things don't work out..."

She walked over and stood in front of me. Brewster lay across both of our feet as he'd done at the Labor Day party. That way neither of us could move without pushing him out of the way. And I swear, he knew it.

"We've both had what I'd call pretty traumatic events happen in our lives, Jess. Yours is more recent than mine, that's all. I think we're both testing the waters. It's going to be a little awkward for many reasons. Maybe I'll have to switch vets if it doesn't work out." She shrugged then touched my hand with her fingertips. "But I have a good feeling about you and I don't think it would be a good idea to—"

"It wouldn't be a good idea to continue seeing each other?" I looked in her eyes and my heart dropped.

"That's not what I was going to say."

My shoulders sagged and I let out a sigh of relief.

"I was going to say, I don't think it would be a good idea to discontinue seeing each other just because you're Brewster's veterinarian. In this instance, I'd like to put myself first, not my dog. I had such a good time when we went out the other night. I don't want to end it."

I hesitantly took her hand in mine but didn't hold it tight in case she wanted to pull away. She didn't. "I feel the same way. I'd like to get to know you better. Like I said, I find you fascinating, intriguing, interesting—"

"Stop it, will you?" She glanced at the floor.

I touched my index finger under her chin and lifted her head so she'd have to look me in the eyes. "It's true. And I'm not going to feel guilty for saying it."

"And I'm not going to feel guilty for wanting to see you again. And maybe again after that. I like you, Jessee. A lot. You're smart and you understand me and you love animals and you're kind and... you're Rose and Harper's grandson. That's enough for me."

She smiled, and I wanted to kiss her so bad. But I knew that was premature and inappropriate. I finished up the examination and walked her out to the lobby where two patients were hiding under their owners' chairs, looking as though they hoped no one would find them.

"Can I call you?" I whispered, knowing Kathy could hear every word. But in a town this size it was stupid to think we could hide our budding relationship. I didn't mind anyway. The Earlham residents' interest in each other was genuine, not meant as fodder for the gossip mill, but engendered by true concern and caring.

She met my eyes, nodded and smiled as Brewster dragged her out the door and down the steps to her car. I watched as she drove away and wondered, not for the first time, what it would be like to kiss her pink-glossed lips.

That night after dinner, Grampa, Nana and I were sitting around the kitchen table having coffee. I'd been sharing with them my experiences during the first month at the clinic, the surgeries I'd performed, the various animals I'd examined and their diagnoses.

"What about retirement, Grampa? Are you enjoying it as much as you thought you would?"

He pushed back his chair and stretched his legs out in front of him. "You know, I'm not sure I'm the type of man who's meant to be retired. Seems all I've done is trade small animal care for larger. I used to examine dogs and cats and rabbits. Now I look after our goat, who has an infected hoof. And occasionally a neighbor's cow or horse." He shrugged. "I went into small animal medicine for a reason. The ones on a farm are too darn big!" He laughed out loud.

I looked at him seriously. "If you want to take back your practice, I'd understand completely. Maybe I could be your assistant. Or better yet, I could set up a practice somewhere near here but not in Earlham."

"Harper," Nana interrupted, slapping him on the wrist none too lightly. "Don't be givin' that boy any crazy ideas about you comin' back to take up where you left off. You should be ashamed of yourself, makin' him feel guilty for movin' all the way out here from California to help you out. And now you're complainin' about the little amount of work you have on the farm? That's just nonsense."

She stood and picked up our dirty plates, brought them to the sink, and turned around to face Grampa. "You've had to look at a couple of animals here and there that weren't doin' too well. Otherwise you've been sittin' in the porch swing, dozin' away, sippin' lemonade and eatin' homemade cookies." She turned her gaze in my direction. "Don't take anything he says seriously. He doesn't know what he's sayin'."

I glanced at Grampa. He winced and rubbed the middle of his chest.

"What's wrong, Grampa?"

He shook his head and stood up from the table. "Nothin'. A bit of indigestion is all. Sometimes the acid in the coffee gives me heartburn. I'm awful tired. Think I'll watch Wheel of Fortune." He ambled out of the kitchen into the living room, and I could hear his lounge chair creak as he raised the leg rest.

"Is he okay?" I asked Nana, frowning.

She patted my shoulder. "When you get to be our age, heartburn is the least of our concerns. Now why don't you go in with your Grampa and watch television. I'll clean up in here then join you in a little while."

I loved this part of the day—dinner and coffee with my grandparents, then sitting on the couch watching a little TV with them. Nana would put on her reading glasses and crochet, glancing up every now and then to see what letters were missing on the Wheel of Fortune board. Grampa often fell asleep in his chair toward the end of the program and invariably missed the winner's answer to the final question.

Living here felt like family and reminded me of the days I was in high school and my mom and dad and I watched TV after dinner. I was lucky to be able to experience that closeness again here on the farm. At times it made me sad and I'd catch myself regretting all the fun times I might have had with Mom and Dad if they hadn't been killed. But I'm a glass-half-full kinda guy. I thanked God I had my parents for as long as I did.

And what fantastic surrogate parents Nana and Grampa were. It was obvious they cared about me and my future, and it warmed my heart to know they were still alive and very much a part of my life. It wouldn't have been the same if they hadn't welcomed me here with open arms. My panic attacks had ceased completely. I loved working at Bradford Vet Clinic. And I'd met Laura and Brewster. Life was pretty darn good.

CHAPTER NINETEEN

The next day I woke at my usual six a.m. I went for a quick run, maybe twenty or thirty minutes, down Chestnut to Main Street, around the park two or three times, up the stairs to the gazebo like Rocky Balboa, where I did stretches and toe-touching exercises, then back around past Oakhurst Lane to see if Laura's car was parked out in front. I don't know why I bothered. At six-fifteen in the morning her Yukon always sat in her driveway. I'd usually return around six-thirty, take a shower, and head down for breakfast by seven.

When I reached the kitchen door Nana was flipping pancakes on a cast-iron skillet. She glanced up. "Would you please go upstairs and wake your grampa? He was supposed to be outta the shower and down here by now. He has to take a look at one of the goats. Her teat's swollen, and she hasn't been givin' much milk the last few days."

The scent of pancakes frying smelled heavenly. In California, breakfast consisted of yogurt and a banana. Since moving here I'd taken up running every day instead of every other day because I didn't want to gain weight.

I kissed her on the cheek. "Sure. Be right back." I took the stairs two at a time and walked down the hall toward their bedroom. The door stood ajar and I pushed it open. Grampa was still asleep on his side, facing the window.

I shook his shoulder gently. "Grampa, wake up. Breakfast is ready, and you don't wanna make Nana mad."

He didn't move so I pressed on his shoulder to turn him toward me. "Grampa," I whispered and waited. "Grampa," I said again, louder.

His eyes were wide open and he had a smile on his face. But he wasn't awake.

My head filled with the same ringing I felt after leaving a loud concert. I closed my eyes for just a second, held my breath and extended my arm toward Grampa's neck. My hand was shaking so badly, I clenched and opened my fist several times to steady my fingers then placed the tips against his neck.

No heartbeat. I leaned my ear next to his mouth. He wasn't breathing. When I pulled back the covers and tried to move his legs, they were stiff and cold. Rigor mortis had already set in.

My Grampa was dead. And had been for at least several hours.

I collapsed to my knees next to the bed, laid my head on his chest, closed my eyes and wept quiet tears that turned into sobs. I'd lost a huge piece of my family, the connection to my past, to my parents, to my present, as well as my future.

I took a deep shuddering breath between tears and suddenly felt a presence. I turned my head and saw Nana standing at the foot of the bed, both hands covering her mouth, tears running over her fingers. She knew.

I stood up and took her in my arms. For the first time in my life my grandmother looked fragile. Nana is a sturdy five-foot six-inch woman of German stock. No pansy, she. But right now she would collapse on the floor if I didn't find a chair for her to sit in.

I turned her away from the bed and set her gently in one of the easy chairs next to the window overlooking the apple tree in the side yard. Then I placed a crocheted blanket over her knees.

"You better call Doc Carmichael," she said.

I knelt down in front of her and took her hands in mine. "I'll do that right away. Can I get you something? Do you want to go downstairs?"

She shook her head and looked me straight in the eyes. "I'll stay right here until Doc arrives. I don't want Harper to be alone."

Hearing her words made my heart ache. My grandparents had been together for fifty years. This farm was my grampa's, passed down from his father's father, and maybe further back. And I believed it would have been my dad's except for his untimely death. Now it belonged to Nana. And I wondered if she could take care of it all by herself.

I walked downstairs to the kitchen to call Doc Carmichael. I figured his phone number would be written in the address book Nana kept in the drawer under the phone. Sure enough, he was listed and when I heard it ringing I took a deep breath before he answered.

"Dr. Carmichael, this is Jessee Bradford, Harper's—"

"Good morning, Jessee. I remember you from when you'd visit Rose and Harper in the summer. How are you?"

I let out a breath. "My grampa passed away in his sleep. Do you think you could come over?" I said the words without crying and relief washed over me. Maybe I could make it through a portion of this day without hiding in my bedroom to sob.

"Be right there." He hung up.

In less than five minutes a light knock sounded on the front door and there stood Doc Carmichael. I barely recognized him. It had been years since I'd been here with my parents, and people age differently. He looked to be about eighty years old, almost completely bald except for little tufts of white hair above his ears. I wordlessly opened the door to let him pass ahead of me and followed him up the stairs.

When he reached the door to my grandparents' bedroom, his pace slowed and I heard a deep intake of breath. I bet he was close to my grandparents, living as long as they all had in the same small town. This had to be hard for him.

He walked over to where Grampa lay on his back and took out a stethoscope and placed it on Grampa's chest, listening intently for several minutes. Then he turned and walked to where Nana was still seated, hands clasped on top of the blanket covering her lap.

"He's gone, Rose." He kissed the top of her head and patted her shoulder. "I have to call the coroner's office in Des Moines. It'll take at least thirty minutes for them to get here. I'll be downstairs if you need me."

We both slipped silently out of the room, and he followed me to the kitchen. I poured each of us a cup of coffee, making sure the burners were turned off under the griddle. A plate of pancakes sat in the middle of the kitchen table, and I moved them to the sideboard before placing the doctor's cup on the table.

He made a quick phone call then took a seat. He stared into his coffee cup for a few minutes before breaking the heavy silence between us. "Harper was one of my best friends."

"He was like a father to me." I coughed to cover up the quiver in my voice. "When my mom and dad were killed in a car accident several years ago, I was so glad I had Nana and Grampa. They called me once a week when I lived in the dorms at U.C., and Nana sent me care packages. Then they welcomed me here when Grampa wanted to retire and I started working at the clinic." I swiped at the threatening tears with the back of my hand.

"Harper told me when your parents were killed. Terrible thing to happen."

The jangling of the phone assaulted the quiet of the morning. I grasped the remote on the countertop.

"Dr. Bradford?" It was Kathy.

"This is Jessee, Kathy."

"Are you sick? You have surgery in a few minutes."

I'd forgotten about my eight o'clock appointment. I pinched the bridge of my nose with my fingers. "Could you please reschedule all of today's appointments? There's been a family emergency."

"Can I help in any way?"

"No, thank you. Uh, Kathy, if you could keep this conversation confidential between us until I call you back, I'd appreciate it."

"Of course, Dr. Bradford."

"My grampa passed away during the night." I heard her intake of breath. "Doc Carmichael and I are waiting for the coroner to arrive from Des Moines. Kathy? Are you still there?"

"Yes." Her voice sounded choked, as if she was already crying.

"I know how close you were to my grampa," I continued. "I'm just trying to make it through this one day at a time. Will you be okay at the office alone?"

She cleared her throat. "Of course, Dr. Bradford." Her voice suddenly got much stronger. "I'll cancel all of your appointments for the remainder of the week and reschedule them. Does that sound like a good idea?"

I couldn't think straight, couldn't remember what day it was, and didn't care about going into the clinic anyway. My heart had been torn out of my chest, and all I wanted to do was go to bed and wake up to find that all of this had been a nightmare.

"Dr. Bradford?"

"Uh, yes, whatever you decide. I'll call you later when I know more." I placed the phone back in the handset and noticed Doc Carmichael had stepped outside.

I walked upstairs to check on Nana and found her exactly where we'd left her, eyes closed, hands folded in a prayer-like fashion, lips moving silently.

I knelt in front of her and took her hands in mine. She opened her eyes, and the corners of her mouth quirked up a bit in a smile. "Jessee," she whispered. "Your grampa's in Heaven now. I can't be completely sad about that. I just hope he and I can be together soon."

I shook my head and looked into her watery blue eyes. "No, Nana. I know Grampa is in Heaven but I don't want you to go. I need you. I love you." I could hear the pleading in my voice and didn't want to make her feel guilty for wanting to join her husband in the afterlife. But I couldn't bear to imagine another loss in my already dwindling family. Nana was the only person I had left now.

I laid my head in her lap, and she stroked my hair. The tears flowed and I couldn't stop them, didn't want to stop them. It was as if all the sorrow stored up since my parents' deaths, Serena and Sofia's disappearance, and now Grampa's death came tumbling down, overwhelming me.

Then I heard a familiar tune and realized Nana was singing under her breath. I recognized the melody from my childhood. "Hush little baby, don't say a word. Nana's gonna buy you a mockingbird. If that mockingbird don't sing, Nana's gonna buy you a diamond ring."

The words were like whispers from her soul, a balm for my aching heart. I picked up my head and looked into her face. She smiled down at me.

"I never knew you felt that way, Jess. Thank you for tellin' me. I love you, too." She wiped an errant tear from my face with one of her embroidered hankies. "Don't worry, love. I'm not goin' anywhere any time soon."

I stood up. She took my hand, and we walked down the stairs. She patted Doc Carmichael on the shoulder as we passed him in the foyer where he was talking with the coroner. Nana and I went into the kitchen.

"I can fix you some breakfast." She grasped the knob under the burner.

"No thanks. I couldn't eat."

She nodded and her mouth pinched together while she put the plates back in the cupboard and wiped off the counter. I sat down at the kitchen table and stared out the window, wondering when this diminishing of my family would stop. Realizing I was feeling a bit too sorry for myself, I stood up, poured myself another cup of coffee and brought it back to the table.

Nana joined me after drying the dishes and patted my hand. "I need to phone Pastor Morris and make plans for people to come over the house after the service."

I turned my palm up and held her hand. "You don't have to do that today."

She nodded and squeezed my hand. "I know that. But I have to do somethin'. I can't just sit here."

"I can call people if you want. Anything to take the burden off your shoulders."

"No," she shook her head. "I have to do it. Your grandfather had a lotta friends. They would expect me to tell 'em myself."

"Okay. What can I do then?"

"Check on the goat's hoof? Collect the eggs the hens have laid?"

I stood up and smiled down at her, patting her on the shoulder. "This will bring back memories from when I was a kid."

She nodded, though I wasn't sure it was in response to what I just said. She stared out the kitchen window at the lawn or the trees or the blue October sky. I wasn't sure. But I sensed she was thinking about Grampa. And wishing she could be with him.

CHAPTER TWENTY

Grampa's funeral was scheduled for Saturday. Word spread within hours of Nana calling friends on the phone. Grampa had been a veterinarian in Earlham for more than forty-five years, so it wasn't surprising that the small church was overflowing with people wanting to say their last goodbyes.

Friends poured through the front door, bearing an unbelievable array of homemade cookies and cakes spread over the kitchen table and counters, along with coffee and alcohol. Grampa liked to have a small glass of good whiskey on occasion. In honor of him I had my first sip. My eyes began to water, and my throat felt as if I'd swallowed gasoline. I finished drinking the small tumbler, thought of Grampa then had to laugh.

"What's so funny?"

I knew it was Laura before I turned around. She stood behind me with a small plate of cookies in one hand and a cup of coffee in the other. When she put her food down and hugged me, my heart lightened for the first time since Grampa died.

"I was just thinking about Grampa. He loved to have a shot of good whiskey on special occasions. I just tried a sip and thought I'd been poisoned." I cleared my throat. "I drank a lot of beer in college but never graduated to the hard stuff."

She patted me on the back and smiled. It was the first time I noticed one of her front teeth slightly overlapped the one next to it. All the words of consolation throughout the day meant to comfort me paled in comparison to the contour of her lips drawn up in a smile.

"I loved your grandfather." She laid her hand on my forearm. "He was one of the kindest people I've ever met."

I nodded. It had been a draining week, accompanying Nana while she talked to the funeral director and the coroner, then keeping by her side while my grandparents' friends stopped by.

"Rose said he died peacefully in his sleep. That's a blessing, Jessee."

I gestured toward the back of the house, and she followed me out to the yard. Several tables were set up under the overhang, and I pulled out a chair for her and sat down.

"The coroner said he died of a heart attack." I shrugged. "He had no history of heart problems. I'm just glad he didn't have to suffer from some lingering disease."

She took a sip of coffee and pushed her plate of cookies in my direction. I selected one of Nana's double chocolate chips and took a bite.

"Sometimes I think about death," she said. "You know, like what type of death I wouldn't want. Cancer scares the crap out of me." She pressed her hand over her mouth. "Excuse my language." Tracing her fingertip around the rim of her coffee cup, she continued. "When I think about how Jeff died... I don't know. It must have been so frightening for him. In the middle of Iraq, surrounded by people he didn't know who wanted to kill him. I wish I'd had a chance to say goodbye."

Talking about him was still difficult for her. Her eyes were the exact same golden color as Brewster's and looked just as sad as his when he'd stare up at me, begging for attention.

"What is it, Jessee? You're looking at me rather strangely. Did I say something wrong?"

Her face was a mask of concern, and I shook my head. "No, it's nothing you said. I was just watching you talk about Jeff. You still miss him a great deal."

Her gaze shifted in the direction of the barn and she looked lost in thought, not answering for several minutes. "The last time he and I talked was on Christmas Day. He was allowed one phone call. Five minutes. And we spent it arguing over whether he'd re-up for another two years." She paused, her eyes glistening in the diminishing daylight.

"I'm sure he died knowing you loved him, Laura. Isn't that the most important thing?"

A tear escaped down her cheek and fell from her chin. "I insisted he come back home so we could start a family." She shook her head from side to side. "Well, he came home all right. They lowered an empty casket into the ground. There was nothing left of him to bury." She swiped at her eyes with her fingertips.

"I know what it's like to lose your spouse." I reached out and took her hand. "The pain, the nightmares, wishing they were still here with you."

Our eyes settled into a fixed stare. Her pupils dilated. My heart thumped in my chest.

Her grasp lightened, and I opened my fingers to let go of her hand. She looked away and sighed. "You're still married. Your wife and child may still be alive."

"I have an appointment with the mayor next week." I paused, not sure how much was too much to say right now, not wanting to scare her away by being too honest. "I'd like to spend more time with you. But if you'd be more comfortable waiting until I'm a…" Here I used air quotes. "…free man, I'll understand."

She looked in my eyes and tilted her head a little to the side. "I don't want to wait. I've enjoyed the time we've spent together. You're a sweet, kind man. I like you a lot." Her eyes shifted to her lap and the white skin of her face slowly colored with a pink blush. "But my heart's still healing. I don't want to get hurt."

I placed my hand on top of hers and held it firmly until she raised her eyes. "I'd never hurt you. I promise." I smiled and she smiled back. "Would you like to go out to dinner again or see a movie?"

"How about I make you dinner? Then you can see my house."

"And your horse," I added.

"Well, that goes without saying. He'll know you're there anyway. Horses sense things that people often miss."

"I look forward to making his acquaintance." I grinned. "Next Friday at six-thirty?"

"It's a date."

I stood up, took her plate and empty cup. "It's getting a bit chilly out here."

"I have to go."

I raised my eyebrows.

"I've been gone for hours and I have to feed Maximus his dinner."

"Maximus? Who's…" I realized she must be talking about her horse. "Is that what you named him?"

"Maximus Decimus Meridius," she answered. "From the movie Gladiator, right?"

She nodded.

We walked around the side of the house to the front yard, and I opened her car door. "I'll come by at six-thirty on Friday?"

"I look forward to it." She slid into the driver's seat, started the engine, and rolled down the window.

"See you then," I said as I backed away from the car and watched her maneuver around the many vehicles parked along the street, toward Chestnut Avenue.

I missed her already.

CHAPTER TWENTY-ONE

By the middle of the week I was getting back into the "work groove". My mind wasn't as cluttered with memories of my grampa's death. Actually, I found it easier to accept his death than to accept losing Serena and Sofia. Grampa was gone forever but I wasn't convinced my wife and daughter were dead.

Not knowing was definitely the harder of the two to live with. Since they went missing I had prayed for closure, but as the months passed it became more and more like an elusive dream.

The plan had always been to move into my own place but my heart said I should remain on the farm with Nana to help her get through this tough time. Treading lightly around the subject wouldn't work with her. She could always read my thoughts before they came out of my mouth. So, I approached her directly during dinner several days after the funeral.

I'd just eaten my last forkful of spaghetti and was wiping my mouth with a napkin when Nana poured another glass of iced tea and looked at me, one eyebrow cocked upward.

"What's wrong?" I asked, seeing that "look" on her face—the one she always used when I was young and had done something wrong.

"Nothin's wrong, Jess, but I get the feeling somethin's weighin' heavy on your mind. You make that... that lip, for lack of a better word."

I looked up at the ceiling and laughed out loud. "I don't make a "lip", as you call it."

"The way you move your mouth and..." She pointed at my face. "You get this look. I can't describe it, but I know I'm right."

"I swear you're psychic. Thanks for the iced tea."

She settled in her chair, hands in her lap, and waited.

"Remember I told you I'd find my own place once I got settled?" She nodded.

"Now that you won't have help from Grampa, I... well, I don't want to move out right now. I mean, if that's okay with you. If you'd prefer to live alone, I can look around for a place but—"

"Jessee," she interrupted. "Of course I'd love for you to stay, but I really don't need any help. Harper was gone sometimes ten hours a day when he was at the clinic, so I'm used to takin' care of the details on the farm. And you're young. You don't wanna live with an old lady. Aren't you and Laura seein' each other?"

I nodded.

"Well, wouldn't you like to take her to your own place, have dinner or talk or whatever young people do these days, without worryin' about whether I'll walk in on you two in my robe with night cream smeared all over my wrinkled face?"

I leaned back in my chair, grinning. Since moving here Nana and I saw each other for breakfast and at dinner if I got home in time. The house was so big it wasn't as if we were running into each other all the time. I understood, though, that she might think she'd annoy someone as young as I.

But I saw my grandmother in a different way. I could talk to her about anything. I respected her feedback. After all these years she had intimate knowledge about the clinic, knew how to run this small farm on her own, and she was family. And, hey, I wasn't some twenty-year-old swingin' bachelor. If my relationship with Laura reached the point where we wanted to spend intimate time alone, we could always go to her house. Plus, Nana's husband of some fifty-plus years just passed away. I knew she missed him something fierce and no matter what, she'd get a little lonely. If I could do something to help her out during this initial grieving period, I was determined to try.

"Nana, haven't we been living together now for several months?"

She nodded.

"Would you rather live alone? Tell me the truth now. You get a look on your face when you're trying hard not to hurt someone's feelings."

She took a sip of tea and patted her lips with a napkin. Nana was a warm, understanding person but she could also be direct.

"I'll be honest with you, like I always am." She took hold of my hand and looked at me. "You're my grandson and I love you like my own son, like I loved your father when he was alive. And I've enjoyed havin' you here. But I don't want you stayin' here out of pity for me, because you feel sorry for your old grandma, and you think I'll be depressed livin' here by myself, that in some way it's your responsibility to make sure I'm happy.

"If you want to stay, I'd love to have ya. With the understanding that if you ever want to get a place of your own, you'll tell me and I'll be one-hundred percent behind you. I'll even make curtains for your new place, crochet you a blanket to throw over your couch." She patted the back of my hand and rearranged the napkin in her lap. "Do we understand each other?"

I closed my eyes for a second, thanking God for this wonderful person in my life. "Then I'm staying. I like being your roommate."

She chuckled and stood up from the table. "Dessert?"

I grabbed my napkin off the table and tucked it under my chin. "Bring it on," I said, laughing.

It felt good knowing I'd still be living on the farm. I needed to be close to family and now Nana was all I had.

CHAPTER TWENTY-TWO

On Friday there were a few cancellations and a couple of no-shows. Kathy rearranged the schedule so my day was over at three o'clock. I sat at my desk, making notes on the daily charts, and thought about what I'd do with the free hours I had before my date with Laura.

Laura mentioned she was busy this time of year. The weather had turned mild, not beastly hot as it had been in the summer, and was a perfect time to use the outdoor arenas for working with the horses. I'd never spent time at her place so I called her and asked if she'd mind me watching her work. She told me she was accustomed to people observing her on the job since the horses' owners wanted to see how she handled their animals.

After changing into jeans and an old pair of tennis shoes, I drove over to her house. Her voice echoed from behind the house and I walked around to the backyard. I assumed the horses were housed in the large rust-red barn located on the left side of the property.

To the right of the barn sat a large open-air covered arena with a gate on the left side near the barn. In front of it stood a small round pen fenced in with wooden boards. I could see Laura's head above the top of the pen and made my way over.

A raised deck jutted off the back of her two-story house with a table, four chairs and an umbrella. Laura had grown up in this house, and I tried to picture how her room would look now that she was older. Had she left it the way it had been when she was a teenager as Nana had done with mine?

Putting aside my mental meanderings, I reached the side of the round pen and laid my elbows on the upper rail. She wasn't aware I'd arrived and I took the opportunity to watch her in her element, pure intensity written on her face.

She wore a pair of skin-tight riding pants with black leather boots, and her white stretch top revealed full breasts and a thin waist. Her black hair was pulled up into a high pony tail, her patrician nose tinged pink from the sun.

I could hear her voice, talking soft and low. Her arm jutted straight out, palm up, fingers touching the nose of one of the biggest horses I'd ever seen. I assumed it was the Friesian she told me her husband had given her. The horse must have weighed fourteen hundred pounds. His neck was regally long, and his hooves were covered in what I knew were called feathers. The tip of his jet-black tail reached all the way to the ground.

The few words I caught were "Maximus" and "good boy". The rest were just soft mumblings only she and her horse could hear. She walked slowly backward and he followed her until she stopped, then he halted also. Her arm and hand struck a pose that simulated holding onto a rope and as she mimed pulling it, the horse followed her as if his head was attached to the lead rope.

When she turned her back to him and he continued to follow her, she noticed me and she walked over to where I stood, her horse following close behind her.

"How long have you been here?" she asked, head tilted, golden eyes shaded from the sun with one hand above her eyebrows.

"Just got here. I didn't want to break into your session with… Maximus, right?"

"Yes." She turned to her right where her horse stood, his head high above her shoulder. He looked right at me. "Maxi, this is Jessee."

"Should I shake his hoof or what? I don't want to offend him. He's a big guy."

"Wanna join us?"

"Are you sure he doesn't feel proprietary about you?" I looked over the side of the pen at the underside of his belly and nodded. "At least he's fixed."

She gave me a withering look. "He's not the jealous type." She gestured toward the gate to my right. "Come on in."

After closing the gate behind me, I turned around and met Maximus. He pushed his nose into my chest, and I stumbled a few steps backward.

My eyes widened. "Not jealous?"

"He can be pushy. We're still working on his ground manners.

He'll be your pal eventually. He just needs to know you're not afraid of him."

I rubbed my hand up and down from his forelock to his velvety nose. "Hey, buddy." I pressed the side of my face against the side of his, near his huge black lips. "You're a big dude, but you're really just a big black lab, huh?"

"He's got the typical breed personality. Pretty mellow, laid back. And he's stronger than any horse I've ever ridden. When I get him to canter it's like riding a locomotive."

"I never gravitated toward large animals in vet school." I shrugged. "But I have an innate sense about the smaller animals. Horses have always baffled me. And riding on top of a locomotive sounds scary."

She nodded. "It can be. But if you're afraid of them, believe me, they feel it. Then again, I treat horses with respect and love. And they feel that too."

"That's for sure. These guys are big, and there's no way you can bully them into doing what you want. They have to want to do what you want them to do."

She tilted her head and smiled. "That's what my training's all about." She bent down to pick up his halter, slid it over his nose and buckled it on the side of his jaw. "Let me just put him in his stall and feed him dinner. Then I can shower while you relax."

I followed her to the barn where Maximus happily entered his stall and waited for Laura as she grabbed two flakes of hay and threw them gently in the corner of his stall. After closing the stall door, we walked to the back of the house and entered through the kitchen.

"Help yourself to something to drink." She gestured toward the refrigerator. "I'll just be a few minutes." She bounded out of the room.

I heard her feet pounding on the stairs to the second floor then the patter of the shower echoing through the walls. After grabbing a glass out of the cupboard, I poured myself some iced tea and strolled toward the front of the house.

Two chairs and an ottoman were stationed directly in front of a bay window that overlooked the front lawn, which was bracketed by a yellow picket fence running along the sidewalk. An overstuffed couch covered in throw pillows sat across from the fireplace. After setting my glass on the coffee table, I took a seat on the couch and leaned my head back and closed my eyes.

The cushion dipped, and I realized I'd fallen asleep. I turned my head. Laura sat in the corner of the couch, staring into the flameless fireplace. Her hair was still wet, parted on the side, and she'd tucked it behind her ears. She'd put on make-up: a slender slash of eyeliner beneath her lower lashes, black mascara. A dab of pink lip gloss enhanced her full lips.

Her expression was serious, and I thought perhaps my presence in her house was making her ill at ease. "Laura?" I whispered. The house was so quiet my voice cracked through the silence.

I heard the heater kick on. October nights could be cold in Iowa, yet it felt comfortable and cozy inside the house.

She shifted her gaze in my direction and gave me a weak smile. "Hey," she whispered.

"Is something wrong?"

She shook her head but I noticed her glassy eyes and cheerless expression.

"I took a tiny stroll down memory lane is all," she said. "It happens sometimes." She grabbed a small pillow and laid it in her lap then fiddled with the stitching.

"I've never told anyone this but Nana and Grampa," I said.

She looked up at me.

Though there was no solid reason for my feeling this way, I believed I could trust her. "Before I moved to Iowa I used to have panic attacks. They'd come on at no particular time, in the most random places. I'd suddenly be overwhelmed with sadness about my wife and child. I couldn't breathe.

"If I was at work I'd hide out in the bathroom and wait until the feeling passed. If I was in a public area I'd run for my car or the nearest restroom." I leaned my head back on the pillows and sighed. "I haven't had one since I moved here." I turned my head and looked into her eyes. "I think they're completely gone."

She reached her hand out and laid it on the cushion seat next to me. I intertwined my fingers with hers, and she gave my hand a tiny squeeze. "Thanks for telling me," she whispered. "When I sit here it reminds me of all the times Jeff would light a fire and we'd snuggle together, holding hands, staring into the flames, talking."

"Should I leave?"

She shook her head and tugged on my hand. I answered with a

tug of my own, and she slowly slid over in my direction. I slipped my arm around her shoulders, and our thighs touched. She laid her hand on my chest and her head near my heart. I could hear her breathing, slow and easy.

"I can feel your heart beat," she whispered.

"This feels right, Laura."

She tipped her head up and I looked down into her face. Our eyes met and my insides gave way. I leaned in and our lips touched, tentatively at first, then she deepened the kiss and our tongues entwined, a slow dance round and round, ending in a warm brush of my lips on hers. She laid her head back on my chest, and I set my chin on the smooth hair on the top of her head.

When my stomach growled, our intimate moment lapsed and she chuckled.

"That's just so romantic," I said under my breath.

She pulled out of my embrace and sat up. "I have vegetable stew heating in a crock pot, and the bread's fresh from the bakery. We can eat any time."

"Sounds good. Can I help set the table?"

"It's already done." She stood and stuck her hand out toward me. I grasped it, and she playfully pulled me off the couch and we strolled through the doorway into the kitchen.

"Sit down and I'll bring you a bowl of stew." She gestured toward a table overlooking the back yard.

I took a seat and watched as she ladled our dinners into oversized ceramic bowls and set them on the table. Then she cut thick slices of French bread and placed them on small plates.

I laid my napkin in my lap and waited for her to pick up her spoon. She tilted her head at me and her lips curved up in a smile.

"What?" I asked, grinning.

"You are such a gentleman." She pointed at my bowl. "Try it. Or are you afraid because there's no meat in it?"

I shook my head and grabbed my spoon. "Of course I'm not afraid of vegetarian food." I took a bite, chewed, and swallowed. To my surprise, the stew was thick and spicy, the vegetables al dente. "This is delicious."

She wiped her lips with her napkin and gave me a withering look. "Don't act so surprised, Jessee Bradford."

My eyes snapped back down to the bowl of stew and I took another bite.

Several seconds of silence passed before she whispered, "Did I say something wrong?"

"Not wrong," I answered, glancing up at her for a second then back down at my bowl. I scooped up a spoonful of stew then laid the spoon back in the bowl and looked at her. "When we were sitting on the couch you said something about taking a little trip down memory lane."

She nodded.

"I guess we both are dealing with a bit of nostalgia. It'll take time, I'm sure."

"Neither of us will ever forget them, Jess."

I reached out and grasped her hand and felt her firm clutch. "I never imagined not having Serena and Sofia in my life."

"And I can't believe Jeff died so young after promising to stand by my side forever."

"Are you okay with this?"

She frowned and cocked her head to the side.

"You know... you and me... seeing each other like this?" I said.

"Jeff's never coming back." She shrugged. "But Serena might."

I set my lips in a tight line and nodded up and down slowly. "You know how you talked about horses having a special sense about people?" I traced the edge of her knuckles with my thumb. "For months I've had this weird feeling in my gut that Serena's alive."

She attempted to pull her hand out of my grasp but I squeezed harder, not letting her go. "I believe with my whole heart that she's out there somewhere, living happily ever after without me. And I hate her for that." I paused, trying to put the feelings into words. "I want my little girl back. It kills me to know Sofia's alive and Serena doesn't have the courage to face me with the truth of why she deserted me."

"One day you'll know, Jess. You've got to believe that."

I shrugged. "Hangin' onto a dream, they call it."

"It's not a bad dream, wanting your child back."

"I'm hoping one day Sofia will demand to know about her father. Maybe she'll even come looking for me."

She nodded her head slowly, a tiny smile gracing her lips. "Hang onto that dream."

"I will," I whispered. "In one of my dreams I promised Sofia I'd never stop looking for her. And I won't. Ever."

CHAPTER TWENTY-THREE

It was nearing Halloween, and already the days in Iowa were much colder than I was accustomed to in California. Earlham was located directly in the path of every storm to hit the heartland. And although it was still autumn, even on relatively calm days, the temperature often rose no higher than the 40's during the day then dipped into the 30's after sunset.

One October day, I had just left the clinic for the evening. The sun was setting and I could barely see through the flapping windshield wipers on high speed. Rain pelted the car, pinging against the hood and roof so hard I couldn't hear the radio. The side of the road dipped toward a wide trench, making it difficult to keep the Mustang from gliding dangerously in that direction because of the gusting wind.

Tense, I gripped the steering wheel with fisted hands, my eyes riveted on the road ahead. A figure suddenly appeared, walking down the middle of the street, and I slammed on the brakes. The back of the car fishtailed, pulling sharply to the left then shuddered to a stop, facing oncoming traffic. Luckily no one was traveling Chestnut Avenue in the storm.

My heart pounded like a drum. I grabbed the door handle, intending to get out and make sure I hadn't hit whoever I'd seen in the road, when a knock rattled the passenger side window. I rolled the window down, and a young girl's head popped through the opening.

"Oh my God, I'm so sorry," she said. "Are you all right?" Rain dripped from the wet hair plastered to her head.

I raised my voice to be heard over the downpour clattering on the car's roof. "I'm fine. What about you? Why were you walking in the middle of the street?"

She swiped at her face, brushing the water onto the passenger seat. "I was afraid to walk on the side of the road. It's so muddy." She gestured behind her. "I didn't want to fall in that ditch."

I nodded. "I saw that too. I was trying to keep to the left so I wouldn't kick up a ton of mud onto the windshield." She was shivering, and suddenly the rain began beating down even harder. "Do you need a ride?"

She shook her head and water droplets flew inside the car. "Thanks for not hitting me and all, but I don't know you. My mom taught me not to talk to strangers." She smiled, and I noticed a silver retainer covering her bottom teeth.

"Look," I said, "I'm a stranger but I'm not strange." I picked my white lab coat off the back seat and pointed below the collar. "See. I'm a doctor. My name's Jessee Bradford. I live with my grandmother just about a block from here."

She glanced down the road toward where I'd pointed then looked back at me.

"Let me at least take you to my grandmother's house where you can get dry."

She gave me a dirty look. "What are you, the big bad wolf or something?"

I laughed out loud.

"Or do I just look like Little Red Riding Hood?" she said.

I chuckled then shook my head in mild exasperation. "Look, it's pouring and it's freezing. I know I probably sound like your mother, but you'll catch your death if you stay out in this storm. And it's getting dark."

She glanced in the back seat then back at me, down at my lab coat before grabbing the door handle and jerking it open. "Okay. But I want you to know I have a knife." She pulled a five-inch pocket knife out of her jeans and opened it. "Don't try anything." She cocked an eyebrow, then squinted at me.

"Don't worry." I started the car's engine. "We'll be there before you can count to ten," I added as I drove down the street toward the farm.

"One one-thousand, two one-thousand," she counted. When I glanced in her direction she had the knife open in her right hand, pointing it toward me, but the sides of her lips were twisted up in a tiny smile. I turned my attention back to the road and grinned. It was obvious she wasn't really terrified of me, but I admired her caution.

We reached the driveway leading to the farm. I turned into the lane, drove through the thick mud, stopped at the side of the house, and turned toward her.

"Ten one-thousand," she mumbled.

"This is it."

"You're very lucky, you know."

I grinned. "Glad you didn't have to use that knife of yours."

She grinned back at me.

"Let me go inside and tell my grandmother what's up. I'll be right back."

She nodded and shivered again when I opened the door. The wind was blowing harder now that darkness was advancing. I ran to the front door and threw it open. Nana met me before I reached the kitchen.

"What's goin' on, Jessee? You should leave your shoes outside on the porch. Shake out your jacket, too," she scolded.

Realizing I was dripping water on the hardwood floor, I stepped back onto the rug. "Sorry. Listen, I have sort of an emergency here. I picked up a girl who was walking in the middle of the street. I almost hit her. I gave her a ride here so she could at least dry off. It's freezing outside."

Without saying a word, she rushed over to the hat rack, grabbed a raincoat and pushed the front door open. I followed her as far as the edge of the porch and watched as she opened the passenger side door of my car and had a conversation with the girl. Within seconds she tucked the young girl under the bright yellow slicker and they both ran to the porch, where I stood waiting for them.

"Can you show Kerryanne upstairs? Get her some towels and I'll find some clothes for her to wear. She can take a hot bath while I finish cookin' supper."

I nodded.

Kerryanne followed me up the stairs to the bathroom at the back of the second floor. At the doorway to the bathroom I turned toward her. "Nana has a big heart. She likes to take care of people."

She looked up at me with wide blue eyes. "She's not the only one with a big heart."

I grabbed two towels and a washcloth out of the closet and handed them to her. She nodded, went into the bathroom and closed the door behind her.

After drying off and changing out of my wet clothes, I joined Nana in the kitchen, where she handed me a hot cup of coffee.

"So did she tell you anything about herself?" I asked. She was busy stirring something in a pan on the stove, her back to me.

"Not much. Just her name and that she's from Little Rock. She thanked me for allowin' her to come inside."

"I wonder what she was doing out there alone in weather like this."

"I don't know, Jess. We'll have to see what she tells us when she gets outta the tub."

Nana finished stirring, then poured what looked like hot chocolate into a mug, placing it on the kitchen table across from me.

I heard footsteps on the stairs. Kerryanne stood in the doorway, her hair just as wet as before, but her clothes were dry.

She glanced down at the coveralls she'd put on, touching the material. "Thank you for loaning me these, Rose. I'll give 'em back to you as soon as mine are dry."

Nana reached out and guided her to the chair across from me where she sat down and looked at the mug in front of her. "Drink it slowly, it's hot. It'll warm ya' up."

Kerryanne reached for the mug and took a sip, then another and another and smiled. "Mmm. This is s-o-o good. Thanks. Is it homemade?"

"My own recipe, handed down from my mama and her mama before her. By the way, I put your clothes in the washer, but it'll take a while before they're outta the dryer. Would you like to stay for supper, hon?"

The girl took another sip then looked intently into her mug. "I couldn't do that." She paused. "You don't even know me."

"Your name is Kerryanne. You're from Little Rock, Arkansas, and I'm Rose, and this is Jessee." She pointed at me. "You're new to this town, and we want to welcome you. Jessee and I are gonna eat supper, and I made plenty so you're welcome to join us."

Kerryanne glanced at me then at Nana. Her hair was drying and it was dark brown and curly. Her blue eyes looked huge in her tiny face. She must have weighed no more than a hundred pounds, and the overalls hung loosely on her petite frame. She looked like a pixie in farm attire.

"Thanks. I'd love that."

Nana smiled and went to the cupboard for plates and glasses.

Kerryanne stood up and brought her empty mug to the sink. "Can I help set the table?"

Nana shook her head and gestured for her to sit down. "You're our guest. You must be tired from all that walkin'. Where were you headed?"

Without lifting her eyes, she played with her napkin, folding it in half then opening it again. "I'm just walking, nowhere in particular."

When she glanced up I caught her eye and smiled. I had the distinct feeling she wasn't telling us the whole story. Then again, we were strangers and I wouldn't expect her to reveal secrets after just meeting us.

"Are you thinking of staying in Earlham?" I asked.

Her head shot up. "Earlham? Is that where I am?"

I nodded. "Earlham, Iowa. Is that where you want to be right now?"

"All I can say is I'm getting tired of hitchhiking in this weather. No matter where I am it's cold and rainy."

"Why'd you leave Little Rock?" I asked.

"I..." she stumbled and her lips set in a tight line.

Nana gave me the "look". "Jessee, would you pull the casserole outta the oven for me?"

I grabbed the pot holders and brought out a bubbling hot tuna casserole, topped with crushed potato chips—my favorite. I brought the dish to the table and placed it on one of Nana's ceramic trivets. "Hope you like tuna casserole, Kerryanne."

The way our young wanderer looked at the steaming casserole told me she hadn't had a hot meal in ages. Her lips parted, eyes riveted on the dish. She leaned forward and sniffed. "It smells s-o-o-o good."

Nana ladled heaping spoonfuls onto our plates, and we waited for her to sit down at the table before digging in. As soon as Nana took a seat Kerryanne jammed her fork into the hot mixture, shoving it in her mouth and swallowing before I'd taken my first bite.

Nana took a quick look at me and nodded. I smiled back. This kid was starving and I knew Nana's heart was bursting at the prospect of finding another "lost puppy" to take care of.

We ate in silence and Kerryanne cleaned her plate within minutes. When Nana asked if she wanted seconds she nodded, accepting another huge ladleful of casserole.

After she polished off her second plate, she looked at us and shrugged. "Thanks for dinner, Rose. I haven't eaten this much in days." She paused and took a deep breath. "Do you know anyone who might need help around here? Like on their farm or anything like that? I need a job. I'm running outta money." She glanced first at me, then Nana. "I'll do most anything. I'm not picky."

I leaned back in my chair, wondering whether I was speaking too soon. What the heck, I thought. "I could use someone at the clinic."

Her eyes lit up. She sat up ramrod straight and raked a hand through her short curls. "You mean like a medical clinic, where sick people go?"

I shook my head and chuckled. "No, not that type of clinic."

Her eyebrows flicked upward.

"I'm a veterinarian."

Her mouth dropped open, and I wasn't sure whether that meant she would love to work with animals or perhaps she was scared of dogs or cats. "Since I was a little girl I've dreamed of becoming a vet. But my parents can't afford to send me to college. Am I qualified to be like an intern or something?"

"Do you have any work experience?"

She nodded, a huge grin on her face. "I've been working since high school at the local grocery store."

"Since high school?" I asked with obvious surprise in my voice. "How old are you?"

"I'll be twenty-one this January." She must have seen the look on my face. "I know, I know, I look about fifteen, but I swear I'm twenty." She patted one of the pockets of her coveralls and produced a driver's license. "See." She handed me a beat-up wallet and pointed to her picture. "Look at the date."

After taking a quick glance at her license, I handed it back to her. "I'm sure you'll do just fine. My assistant Kathy and I can teach you the ropes. You could start tomorrow."

Delight spread across her face, and she bounced up and down in her chair like a toddler. "Thanks, Doctor—"

"It's Jessee," I interrupted.

"Thanks, Jessee."

I caught Nana's eye, and she gave me a satisfied grin. I could tell she thought I'd "done good", as she'd call it.

Everyone needed a break, I thought. Maybe I'd just given Kerryanne hers.

CHAPTER TWENTY-FOUR

Kerryanne said she was tired so Nana showed her the extra bedroom upstairs after we finished eating. I was cleaning up the dishes when Nana came downstairs.

"That was nice of you to offer her a job, Jess. You remind me so much of your father. And your grampa, of course. Always helpin' others, whether animals or people."

I grabbed a towel to dry the plates and glasses. "Thanks for the compliment, but I really need the help. Like I told you, it's been hard for Kathy to answer the phones, do the intake evaluations, pay the bills, clean up, assist me in surgery.

"Kerryanne can help out with the front desk and cleaning the kennels. More and more people are taking advantage of our boarding service. And when there are newborn puppies, it would be great to have a third person to share night duty."

She patted me on the back and took the dish towel out of my hands. "I know you work hard, just like your grampa. And it looks like Kerryanne could use the money. After I washed her clothes they practically fell apart when I took 'em out of the dryer. She musta been wearin' 'em for months."

I poured her a cup of coffee, set it on the table and leaned back against the counter. "I think she has a past she doesn't want to reveal to us. At least not yet."

Nana lowered herself in a chair and took a sip from her mug. "Maybe she's been hurt and can't trust us with the information. We'll find out down the road."

I stretched my arms toward the ceiling. "I'm gonna hit the sack. Tomorrow will be a busy day, getting Kerryanne settled in her new job. I'll see you in the morning." I bent down and gave her a kiss on the cheek. "Oh, I forgot to tell you. I have an appointment with

Mayor Morrison tomorrow to discuss my divorce. I may be a little late getting home for dinner."

"Will you be droppin' Kerryanne off beforehand?"

I thought about my schedule the next day. "Yeah, I can do that." I lowered my voice. "Do you think she'll be staying long? I didn't mean to spring her on you like this, but what else could I do? When I think of how close I came to running her over out there in the storm—"

"Stop worryin' about it. We'll take it day by day. It's no trouble havin' her. She's a tiny thing, doesn't take up much room. We can't have her livin' on the street, can we?"

I shook my head and gave her a hug. "You're the best."

She gave me a friendly slap on the arm and shooed me out of the room.

* * * *

I got up bright and early the next morning. The sky had cleared and I decided to take a quick run around Earlham. Laura was already up, the lights on inside her house. My heart fluttered. And it wasn't from the exercise. I enjoyed our evening together, getting to know her better, and made a mental note to call her so we could go out on another date.

When I got back to the farm Nana was dishing up scrambled eggs onto Kerryanne's plate. After a quick shower I joined them for breakfast.

"More coffee, Kerryanne?" Nana asked, hovering near the table, coffee pot in hand.

"No thanks, but..." She paused and gazed into her mug.

"What is it?"

Kerryanne chewed on the side of her lip and glanced up at Nana. "Do you think I could make a long-distance phone call? I'll pay you back for the charges as soon as—"

"Yes," Nana interrupted her. "Don't worry about it, sweetheart. You can use the phone upstairs in the hallway if you'd like. It's a little more private."

"It'll only take a minute." Kerryanne placed her dishes in the sink and scooted out the kitchen door.

"What do you think that's all about?" I asked.

Nana shook her head, looking thoughtful. "I have no idea. Maybe she'll open up to us later. It's still early days, you know. We can't expect her to tell us everything just yet."

Five minutes later, Kerryanne bounded down the stairs and we headed to the clinic. We arrived by seven thirty, and Kathy was already at her desk, organizing the patient files for the day.

"Kerryanne, this is Kathy, my assistant. Kerryanne and I met yesterday. She'll be working here, helping us out with filing, answering phones, cleaning the kennels, that sort of thing."

Kathy's smile went from ear to ear. This would give her some much needed time off from the long hours she worked.

"Nice to meet you," Kathy said. "We sure need an extra hand around here. You're a godsend, Kerryanne." She opened a drawer and took out a file. "Here's a form you'll need to fill out. You know, for taxes, social security and stuff, so I can cut you a check in two weeks."

Kerryanne took the paper and looked it over. She frowned and chewed her bottom lip, looking a bit nervous.

"Yeah, sure." She turned back to me. "Thanks again, Doc, for hiring me."

I left her with Kathy to show her around. The girl's reaction puzzled me. Maybe, as Nana had suggested, she just felt uncomfortable answering questions about her personal life. But she must have realized she'd need to provide at least her full name and social security number for any job she took.

Later, after eating lunch at my desk, I took a moment to call Laura and asked her out for dinner next weekend, on Halloween. I told myself I didn't want to be stuck handing out candy to little kids although, if I was honest, that wasn't the real reason for my discomfort.

Passing out treats to children would only serve as a reminder that Sofia would be a year and a half by now. Was she missing out on one of the most exciting nights in most kid's lives due to an early death? Or was she holding Serena's hand, canvassing a neighborhood somewhere, stuffing a pillowcase with treats? Where were they? My mind would never wrap itself around their being gone forever.

That afternoon I dropped Kerryanne off at the farm before

meeting with Mayor Patrick Morrison. Being a distant relative of John Wayne's, I expected a robust, hearty looking guy.

His secretary informed him of my arrival, and the man stepped out of his office—a total surprise. Maybe five feet six inches tall, he was thin with thick tortoise-shell glasses, a pointy nose and large ears. He looked like a character out of a comic book.

"Dr. Bradford." He had an unexpectedly deep voice. "Come in."

I sat in a leather chair across from his huge, glossy wooden desk. The walls were covered in bookshelves lined with legal tomes, and a bay window behind his desk overlooked the town's park and gazebo.

"Laura Driscoll referred you, is that right?"

"Yes, she did."

He leaned back in his chair and asked, "What can I help you with?"

"Last January my wife and child went missing from our home in Santa Barbara, California."

He nodded and swiveled his chair slowly, left to right, while I explained.

"Of course, the FBI and local police were involved, but they haven't found them. In fact, the agent in charge thinks my wife left me. I got a custody order, so if she's ever found I'll get my daughter back right away. But I have a question. If I wanted to, could I file for divorce if Serena's... body hasn't been found?"

He leaned forward, elbows on the desk, and steepled his fingers. "I can handle all of this for you, Dr. Bradford, but I'd like to ask you a few questions first, if you don't mind."

I nodded and sat up straighter in the chair.

He grabbed a legal pad and pen. "What are the names of your wife and child?"

"Serena. And Sofia is my daughter."

"Maiden name?"

"Serena kept her maiden name. It's Middleton."

I noticed his eyebrows drift up a bit. "Rich family in Southern California? Philanthropists?"

"Yes," I said.

He chewed on the end of his pen before scribbling something on his notepad. "I read about that in the newspaper. Her parents offered a substantial reward." He pointed the pen at me. "You're the husband?"

"That's me."

He stared at me as though he couldn't believe I was sitting in front of him.

"Do you anticipate a problem, Mayor?"

"Did you sign a pre-nup?"

I shook my head side to side.

"Had you drawn up a will?"

I nodded.

"Combined your assets?"

"Yes."

He shrugged. "Well, money talks, son. You ought to know that by now."

I squinted at him. "What's that supposed to mean?"

He dropped his pen on the desk and sat back in his chair. It tipped so far back I was afraid he would fall on the floor. "It means," he continued, "that if a certain party wants to make this difficult for another party, i.e. you, Dr. Bradford, let's just say we may find ourselves at the bottom of the court docket for months, even years."

I frowned. "But why?"

"What is your relationship with your in-laws?"

I leaned back, resting my foot on my other knee. "They think I had something to do with her disappearance. They'd never met me before this happened."

He nodded. "California is a fifty-fifty state. You and your wife would split all money and assets right down the middle if you were to divorce her." He paused. "That's a lot of money, doctor."

"I never really thought about that before now. But you're right. Serena acquired the majority of what would have been her inheritance, when she turned twenty. Since then her father's been investing it for her."

He looked more like the cat who caught the mouse. "Bingo, my boy."

I shook my head. "You've lost me, Mayor."

"Mr. Middleton could not only stall proceedings in court, he may well have something up his sleeve to prove coercion on your part with regard to the pre-nup and the will you and your wife had drawn up, that sort of thing. You get my drift."

I put both feet on the floor and leaned nearer to his desk. "Well, what if I refuse all claims to any of her assets? That would make a difference, wouldn't it?"

He tipped one eyebrow up and smirked. "And add more credence to the statement that you purportedly were never involved in their kidnapping."

I stood up so quickly I must have scared him. His chair came down with a thud onto the floor. "I didn't have anything to do with my wife and child's disappearance, Mayor." I turned to leave.

"Wait a second, Dr. Bradford," he called out.

I turned back around and gave him a withering look.

"I just needed to know," he said in an even tone.

"Know what?" I didn't try to hide my irritation.

"I wanted to gauge your reaction, see what you'd do if I goaded you." He gestured with his hand. "Sit down. Please."

I sat back down in the chair, my heart tripping in my chest. "Well, your little ploy worked, Mayor. They dropped me as a suspect months ago."

He opened a drawer, took out several sheets of paper and handed them to me. "Fill out these forms, bring them back to my office, and I'll contact the authorities, deal with the appropriate legal offices in California. My secretary will explain my retainer, and I'll be in touch with you soon."

He stood up and came around to the other side of the desk. "I'm sorry for pushing your buttons. I'm an excellent judge of character. I had to know how you would react."

I nodded but my mouth was set in a tight line.

"It may take several months. And, depending on how busy the legal system is in that crazy state you're from, it could be longer."

I cleared my throat. "Well, I haven't decided to go through with the divorce yet. I just, uh, wanted to get as much information as I could before proceeding."

Pursing his lips, he looked at the ground then back up at me. "You mean, if your wife is found alive you may not want to pursue the divorce?"

I stared over his shoulder out the window. "If she's found, I doubt I'll be happy about what I find out. I can't think of one logical reason for hiding my baby daughter from me." I turned my gaze back to him. "From what I understand, she'll be prosecuted to the full extent of the law."

"That's right. Parental abduction is a felony." He shook my hand

and walked me to the door. "Say hello to your grandmother for me." He patted me on the back.

"I'll do that." I paused. "Keep me apprised of what you find out."

"You can count on it," he answered, shutting the door behind me.

I concluded my business with his secretary and drove home. I'd pegged the mayor of Earlham for a nerdy, small-town, home-boy politician. He turned out to be a pretty crafty fellow, a serious, no-nonsense lawyer. Proof that looks didn't mean anything in the arena of intelligence.

I looked forward to getting more information about this matter in order to make an intelligent decision about divorce proceedings, when the time was right. I felt a tug toward my future and knew I wouldn't be able to pursue it until I dealt with the past. If I decided to go forward and if that meant relinquishing any claims to Serena's fortune, then so be it. Money had never been that important to me anyway. I just knew that soon enough I'd want to get on with my personal life.

CHAPTER TWENTY-FIVE

Kerryanne was a hard worker. She never complained about cleaning out the kennels, she spent hours arranging the filing system, quickly mastered use of the computer, and was unfailingly polite to anyone who phoned. She and Kathy got along well, too. I often heard them talking and laughing. Sometimes they took lunch breaks together. The office was running more efficiently than ever before, and I attributed it to Kerryanne's arrival.

At the end of her first week I buzzed her on the intercom and asked if she'd come to my office.

"Yes, Dr. Bradford?"

"Sit down, Kerryanne," I gestured to the chair in front of my desk. "I want to thank you for all the help you've given me and Kathy since you arrived."

She stared at me, her pupils dilated, mouth turned down. "You don't need me anymore. You're letting me go." She pushed herself out of the chair.

"No," I said, a little too loudly. She sat back down and I leaned toward her. "Of course I'm not firing you. I'd actually like to give you a raise."

She looked at me with wide eyes. "Seriously?"

"Seriously. Let's just say your one-week probation period has ended. Your first paycheck will include a substantial increase for the second week of work."

She shook her head and blinked several times. "Are you for real?"

I sat back in my chair and smiled. "Yes, I'm for real. You're a good worker."

She still didn't look pleased. Her eyes shifted from my face to her folded hands in her lap then back to my face. "Did you need references or something?"

"Stop." I put my hand up, palm facing outward. "I'm not asking you for anything. This was supposed to be a two-minute discussion about your raise. That was all." I paused, afraid of making her more scared than she already appeared. "Are you in some sort of trouble?"

She shook her head but wouldn't look me in the eyes. "Is someone looking for you? Someone you're afraid of?" Another shake of her head. She twisted her hands in her lap like a pretzel.

I came around to the other side of the desk and sat down in the chair facing her. "If you ever want to talk, I'm here. I know what it's like to be hurt."

Her head came up and she met my stare. "Whaddaya mean?"

"My wife and child went missing January fifteenth of this year. I don't know whether they were kidnapped and murdered or if my wife took my little girl and left me. Every night I'm afraid of the day I'll find out the truth. Both scenarios scare me to death."

She laid her hand on top of mine. Several moments passed. "I'm afraid my father will hire someone to track me down." She looked down at the floor. A tear fell from her chin. "I wrote down a fake social security number. God, I'm so stupid. What was I thinking?"

I squeezed her hand and gave it a little tug so she'd look at me. Her head popped up. "It's okay. We'll work something out. Maybe I can pay you cash until your life straightens out." I looked up at the clock on the wall. "It's time to close up shop. Why don't we go home for dinner? I'm sure my grandmother will be fixing something extra special."

She smiled and swiped at her wet cheeks with her fingertips. "Okay."

Nana had indeed outdone herself—fried chicken, mashed potatoes, corn on the cob, and cherry cobbler for dessert. I didn't want to eat again until the next night when Laura and I were supposed to have our date.

When Kerryanne went upstairs to her room I took the opportunity to tell Nana about the conversation I had with her at the clinic.

"I wonder why she's afraid of her father?" she asked, handing me a wet plate.

I wiped the plate with a towel. "I don't know. I didn't want to pressure her. I was surprised she opened up to me at all. But I guess she had no choice. She wrote down a fake social security number on the job application."

She made a tsk-tsk sound and shook her head. "Poor little thing. To be so afraid of your father?" She shut off the water and glanced at me. "I think she'll talk to me. Not tonight but maybe tomorrow I'll bring up the subject. We've never discussed how long she'll be stayin' here. It would be an easy way to start the conversation."

I put my arm around her shoulders and gave her a squeeze. "Good luck with that. Tomorrow night I'm taking Laura out for dinner. That leaves you to deal with the trick-or-treaters. I hope that's okay."

A smile lit up her face. "Of course. And good for you goin' out on a date. You know, for such a young person, Laura's had her share of sorrow."

"I know. But she seems to be doing okay."

She nodded. "Of course she does. She just had to find that right someone at the right time."

"I'd like to think so." I watched as she emptied the dishpan of soapy water and wiped down the counter. She took the towel I was holding and dried her hands. "I like her a lot."

She grinned and gave me a kiss on the cheek. "No doubt. Your grampa predicted as much 'fore he passed, you know."

I tilted my head and our eyes met. "He did? He never said anything to me."

"He didn't want to interfere. Harper would never meddle. Now why don't we watch some television before bed, or are you plannin' to read?"

I put my arm around her shoulders and we walked into the family room to sit in our favorite spots: Grampa's Barcalounger for her and the couch for me. At the end of Wheel of Fortune I climbed the stairs to bed, grateful once again for having my grandmother alive and well. She was one of the kindest people I'd ever known and I felt lucky to have her in my life.

* * * *

The following day, the phone rang after breakfast and I heard Nana answer it just as I headed out to the barn to collect the eggs.

"Jessee, it's Laura on the phone."

I returned to the kitchen and picked up the extension.

"Good morning. The chickens are waiting for me in the barn. What's up?"

"I'm sorry." Her voice sounded as though she was squeezing her nose with her fingers. "Can we change our date to next weekend?"

"Do you feel as bad as you sound?"

"Worse," she answered. "You do not want to be around me right now. I'll just stay in bed this weekend."

"Can I bring you anything? Soup, aspirin?"

"No, thank you. I was looking forward to this evening, though."

"You better shut off all the lights in your house. Remember, it's Halloween."

I heard her gasp. "You're right. I forgot all about that. I didn't even buy any candy. I've been so busy with the horses and... I don't know. I lost track of time, I guess."

"The weather's been horrid. And you probably worked right through it, rain or shine, huh?"

"There's a covered round pen at the back of the barn. I work there when the weather's bad, but the wind can be brutal."

"Well, I hope you're better by next weekend. I've picked someplace special I want to take you."

"It's a date. Talk to you soon."

I hung up the phone and heard someone step into the kitchen. It was Kerryanne.

"Can I help hand out candy tonight?" she asked.

I had to mentally shift gears. I hadn't planned on handing out treats this evening but now I had no excuse for evading the inevitable. "Nana's in charge of that."

"Just a second, Jessee." Nana stepped around Kerryanne. "It was always your grampa's favorite day and now that you're the man of the house, the job's all yours."

I laughed and glanced at Kerryanne. "She has spoken," I said in as deep a voice as I could.

Kerryanne snickered. "I could make cupcakes. Do you have any idea how many kids will stop by?"

Nana tapped a finger on her chin. "I'd say thirty or forty. I'll help ya' decorate, Kerryanne." She took Kerryanne by the hand, and they sat down at the kitchen table with Nana's recipe box. "One of the wonderful things about living in a small town. I've watched most of these younguns go from barely walkin' to teenagers. Everybody 'round town knows we always hand out homemade cookies or cupcakes. No one has to worry about razor blades or drugs inside of 'em like they do in the big cities."

I headed outside to the barn, and spent most of the day doing chores so Nana and Kerryanne could bake, frost, and decorate four dozen chocolate cupcakes. After feeding the chickens and goats, I mowed the front lawn and fertilized the flower garden.

As the sun set, purple and orange streaks lit up the sky. I turned on the outdoor lamps and within minutes the sounds of "Trick or treat?" could be heard through the screen door. Nana sat in a chair on the front porch, cupcakes lined up on a cookie tray on a table beside her, along with a pitcher of hot apple cider with tiny paper cups. Each cupcake was decorated with a different Halloween design drawn in frosting: an owl or a goblin or a witch or a pumpkin. It wasn't hard to guess why this farm was so popular with the young ones.

Kerryanne and I sat on the porch swing with a bowl of candy between us. Having never handed out treats on Halloween before, the costumes amazed me. They were so different from those when I was young. There was Freddy Krueger, Michael Myers, Jason Voorhees. Unbelievable.

What wrenched my heart were the littlest ones of the bunch, toddlers whose parents prodded them up the front stairs, reassuring them it was okay to walk up to Nana and get a cupcake. Then Kerryanne would lure them over to the porch swing with handfuls of Tootsie pops and Milky Way bars.

One little girl, dressed up as a ballerina with a pink tutu, tights and slippers, walked over to where we were sitting, a huge paper bag dangling from her tiny hands. She had long blond curls, a tiny bow-tie mouth, and fat cheeks.

My mind lurched at the resemblance between her and my mental image of Sofia at this age. The little girl could have been Sofia's clone. Reaching out to hand her a sucker, my heart stopped. Moms and dads waited at the bottom of the stairs, and I scrutinized each of the women's faces. Could one of them be Serena? Feeling the tug on my fingers, I realized the little ballerina was trying to grab the sucker out of my hand. I stared at her, mesmerized, wishing this were my little girl.

"Suzie, hurry up." A woman who looked to be in her early forties with short dark hair ran up the stairs and grasped her little girl's hand. "Say thank you," she prodded.

The little girl turned toward her mom and hid her face in the folds of her coat.

"That's okay," I said. "Happy Halloween."

But they were already headed down the stairs, and my heart plummeted to my feet. Would I always imagine that every blonde child who was Sofia's age might be my daughter? Until they were found, I surmised that would be the case. I stood up on the pretense of getting a drink of water and went into the kitchen to sit at the table, glancing every now and again out the window at the trick-or-treaters.

The front door slammed, and Kerryanne entered with the empty tray. "We're all out of cupcakes. Your grandmother wants me to grab another bag of candy. She said it's on the counter." She paused. "What's wrong?"

I closed my eyes, trying to rid myself of the compulsive need to examine every toddler's face. When I opened them, Kerryanne had taken a seat across from me.

She placed a hand on my forearm. "What is it?"

I met her sympathetic gaze. "It's nothing. Just my imagination going wild."

She patted my arm. "You're looking for your daughter, aren't you?"

I nodded. My heart twisted for the millionth time since they went missing. "I sense Sofia's out there somewhere. She's not dead. I just know it."

"And your wife?"

I shrugged. "My gut tells me she's alive, too. I can't explain it. There's no logical reason for my feelings."

"One day you'll find out. You've gotta believe that."

"There are days when I think it's just a matter of time before they'll walk through that door. Then again, Serena doesn't even know I moved here."

"All she has to do is contact any police station in the United States. The FBI knows where you live, don't they?"

"Yeah, you're right. She could find me pretty easily. I just wish someone would find them." I paused. "Can I ask you a personal question?"

She nodded, her brows arching upward.

"Have you been in touch with your mom? To let her know where you are, that you're okay?"

"I've called her twice. With Rose's permission," she added, looking guilty.

I shook my head and smiled. "It's okay. You can use the phone any time you want. I was worried your mother would be concerned about you."

She nodded her head slowly up and down and pursed her lips. "I told her I was staying with you guys here in Earlham. And that I have a job."

"She must have been relieved."

"Yeah."

Silence ensued. I assumed she was uncomfortable telling me more about the conversations with her mother so I stood up and grabbed the bag of candy off the kitchen counter. "Let's go out and help Nana."

She followed me to the porch swing and before long, the flood of kids dwindled. We went inside and turned off the porch light, then blew out the candles inside the pumpkins.

I climbed into bed, depressed. Most of the time I pushed my mental meanderings about my missing wife and child to the back of my mind, tried not to dwell on terrifying guessing games, the why's and where's of their disappearance.

But tonight was one of my bad spells. I tossed and turned until morning. It was Sunday and I could have slept in, but I decided to help Nana with the morning chores, then planned to visit Laura to see how she was fairing.

I drove over to her house later that morning and knocked lightly on the front door. Brewster's deep bark resounded in the foyer. I heard shuffling. The door cracked open a tiny bit.

"Jessee, what are you doing here? I don't want you to get sick." She sounded a bit better than she had the day before on the phone.

"I came bearing gifts from Nana and me. I'll only be here a second and I'll keep my distance."

She pushed the screen door open and grinned when she saw the bouquet of flowers I'd picked from Nana's garden along with a casserole dish. "Rose's tuna casserole with potato chips on top?" she asked.

I grinned and scratched Brewster under his chin, then kissed Laura on the forehead. "She must have given you one of these on another occasion, right?"

She nodded and took the casserole into the kitchen, setting it on the counter.

I followed her and asked, "Feeling any better?"

"Yeah, I am. I slept most of the day yesterday and even though I still have a stuffy nose, my throat's fine." She paused and took a seat, gesturing me to join her. "I got a call from my mom yesterday."

"They live in Des Moines, right?"

She nodded and tucked her robe tighter across her chest. "She has a show at a pretty well-known gallery this coming weekend. She invited me to come opening night. Would you like to join me? I know we said we'd go out to dinner, but I'd really like you to meet my parents."

My insides tipped a little in my gut. I never had the chance to get to know Serena's parents. I shook my head and looked down at the table, remembering the past and how much they'd hurt me.

"You don't want to meet them," she whispered.

When I glanced up her eyes were welling with tears and suddenly I realized I'd given her the wrong impression. "No, no that's not it at all."

"Then what is it?"

I covered her hand with mine and gave it a tight squeeze. "I'd be honored to meet your parents. In fact, it's one of the nicest things you could ever ask me."

She tilted her head, eyebrows scrunched together.

"My wife's parents wanted nothing to do with me, never wanted to meet me. I'm sure they wished it had been me who went missing instead of their daughter, so they could marry her off to one of their rich friends' sons."

She turned her palm up and intertwined her fingers with mine. "I'm so sorry. You don't deserve that kind of treatment. But money can make people do the strangest things." She paused, and her eyes lit up. "When I told my parents about you, they couldn't wait to meet you. Would you like to go with me to the opening, then?"

I looked at her and smiled. "I'd love to." I stood and pulled her up to hug her. She wrapped her arms around my waist. I loved the feel of her body close to mine, the smell of citrus shampoo in her hair. Even though she was sick, without make-up, and her hair askew, I thought she was beautiful.

I walked with her to the front room and settled her in front of the television with a fresh glass of orange juice and the remote control, then kissed the top of her head. Brewster escorted me to the front door. I felt on top of the world and looked forward to meeting her parents at the gallery.

That's when it hit me. Serena never had a showing of her paintings in any gallery. I never dreamed my first experience would be with someone other than my wife.

CHAPTER TWENTY-SIX

The following week was a whirlwind of overtime and emergencies, our kennel bursting with boarders, and we'd acquired several new patients. The clinic was thriving and each day I was thankful I'd hired Kerryanne.

We established a routine at the farm. Kerryanne and I rode home together, Nana fixed dinner, we ate together and chatted about the animals that came in that day. Nana sat at the table, enthralled with our stories. Sometimes a glassy look veiled her eyes as she listened to our tales. This scenario probably reminded her of when Grampa returned home each day.

One evening Kerryanne went up to bed earlier than usual, and Nana and I were left at the table, relaxing over cups of coffee.

"Did you ever talk with Kerryanne about her father or ask if she has any intention of getting a place of her own?"

Nana glanced toward the hallway and went to close the kitchen door. "I invited her to stay here, and she insisted on payin' rent for her room. That's fine with me. Teaches her responsibility and all that." She lowered her voice to a whisper. "Seems her father abuses her momma. And her momma wouldn't leave although Kerryanne wanted to help her move out. I don't know much about spousal abuse, but this is pretty typical. The wife always believes her husband's false promises that he'll change, that it'll never happen again. Finally Kerryanne couldn't stand to watch it any longer and she ran away."

"Did her father ever abuse her?"

She shook her head. "I don't think so. But she thought she'd be next in line if she was caught tryin' to run away with her mother in tow."

"She told me she thinks he might try to track her down."

She nodded. "Legally she doesn't have to go back home. She's twenty years old. She called him a psycho."

"He sounds frightening. Do you think she's telling the truth?"

"I believe her, Jess. You hear about this kinda thing all the time. There are movies on the Lifetime channel about it, for Heaven's sake. If I can help in some small way by givin' her a loving home while she's learnin' to make her own way, then I'm happy to do it."

"She told me she phoned her mom a couple of times. At least she knows her daughter's safe."

"She told me that, too."

I looked into my grandmother's eyes and smiled.

"You're a good person, Nana, taking in lost souls like Kerryanne and me."

She stood up and patted me on the shoulder. "Thank you for the compliment, but it's nothin' that you or Harper wouldn't do. I guess I love takin' in stray cats and dogs... and sometimes humans, too."

We both laughed, and I went up to bed. I was happy living with my new family. Nana and Kerryanne and I got along so well, I couldn't ask for better housemates. Every day I was thankful Grampa had allowed me to take over his practice in Earlham. This little town was nothing like Santa Barbara, but the people made up for anything I missed on the West Coast. I was rapidly considering this home.

On Saturday I dressed in a dark suit and tie in preparation for the opening at the gallery in Des Moines. Brewster's bark announced my arrival and when Laura answered the door my stomach flipped. She looked like a model on the front of a fashion magazine. Her hair was parted on the side and held up with a fancy diamond-like barrette. Her bangs hung just below her eyebrows, setting off her golden-colored eyes.

She wore a short, body-hugging black cocktail dress that criss-crossed over her breasts, showing an abundance of cream-colored cleavage.

"Wow," I whispered. A reddish tint bloomed on her porcelain cheeks. "That dress is..."

"You like it?" She slid her hands down along her sides. "I bought it especially for this evening. My mom and dad think all I ever wear are riding breeches and leather gloves." She grinned. "They probably expect me to arrive with a dressage whip in my hand."

I laughed out loud. "I could go back and put on my cowboy hat. And I think I could probably rustle up a pair of overalls that would fit me."

She yelled goodbye to Brewster and locked the door behind her. Conversation flowed easily on the thirty-minute drive to Des Moines. When we reached the city limits, I glanced over at her, still tongue-tied at how strikingly beautiful she was.

"Is there anything you'd like to warn me about before I meet your parents? Something I should know? Subjects I shouldn't bring up?"

She smiled and shook her head. "No. Actually, there's nothing I have to tell you. Remember, they used to live in Earlham too. They're pretty down-home people, no airs, just honest, loving parents. I'm proud of them both. Daddy has a great job so Mom can do what she loves most in life: paint. I don't know what type of art you enjoy, but I'm betting you'll like her work."

"I'm sure I will." I pointed at the next street sign. "Here?"

"Make a right, then park behind the gallery. It's up there on the left side of the street. You'll see the banners in front, with the sign announcing the grand opening of Colleen Pratt at the Persoll Gallery." She wiggled around nervously in her seat. "I can't wait. This is so exciting for her. She's dreamt about this for years."

I parked and ran over to her side of the car, opened the door and clasped her hand. We strolled around to the front of the gallery where people gathered on the steps, talking and laughing. She tugged on my hand, and we entered the foyer. The building reminded me of a Greek temple with ceiling-to-floor columns and marble floors.

"Let's get something to drink," she suggested, "then we can make our way around the gallery. My parents are here somewhere."

At the side of the foyer, they served champagne and punch. We each took a glass of champagne and wandered to the interior of the building. Paintings of all sizes lined the walls of the dimly lit gallery. Each frame had its own special light placed strategically above it to capture the essence of the colors on the canvas.

I was overwhelmed by the pastel colors. The motion and swirls of the oil paint were mesmerizing, the scenery and portraits captured on the canvas in strikingly realistic detail.

"What do you think?" Laura whispered as she squeezed my hand.

"I... I don't know what to say," the words stumbled from my lips.

She turned and looked up at me with those deep golden eyes. "You don't have to like them just because they're my mom's. Give me your first impression."

I shook my head to clear it of the whirlwind of memories clouding my brain. "It's like going back in time."

"You mean like one of the artists of another century?"

"No, no. It's like seeing Serena's paintings, the way your mother draws your eye into the landscapes. They're just so similar in style to my wife's."

A dark curtain drew down across her face, erasing the cheerful expression that had been there before I opened my mouth. We both knew I was still married, that I had a child out there somewhere who was either dead or living in seclusion with her mother. And though I explained to her I met with Mayor Morrison concerning my divorce, it could take several months for him to gather the necessary information. She obviously felt uncomfortable about my situation, a classic example of one of those awkward moments.

She slowly unclasped her hand from mine.

"Laura?" I touched the underside of her jaw with my finger and turned her face toward me. "I'm sorry. That was an insensitive thing to say. It took me by surprise. I didn't mean for you to feel uncomfortable. I—"

"Stop. I wasn't expecting you to say what you said either. I reacted spontaneously and I shouldn't have. It's not your fault your wife and child went missing." She paused and looked down at the floor. "That may never change."

I placed a hand on each of her shoulders, bringing her closer to my chest. "That thought is never far from my mind either. And I wouldn't blame you for putting an end to our relationship right now. I'd be sad but I'd understand."

"Laura, honey." The words came from somewhere nearby and we both turned in the direction of the voice.

"Daddy!" Laura's smile lit up, and she rushed into the arms of a handsome older man, with silver-white hair and a clean-shaven face, dressed in a dark suit and tie. He towered several inches above me, and I'm six-feet-two-inches tall.

He stretched out his arm. "Paul Pratt, Laura's father. You must be Dr. Bradford."

I shook his hand and smiled. "Please call me Jessee."

He nodded and smiled, showing perfectly straight teeth. "You must meet my wife, Colleen." He made a sweeping gesture with his arm. "This is all her work. Impressive, isn't it?"

"Definitely, Mr. Pratt. Her paintings are beautiful. Really captivating."

"And it's Paul, Jessee. I'll let Colleen thank you for the compliment, if I can find her." He glanced around the room before his eyebrows shot up. "She's right over there." He pointed to the other side of the room and waved. "She's heading our way."

A slim, dark-haired woman walked in our direction. Straight hair flowed past her shoulders, reaching almost to her waist. She had the same full lips as her daughter, highlighted in red gloss. She was a striking woman, as she glided into our little circle on her five-inch heels and wrap-around turquoise dress, tied at the side of her slender waist.

"You must be Dr. Jessee Bradford." She smiled. "It's nice to meet you. Thank you for joining us."

I shook her hand. "Thank you for inviting me, Mrs. Pratt. I'm glad to be here."

"It's Colleen. And thank you for accompanying our daughter to Des Moines."

"And it's Jessee. I love your work, Colleen. And I'm particularly fond of oil paintings, especially the pastel colors you use. I noticed the portrait of Laura," I pointed to my right. "It's for sale, right?"

She nodded. "It was almost impossible for me to make a decision about whether to sell it or not. But if you're thinking of purchasing it, of course it would make it that much easier to let it go." She grinned and her brown eyes crinkled at the edges.

A couple came up behind Colleen, and the woman tapped her on the shoulder.

"Excuse me," Colleen said. "Hope to see you again soon, Jessee."

"I look forward to it."

Paul shook my hand and rushed off behind Colleen, leaving Laura and me alone in the midst of hundreds of people.

I lightly touched her arm with my fingertips. "Where were we?"

"You said you'd understand if I didn't want to date you any longer."

I looked into her eyes, which glistened with unshed tears. "I don't want to hurt you. Ever. I won't have full closure until my wife and daughter are found, but that doesn't mean I have to stop living. And I'd like to live my life with you in it."

"For now." A tear escaped down her cheek.

I wiped it away with my finger and tipped her face up with my hand. "I think I'm falling in love with you." I heard a tiny gasp escape her lips. "I don't say those words lightly."

"I don't say them lightly, either."

I furrowed my brows. "What's that supposed to mean?"

"I'm falling in love with you, too, Jessee Bradford."

Once again, my heart tumbled round. The way she spoke my full name transported me back in time to that first day I met Serena. I contemplated, once again, if this relationship was meant to be—some sign that Laura and I were supposed to be together.

"Do you want to look around some more?"

She shook her head, her eyes never leaving mine. "I'd like to go home."

I nodded, took her hand, and headed for the nearest exit.

On the drive back to Earlham we listened to a soft jazz station and thirty minutes later I pulled up in front of her house and turned off the ignition.

"Do you want to come inside?" she whispered, her words like a megaphone announcement in the silence of the car.

My gut told me where we were headed. It felt right sitting here with Laura, surrounded by a blanket of darkness, the only sound the tick-tick of the engine as it cooled.

I leaned over the console as she came toward me. Our kiss was tentative and soft, her lips smooth. The taste of strawberry lipstick lingered on my tongue.

I came around to her side of the car, opened the door and put my arm around her waist as we strolled to the front door. Brewster greeted us with jumping enthusiasm, and we scratched his head and belly until he rushed back to his bed.

Laura shut the door and turned around. Leaning her back against the door, she looked up at me. I wrapped my arms around her and pressed my body into hers, feeling her legs against my thighs, her breasts pressed against my chest.

Our kisses turned frantic as she slipped the back of my shirt out of the waistband of my slacks and slid her hands up my bare back, her nails lightly scraping my skin.

Our breathing was the only sound to break the quiet of the darkened hallway. I knew where I wanted this to end but needed to be sure of her intentions for inviting me inside. Slipping my arm under her thighs, I lifted her and was about to carry her upstairs then stopped after the first step.

"Are you sure about this?" I whispered.

"Not really. But please don't stop."

That was all the answer I needed. I slowly walked up the stairs to the second floor. Turning to the left, I noticed the first door open and guessed it must be her bedroom. I carried her to the bed and laid her gently on top of the comforter and draped my body over hers.

Her eyes were half-open and a small smile graced her lips. We undressed each other one piece at a time, my shirt, her dress, my boxers, her panties, until we lay naked, the only light coming from the window where a full moon shone through the glass.

We touched and kissed and caressed our way around and over each other's legs and arms and chest and breasts until we were breathing as if we'd just run around the track.

"I want you, Jessee. Make love to me."

She only had to say it once. I instantly put my heart and soul into the task of granting her request.

It was mind-altering, otherworldly, passionate. Afterward, she lay on her side facing me, her head propped up on her hand, a quizzical look on her face.

I reached out and tucked a strand of silky jet-black hair behind her ear. "What are you thinking about?"

"Can I ask you something?"

I nodded.

"You don't have to answer me if it makes you uncomfortable…"

"My life is an open book, Laura."

"What was Serena like?"

I scrunched the pillow under my head and stared at the ceiling. "She wasn't a strong woman like you." I turned my gaze in her direction and smiled. "You've impressed me since the day I met you."

"Oh, come on."

"No, I'm serious. Your life experiences have made you a stronger person, you know? You've had to endure the death of a spouse, you run a business that can be very dangerous, training these huge animals. You're a survivor, Laura. I admire that."

She glanced down and fiddled with the edge of the pillow case. "Thank you for saying that."

I tipped her head up with my finger so she looked me in the eyes. "I wasn't trying to flatter you, just describing how I see you. Serena was, or is, an emotionally delicate woman. I'd never met anyone like her, which was the big attraction, I guess. Back then, I wanted to take care of her. And she was a loner, too. No friends, spent most of her time in her studio, painting."

"You had a good relationship though?"

I nodded. "I thought so. Kind of the opposites attract thing goin' on. But after she had Sofia she... I don't know. She became more reclusive, but at the same time, more needy. I worked long hours at the clinic. She was at home with the baby. She felt neglected, became emotionally clingy when I wasn't there, but when I'd come home she'd clam up and shun me." I shook my head. "When I think about it, I should have seen it coming, her leaving me, that is. Maybe I was hiding my head in the sand. I don't know."

"Why didn't she just divorce you?"

"Her father would have had a fit if I got any of Serena's money . But she refused his suggestion that I sign a pre-nup and insisted we commingle our assets." I shrugged. "Maybe he had something to do with the whole thing. I might never know."

"I'm sorry this is happening to you."

I kissed the tip of her nose and she smiled that beautiful smile of hers. I tickled her sides and she burst out laughing. We ended up wrestling on the floor which segued into another opportunity to make love.

I wasn't falling in love with her after all. I was already in love with her.

CHAPTER TWENTY-SEVEN

It was almost Thanksgiving, the first time Nana would be celebrating the holiday without Grampa. Nana, Kerryanne and I were watching Jeopardy one evening when Nana broached the subject.

"Do you like turkey, Kerryanne?"

Kerryanne laughed. "Who doesn't?"

Nana turned her head in my direction and smiled. "Jessee always had to have the drumstick. Remember, Jess?"

I lowered the volume on the TV. "What sticks out in my mind is how disappointed I was when I got the short side of the wishbone."

Nana leaned back in her chair, eyes focused on some distant point above the television. "Harper told me he always tried to grab it really low so you'd get the longer side so you'd get your wish."

"It never worked." I grinned. "Nana?" She brought her attention back to our conversation. "What would you think about inviting Laura and her parents for Thanksgiving dinner?"

She gave me a withering look. "Now, Jessee, what do you think I'd think about it? Of course you can invite them." She glanced at Kerryanne. "What about you, Kerryanne?"

Kerryanne looked from Nana, to me, then back to Nana and frowned. "You're asking me to come for Thanksgiving dinner?"

"You live here, don't you?" I took a quick peek at Nana. "You're like family to us."

"He's right," Nana added. "You've become a real part of this household. Is there anyone you'd like to invite to dinner?"

Kerryanne looked down at her hands. "If I got the longer side of the wishbone I'd wish my mom could come."

Nana and I looked at each other, and I gave Nana a slow nod.

"What if you contacted your momma, Kerryanne?" Nana said. "Is there a possibility she'd leave your father?"

"You mean, like, for Thanksgiving dinner?"

Nana smiled at her. "No. I mean would your momma leave your father for good... move here to Iowa, away from your father and the... the abuse you told me about. If she had a place to live, with us, here in Earlham?"

The look on Kerryanne's face was priceless. Her jaw dropped half-open, and her eyes grew wide as silver quarters.

"You're not serious," she whispered. Both Nana and I nodded.

"Nana and I were talking about it the other day," I said. "We know you miss your mom and we'd like to help. We wondered what we could do for you, besides telling you how sorry we are that this is happening in your life. We could help your mom escape from your father's abuse, reunite the two of you."

Several tears dropped off her quivering chin. She stood up and leaned over to hug me then walked over and put her arms around Nana's neck and kissed her on the cheek before sitting on the floor in front of our chairs.

I stared at the floor for a few seconds. "We'd have to come up with a plan first."

Nana glanced in my direction and nodded. "You're right." She turned toward Kerryanne. "Could you call your momma and see what she thinks about it?"

"And if she agrees," I said, "maybe we could set up a rendezvous, somewhere safe where we could pick her up without having your father find out."

Kerryanne gnawed at her bottom lip, staring across the room. "That might work."

I rubbed at my chin, looking at the ground, and tried to come up with a foolproof scheme. "Does your father ever work on the weekends?"

"He works every Saturday 'cause he gets overtime." She nodded, looking pensive. "Eight to five-thirty. And it never changes. Ever."

"Then your mom could leave the house and walk to, say, a park or someplace where no one she knows would see her." I paused for a second. "I'm thinking out loud here."

Kerryanne's face changed right before our eyes. A smile formed on her lips, showing her bright silver retainer. "I have the perfect idea."

Nana leaned forward and focused on Kerryanne. "What is it, dear?"

"There's an abandoned gas station about a mile or so from my house. You can go around the back and the restroom doors are always open. And you can't see them from the street. She could hide there."

"And we could drive around to the back, pick her up, and no one would ever know," I interjected.

Kerryanne stood up and rubbed her hands together. "I'll call her." She paused. "If that's okay."

Nana smiled and nodded. "Of course. Oh, does your momma have a cell phone so we could get in touch with her when we reach Little Rock?"

Kerryanne shook her head. "My dad won't spend that much money on her. He'd rather waste it on alcohol and cigarettes."

Nana tapped her finger against her chin. "Well, I have a good feelin' about this. I think everything's gonna work out just fine and dandy."

Kerryanne's eyes looked glassy and her bottom lip trembled. "You guys are too much."

"Well. I guess that's better than being too little." Nana laughed. "You and Jessee can drive to Little Rock together in the truck—"

Kerryanne shook her head. "I'm really not so sure about that, Rose—"

"Call me Nana. Lots of people do. And they aren't related to me either."

Kerryanne smiled. "Thanks." Her face tinged rosy pink. "I don't know if Mom would come back here with me and Jessee." She turned in Nana's direction. "If you came with us, though..." She glanced at me. "Nothing personal. I just think she'd be uncomfortable because you're a guy. She's really scared of—"

"I understand. No harm done." I turned to Nana. "I agree with her, you know. We don't want her mother to change her mind when she sees me. I'll drive all of us there. The truck fits four people comfortably, Nana." I raised my eyebrows.

Nana worked her mouth back and forth, looking serious. She clasped her hands together. "Okay. Let's do it. Or, as you always say, Jessee, bring it on."

Kerryanne and I jumped up and hugged each other while Nana sat in her Barcalounger, laughing.

"Go call your mom," I said, "and ask her if we can pick her up the Saturday before Thanksgiving between two and three in the afternoon."

Kerryanne ran out of the room and within five minutes she returned with a wide grin on her face.

"She'll do it," she shouted then covered her mouth with her hands, tears running down her cheeks. "I guess he got super drunk just the other night. She said she thought he might have broken her jaw but she said it feels better today."

Nana stood up and embraced Kerryanne. "Then I'm glad we decided to do this." She pulled back to face Kerryanne. "Right, sweetie?"

Kerryanne sniffed then her lips quirked up in a tiny smile. "Yeah, I'm glad, too... Nana."

* * * *

We left for Little Rock at five in the morning that Saturday. I Googled the street address Kerryanne provided and knew it would take about nine hours to get there. We stopped several times along the way to stretch our legs, but Nana packed us a lunch and we ate in the truck. We didn't want to spend the night in a hotel and we hoped not to run into any problems once we got to Little Rock.

"So your mother's name is Julia?" I asked, eyes riveted on the endless white line separating the two lanes of the highway.

Kerryanne hung her arms over the front seat. "Julia Otten."

"Julia Otten," I said to myself. "And your father's name?"

I glanced in the rearview mirror and noticed her lips drawn in a tight line. "William. Bill Otten."

"Where does he work? Close to home?" Nana asked.

"He works at the quarry not too far from our house. On Saturdays he always stops at the bar in town with his buddies after work." She paused and I saw her gaze out the side window. "That's when it starts—the drinking. And by the time he gets home, he's smashed. Then he purposely starts an argument with Mom. They end up shouting. Then he pushes her, slaps her around." Tears brimmed in her eyes. "He's broken her nose three times. And once he kicked her out of the house. It was in the middle of winter, thirty-five degrees outside. She almost froze to death."

I heard the rustling of Nana's dress as she turned toward Kerryanne. "Your momma never has to experience that horrible abuse again."

"Mom said if she left him she didn't want me to have to live on the run, always searching for the next place to hide. Part of the reason I ran away was because I thought it would be easier if she tried to leave on her own, without me tagging along. But she's scared of living in shelters and she didn't know anyone who'd take her in."

I glanced at Kerryanne. "Until now." She smiled. "And once she gets to Earlham, she can hire an attorney, get a divorce. Then she'll be free."

Kerryanne nodded. Of course, we all hoped our plan would work and that everything would go smoothly. But what if Bill came home unexpectedly? What if for some reason Julia changed her mind at the last minute? I didn't think any of us was totally sure, even Kerryanne. The outcome was unpredictable.

There weren't many cars on the freeway leading to Little Rock on a Saturday, and we arrived at the abandoned gas station a little after two in the afternoon. I pulled the truck around to the back of the small rundown building, parked close to the bathroom doors and turned off the engine.

A glance in the rearview mirror at Kerryanne showed me that she was nervous, biting her lower lip and never taking her eyes off the restroom doors where we hoped her mother was hiding.

The paint on both doors was peeling from top to bottom and the door knob on the women's side hung about two inches from where it should have been attached. Both stood ajar and I could only surmise how filthy they were inside.

"Should I go check to see if she's inside?" I said.

Kerryanne's voice sounded firm and strong. "I'll go."

Nana opened the truck door and pushed the seat forward so Kerryanne could jump out. At that moment, the women's restroom door drew open a couple of inches. A tall slender woman with short brown hair peered around the edge of the door frame.

Kerryanne raced round the front of the truck and she and her mother hugged for several minutes, rocking from side to side. Julia carried a small duffel bag which Kerryanne took, grabbed her mother's hand and pulled her to Nana's side of the truck. They climbed into the back seat after throwing the duffle bag in the truck bed. I waited for Nana to shut her door before I turned the key in the ignition.

"Ready to head for Earlham?" I asked, turning to look in the backseat.

Julia's hair was cut as short as her daughter's but spiked out in all directions as if she hadn't run a brush through it in days. She had the same big blue eyes as Kerryanne, but without the wide-eyed look of curiosity always evident in her daughter's face. Instead, tiny wrinkles spread from the sides of her sad-looking eyes, and her skin had a pinched quality to it, making her look older than her forty-plus years.

Julia's arm draped around Kerryanne's shoulders, and their faces were wet with tears. "Thank you," she whispered. She leaned forward over the console and looked at Nana and me, her lower lip shaking with emotion. "Thank you both for taking in my daughter." She laid her head against the back of the seat, tears streaming down her face.

I pulled away from the rear of the gas station and smiled to myself. Nana reached over and patted my arm.

We were good at rescuing strays, I thought. Animals and humans.

CHAPTER TWENTY-EIGHT

Once we were on the road, I glanced in the rearview mirror and noticed a cut above Julia's eyebrow along with bruises under her jawline on her neck. Nana turned on the radio to allow Kerryanne and her mother to have a conversation without us hearing, then she laid her head back on the headrest, closed her eyes and let out a big sigh. It was evident this rescue had taken its toll on Nana. For days she'd been worrying, anticipating the worst case scenario. I was relieved our plan had gone off without a hitch.

I figured we'd arrive in Earlham after midnight, and by six o'clock I was getting hungry. Nana leaned her head against the car window, dozing, and I glanced in the rearview mirror and saw Kerryanne's head resting on her mother's shoulder. They were both asleep as well and I decided not to waken them. Nana, Kerryanne, and I had been up since four, and I couldn't imagine the emotional toll this had taken on mother and daughter as well as Nana.

I continued driving one more hour then another. Everyone was still asleep. By ten p.m., I decided to pull off the road to eat. The moment I turned into the fast food chain's parking lot, everyone woke up. After a short stop at the drive-through, they fell back to sleep, and I continued the rest of the way to Earlham, reaching the farm about one the next morning.

When I shut off the ignition the silence enveloped us like a cloak. I opened the car door, and white clouds of vapor swirled around my face with every breath. Three heads popped up. I helped Nana out of the truck then Kerryanne and Julia climbed down, groggy from sleep.

We entered the house and trudged up the stairs. Kerryanne and Julia planned to share Kerryanne's room which had two single beds, and we all mumbled good night before heading to our respective bedrooms.

I slept for nine hours straight until the scent of bacon drifting upstairs woke me from a deep sleep. It was almost 10:30 in the morning. After splashing cold water on my face and brushing my teeth, I went downstairs for breakfast.

Everyone had eaten and they were sipping coffee when I entered the kitchen.

"Good morning," I chirped.

Three heads turned in my direction and Nana popped up to get me a cup of coffee.

"Did you sleep well, Julia?" I asked.

"Yes, thank you, I did. I want to tell you again how much I appreciate your driving all the way to Little Rock just to..." Her eyes welled up with tears.

"No need to thank me." I gestured in Nana's direction. "We just wanted to reunite you with your daughter. And Nana likes it when her house is full. Isn't that right?"

Nana's smile stretched from ear to ear. "We'll enjoy havin' you here, Julia."

"Kerryanne and I were talking," Julia said. "I'd like to pay you back for all you've done for my daughter."

"You don't have to worry yourself about that," Nana replied. "We're happy to help. As Jessee will tell you, Kerryanne's really come to their rescue at the clinic."

I nodded. "She's been great, Julia. I couldn't run the clinic without her." I paused, wanting to address the elephant in the middle of the room. "How will your husband feel about you leaving?"

She glanced out the window. "He'll find me, you know?" She turned to look at Nana and me. Kerryanne laid a hand on her mother's back.

"And if he does," I said, "he'll have to deal with all of us, Julia."

"He gets violent when he drinks."

Nana patted Julia's arm. "Then we'll make sure you're never alone."

Julia shook her head. "It's not fair to y'all." Her gaze flowed from Nana to Kerryanne then to me. "I was so happy that Kerryanne found good, solid people to live with, here in Iowa. I missed her but at least I knew she was safe." A tear rolled down her cheek. "Now she won't be safe. Because she's with me. I'll worry every single day." She took in a shuddering breath. "The only way she and I will ever be truly safe is when he's dead."

"Don't even think that way," Nana scolded. "What you need is a good lawyer, Julia. Maybe you can file for a legal separation or a divorce or get one of those restraining orders or something."

"I can't afford a lawyer, Rose. Bill never even let me have my own ATM card or credit card or a cell phone or more than a few dollars at a time. He knew I could never leave."

"But you did," I said. "And we'll help you, Julia. The mayor of Earlham is an attorney. Perhaps you could speak with him." I paused, smiled. "First things first, okay?"

"I'll need to find a job, too."

"Nana and I will ask around town."

"The holidays are comin'." Nana beamed. "Store owners always need a helpin' hand at this time of year."

Julia nodded and put her arm around Kerryanne's shoulders. "Thank you, Rose, Jessee. For everything."

"Thanksgiving's in a few days." Nana smiled across the table at Julia. "I'll need help bakin' pies and makin' casseroles."

Julia grinned and let out a sigh. "That sounds like Heaven. While those two are at work this week I can help with whatever you need done here, Rose. It'll keep my mind off... other things."

I was interested to know more about Julia's situation with her husband Bill. It was obvious she feared he'd find her in Iowa. I'd seen the cuts and bruises on her face and neck when she entered the truck in Little Rock. There was a lot more to her story than she was telling us right now.

* * * *

We had a short week at the clinic because of the holiday. Trying to cram five days of examining animals into three days before Thanksgiving meant longer hours. But I looked forward to dinner on Thursday with Laura and her parents as well as Nana, Kerryanne and Julia.

When Thursday morning arrived, the scents emanating from Nana's kitchen made my mouth water. I always loved Thanksgiving, and my mom and dad and I travelled to Iowa several times to join Nana and Grampa for this holiday when I was younger.

Laura and her parents arrived at two o'clock, and Nana instantly made them feel at home, offering drinks and talking about the people of Earlham whom they all knew.

When Laura and her father walked into the kitchen to look at the turkey, I turned to Colleen.

"I wanted to ask you about the painting of Laura I saw at your opening at the Persoll Gallery. I'd like to purchase it."

"I'd be happy to sell it to you." She smiled. "Where are you thinking of hanging it?"

"For now, I'd like to hang it in my office at the clinic. It would really brighten up the place."

"I'm flattered, Jessee." She paused and worked her lips into a tight line. "Did Laura tell you about—"

"Jeff?"

She nodded.

"Yes, she did. What a tragic thing to happen. One of the many casualties of war."

Her face took on a look of sad resignation as she shook her head from side to side. "All the wives and children of those who died over there, their lives forever changed because of the fighting and bombs."

"Laura's still hurting from that, I can tell. When I met her—"

"She told us about how you saved Brewster. That's the only living tie she has to Jeff, you know. They planned on having kids just as soon as he got out of the service." She put her drink on the coffee table and leaned back on the couch. "Laura speaks very highly of you."

That warmed my heart and I smiled. "Thank you for saying that. I really like her too."

She stared at me with a serious expression. "She's still healing from Jeff's death. Paul and I weren't sure she'd ever recover. We were against Jeff re-upping for another stint in Iraq, and Laura was so frightened something would happen to him. Then—"

"Then something did," I completed her sentence. "You know, Colleen, I won't hurt your daughter. She means a lot to me. She's a fantastic person."

She lowered her voice to a whisper. "I'm sure you mean that. Jeff promised us the same thing before the two of them were married. But Laura told us that—"

She hesitated and I jumped right in. "That I'm still married. But I'm assuming she explained the story to you."

She nodded.

"The Mayor's my attorney now, and he's working on getting information regarding my divorce."

"Yes, her father and I understand that but we're still concerned—"

"That if my wife and child are found, I'll leave Laura?"

"Yes. You've hit the nail on the head. Do you blame us?"

"Of course not. Any parent would feel the same way. But I promise you, I mean to get on with my life. It kills me to admit this, but the FBI doesn't believe my wife and child were kidnapped." I paused, feeling that familiar twisting sensation in my gut. "It took me awhile, but I agree with them. They think she left me. For some reason I may never know. And, if that's true, I wouldn't want to be married to her if she came back."

She nodded her head up and down slowly, her lips pursed. "Makes sense." She sat up and tilted her head. "We'd love to have you over for dinner sometime."

I grinned. I had a feeling she liked me, that she knew I had no intention of causing her daughter any more sadness than she'd already experienced. "Anytime is good for me."

Laura and her father returned to the front room and sat down. Laura wore a red silk dress and leather boots. Her hair looked like shiny black marble against her fair skin.

"What are you two talking about?" She looked from me to her mother and back.

I shrugged. "I was telling her about the farm. Nana's thinking of buying more chickens. The local grocery store can't find enough fresh eggs to keep up with the demand here in Earlham."

Laura laughed. "Stimulating conversation."

"We were just discussing you two coming to dinner at our house," Colleen piped up.

Laura raised her eyebrows, inviting me to answer. "I said yes, of course." I laughed.

"I'm glad to hear that." Laura smiled. "Dinner's almost ready. Julia and Rose are just putting it on the table in the dining room."

Everyone enjoyed themselves during the meal. The conversation leaped from Nana's newest idea of purchasing more chickens to Kerryanne's job at the clinic and Julia's search for a job.

"Have you ever been a waitress?" Laura asked.

Julia nodded. "It's been years but yes, I worked in a small cafe when I was a teenager."

"They're always looking for good wait staff at the local diner, especially around the holidays. You might try Billy's."

"If your daughter wasn't so efficient at her job at the clinic, I'd hire you, but I'm about to give her another raise. She's great with clients. Never complains about working late, which happens fairly often."

Kerryanne's cheeks reddened at my praise.

Julia smiled. "I'm proud of her, too. She deserves to be happy."

After dinner Colleen and Paul left to visit a few friends who still lived in Earlham. Nana and Julia were busy cleaning up in the kitchen, and Laura and I stole a few moments alone in front of the fire.

"So my mother invited you to dinner."

I nodded.

"That means she likes you."

"And I like her. And your father, of course. They're good people."

"They are. And very protective of their only daughter."

"I talked to the Mayor the other day and he'll be getting all the information about filing for my divorce. But he said it may take months."

"It's a long process."

"He said it can be. I plan on waiving any claim to Serena's money though. Otherwise it could take even longer. I never cared about her money and I don't want to enter into a court battle with her parents over it."

"I'm sorry." She placed her hand on top of mine.

I turned my palm up and intertwined our fingers. "I never dreamed the day would come when I'd be talking about divorcing my wife."

She looked me straight in the eyes. "Are you sure you want to go through with it? You love her very much."

"She'll always have a place in my heart. I admit there are days I feel guilty talking about divorcing her, but how long is long enough when it comes to emotional suffering? And the waiting is killing me."

She squeezed my hand, her eyes glistened. "There's no set time. I believe you just know in your heart."

"You're ready to move on, aren't you?"

"It took me over two years before I met you."

I gave her hand a little tug and bent my head toward her. Our lips met in a languorous kiss that left me wanting much more.

"I should go, Jess. I have to work tomorrow."

I pulled back in mock horror.

"My horses don't know it's Thanksgiving. I have a young foal arriving tomorrow morning. I have to get some sleep. I'm no good to anyone, least of all the horses, if I'm dragging my body around like a ten-ton weight."

We went into the kitchen where she thanked everyone for dinner. I walked her to the car, and we kissed one more time before I opened the car door and she slid inside. I held the door open, gazing down at her. "That dress looks great on you."

"Thank you. I was hoping you'd like it." The edges of her lips curved upward.

"I like you in it." I paused. "And I'd like you out of it, too."

The color of her cheeks flared. "Then it was worth every dime I spent." She smiled and closed the car door.

As I watched her car disappear down Chestnut Avenue I realized once again that I loved her, even more now than I had just a few weeks ago. My life was back on track when I was with her, all the gloom I experienced since Serena and Sofia went missing slowly fading away. Laura was becoming a part of my new life or, better said, Laura was making my life new again.

CHAPTER TWENTY-NINE

December barreled in with a blast of snow and freezing rain. Laura and I drove to her parents' house for dinner, and Nana let me take Grampa's GMC Sierra. In this weather, a four-wheel drive would be a safer vehicle than my Mustang.

Both of us dressed casually in pants, boots and jackets. Colleen told us dinner was an informal affair and we should come prepared to have a relaxed evening together.

I knew how to negotiate a vehicle in the rain, sleet, and snow, and it still took more than an hour to reach her parents' house in Des Moines. Colleen met us at the front door as we stepped out of the truck. We raced to the house just as the clouds unleashed more buckets of freezing rain.

"I should have rescheduled our night together." Colleen frowned as we rushed past her into the foyer.

We shook the rain from our jackets and rubbed our hands together.

"Don't apologize, Mom. If we thought it was too dangerous we would have cancelled." Laura gestured in my direction. "He's used to this Iowa weather by now, aren't you, Jess?"

"Oh yeah, I'm a regular veteran," I teased. "Thanks for inviting us, Colleen. I was hoping to pick up my painting tonight."

She winked at me. "It's wrapped and ready to go. I got your check in the mail last week. Thank you."

Laura looked at me quizzically. "What painting are you talking about?"

"When I first met your parents at the Persoll Gallery, I fell in love with your portrait, remember?"

Her eyebrows rose up past her long black bangs. "I thought you were just being nice. You bought it?"

I nodded.

"What are you going to do with it?"

I gave her a mock dirty look. "I plan to hang it in my office at the clinic, silly. Then I can see your beautiful face all day long."

She shook her head, looking befuddled, then grabbed my hand. "Let's go find Daddy. He's probably in the kitchen."

I smiled at Colleen as I passed her, and she gave me a friendly pat on the back.

From what I'd seen so far, their house was tastefully decorated with paintings and comfortable-looking couches and chairs in mauve and cream colors.

Paul Pratt stood in the kitchen with a white apron tied around his waist, stirring something on the stove. He turned around to greet us, holding a large spoon covered with red sauce.

"Jessee, nice to see you again. Hope you like Italian food."

Laura kissed her father on the cheek and bent over the pot, taking in a big breath. "This smells delicious."

"It does," I agreed, giving Paul a firm handshake. "Thanks for inviting us."

"Why don't you help me with the final touches, honey, while Jessee looks around?" He turned and waved his hand toward the front room. "You might enjoy looking at some of the artists in our collection."

I thanked him and walked into a huge parlor with antique furniture, a fireplace, and a dining room table at one end. I had just entered the room when Colleen joined me.

She pointed at a painting hanging above the mantel. "This is my inspiration."

The colors on the canvas were a mixture of intense blues for the ocean waves, shimmering white foam, the sunset a striking blend of yellow, pink, and orange oil colors.

"It reminds me of Santa Barbara. I miss the ocean." I noticed a white squiggle in the bottom right corner and leaned closer to get a better look. "A snake?" I glanced at Colleen with raised eyebrows.

She nodded. "That's right. It has two tiny eyes and what looks like a rattler. But the artist's name, believe it or not, is She."

"She?" I asked, gazing intently at the signature, my nose practically touching the canvas.

Colleen chuckled. "It reminds me of that African American singer who plays the guitar—"

"Prince?"

"That's the one. He changed his name to a symbol. Anyway, She's supposed to have a showing at the Persoll Gallery on Christmas Eve. Maybe you and Laura would like to go."

I stood back to get a better look at the painting. "Yeah. I think I'd enjoy that. You say this artist was your inspiration?"

"When I saw this at a gallery in the city it jerked me out of the doldrums. I stopped painting for months and what I'd been doing was just so dark. After seeing She's paintings, I started mixing the darker oil paints with white to get the pastel colors. Suddenly the enthusiasm I had years ago came back." Colleen stared at the canvas with a wistful look in her eyes then shook her head. "So that's my story."

"I'd like to see more of She's work. When I met my wife in college the ocean was the only thing she painted. She spent most of her time at the beach between classes."

"You must miss her."

My eyes were glued to the canvas. "The memories are less sharp. What bothers me the most is every toddler I see on the street reminds me of Sofia. That's my daughter. I dream about finding her. She was only nine months old when they both went missing."

Colleen laid her hand on my forearm. "That must be tough."

"Hey, what are you two doing?" Laura called from the doorway.

I walked over and gave her a chaste kiss. "Your mother was pointing out her inspiration. The artist, She, has a showing at the Persoll on Christmas Eve. Do you want to go?"

"I'd love to," Laura said. "Dinner's ready. Why don't you sit down? Daddy and I will serve."

It was a fabulous meal with homemade sauce over al dente pasta, crusty French bread, a fresh salad, and ice cream for dessert. Just as Laura told me, Colleen and Paul were the kind of people who didn't put on airs, very down-to-earth, but full of interesting stories. They'd travelled all over Europe, and I enjoyed listening to their tales of mishaps and wanderings during their journeys.

It felt as if only an hour had passed, but when I looked at the clock it was close to midnight and we had to get back to Earlham. The rain finally let up so we carefully laid the portrait in the back seat of the truck and headed home.

When I pulled up in front of Laura's house she turned and smiled at me. "Do you want to go riding sometime?"

I pulled back in surprise. "Me? Ride?"

"Yes, you. It might be cold but I have a covered arena and when it's not raining or snowing it can be extraordinarily invigorating."

I nodded my head, slowly. "O-kay. But the only time I've ever ridden a horse was when I was a kid on a trail ride. I already told you, large animals aren't my forte. Are you certain I won't fall off and break my neck?"

She patted my arm and leaned over the console. "You'll be just fine. How about tomorrow morning?"

I waggled my eyebrows up and down. "You could easily talk me into it."

She grinned. "Would you like to spend the night?"

"I thought you'd never ask."

* * * *

The next morning a warm wet nose nuzzled my arm pit and I turned my head to find Brewster standing next to the bed, tongue lolling to the side, hot breath wafting across my bare chest. The clock on the bedside table read seven a.m., Laura was still asleep, and I figured Brewster had to go outside and do his business.

After opening the back door and letting him out I turned the thermostat to seventy degrees and crawled back in bed. Laura snuggled up against me and murmured something unintelligible.

I kissed her neck. "What did you say?"

"It's not raining or snowing, is it?" she mumbled.

"No, why?"

"Then it's the perfect time to ride."

I pressed my body closer to hers. "It's too early. The horses are still sleeping."

She pulled the covers back and hopped out of bed like the Energizer Bunny. "The horses are early risers, just like me." She grabbed my hand and gave it a tug. "Now get up. The early bird and all that."

I sighed as loudly as I could for effect, then tugged on my jeans, boots, and jacket while she dressed. By the time we finished drinking a quick cup of coffee, I was awake and ready to try my hand at riding.

As we made our way through the icy slush to the arena, whinnying sounds emanated from the barn.

"How many horses are you boarding?"

"Four. Maximus, of course, and Carmel, Jazz, and Lido."

"And which horse will I be riding?"

"I think you should start with Carmel. Jazz is a bit unpredictable, and Lido's way too much for you to handle."

"What type of horses are we talking about here?" I asked as she grabbed the handle to the barn door and yanked it open.

"Jazz is a Missouri Foxtrotter and Lido is another Friesian brought to me last week for training."

"And Carmel will be perfect for me because…?"

"Because he'll be an easy introduction for you to the art of riding in an English saddle. He's not too big and not too small. He's perfect for you."

"So he's not a Western pony?"

"Oh, you could ride him in a Western saddle but I think you'll enjoy less paraphernalia if I put an English saddle on him. I actually don't have a Western saddle for him." She gave my wrist a light slap. "Stop worrying. You'll do just fine."

She ambled to the first stall and opened the door. I watched as she led a butterscotch-colored horse into the pathway running down the middle of the barn and tied his lead rope to a large round hook sticking out of the wall.

"Can you go into the tack room over there?" She pointed toward a doorway at the back of the barn. "Grab the black saddle hanging on a wooden peg on the wall with Carmel's name below it. There's a light switch on your left as you enter."

I immediately found the saddle with the bridle hanging next to it. After bringing it to Laura, she showed me how to tack up Carmel, including pulling the bridle over his head, inserting the bit, and tightening the girth that held the saddle onto the horse. We were ready to go after she tacked up Maximus.

I stood on the mounting block and threw my leg over Carmel's back, then settled deep into the saddle.

"Ready?" Laura asked, smiling.

"Too late to turn back now." I felt uneasy about this excursion. Though happy not to be sitting as high as Laura on her over-sixteen-hand Friesian, I was still scared. If Carmel bolted across the arena I wouldn't know the first thing about stopping him.

"Follow me out of the barn into the arena. I left the gate open. Just squeeze Carmel a couple of times with both your legs to make him walk, hold the reins lightly in your hands and don't jerk on his mouth. You'll be okay."

I nodded although she couldn't see me. I was so nervous my mouth went dry, but I was determined to tough this out and not act like a two-year-old.

I squeezed Carmel with both legs once and he walked behind Maximus quietly until we arrived at the covered arena. Small clouds of frosty air emanated with each breath I expelled, but the heat coming from Carmel's body kept me warm along with the adrenaline racing through my veins.

We passed the gate leading into the arena, and Laura and Maximus turned around. She leaned over and closed the gate with one hand. I followed her around the edge of the arena, what she called "the rail". All of this was new to me and should have been exciting, but my gut clenched like a ball in my mid-section, and my clammy hands slipped back and forth through the reins.

Laura turned in her saddle and looked back at me. "Do you want to do a little trot work?" I twitched one eyebrow upward.

"You can just sit the trot for now, Jess. I can teach you how to post some other day."

"Post?"

"Sorry. When a horse trots, you can move your lower body up and down with the rhythm of the trot so your butt doesn't plop up and down on the saddle. But we won't worry about that today."

"I guess I'm game," I answered, lying through my teeth. There was something about backing out that made me feel like a wuss so I sat up straighter, gritted my teeth, and endeavored to appear at ease.

She gave Maximus a light tap on his haunches with a long thin whip and up he went into what looked like a faster walk. Carmel immediately followed. It felt as if I were sitting on a small locomotive, hurtling forward out of control.

I knew we weren't moving very fast, but I bounced up and down on the small pad of leather like a rubber ball. My legs hugged Carmel's belly in a vise grip, and my hands held the reins so far away from the bit that the reins were flapping in the air along the sides of Carmel's neck.

"Hohohohohoho," I yelled after riding down the long side of the arena at what felt like lightning speed.

Maximus came to a halt, and Carmel stopped abruptly right behind him.

Laura turned her horse around to face me. "How did that feel?"

I gave her a stinging look and let out the breath I'd been holding since we began trotting.

Her eyes met mine and she frowned. "You didn't like it."

"You could have warned me I'd be bouncing up and down on this... this scrap of leather you call a saddle. My head feels like it might fall off my shoulders."

"Maybe we should have just walked around the arena and not progressed to the trot." She covered her mouth with one hand, and the edges of her eyes crinkled.

"Are you enjoying my pain?" I asked, not happy seeing her obvious delight at my lack of equitation skills.

She tilted her head back and let out a loud laugh. "Every time I turned around to make sure you were still on Carmel, your facial expression was…I'm not exactly sure."

I shook my head and chuckled. "I think it would be best if we begin with lessons in the smaller round pen. That way I can work myself up to the trot."

She nodded but I still thought I saw a little smirk on her lips.

"Good idea," she said. "But hey, you didn't fall off. You weren't even close, right?"

I squinted at her. "Only Carmel and I are privy to that information. For now, I think I'm through for the day. I have to go to the office and catch up on some paperwork."

She leaned toward me and gave me a light kiss on the mouth. "You go, cowboy," she whispered in a low, sexy voice.

I couldn't help but laugh. I must have been quite a sight, especially to her, since she was such an accomplished rider. If she gave me a few private lessons perhaps we could go out on the trail in the Spring. I looked forward to that. But for now, I slid off Carmel's back, gave him a pat on his haunch and walked him back to the barn.

CHAPTER THIRTY

The next day was Sunday and I had just sat down in the kitchen to have a cup of coffee when Julia opened the side door. The hood of her slicker covered her head, and she stomped her feet on the outdoor mat before she entered.

"Good morning," she chirped, pulling off her bright yellow jacket and hanging it up on the hook near the back door.

Her short hair looked the same as the day we met, poking out in all directions as if she'd just gotten out of bed. But her face appeared less strained, her blue eyes brighter, the look of sadness replaced with a wide smile.

I gestured toward the basket draped over her arm. "That's more eggs than usual."

"Those new chickens your grandmother got last week are really great egg-layers." She set the basket on the counter and washed her hands at the sink.

I poured her a fresh cup of coffee, and she sat down across from me. After blowing on the edge of her mug, she took a tentative sip and smiled. "I can't thank you and your grandmother enough for taking me and Kerryanne into your home."

I nodded and smiled back. "It's our pleasure."

Julia's eyes lit up. "I got a job."

"No kidding. Where?"

"In town, at Billy's diner. I start Monday morning. I'll be working the morning and lunch shifts and he's gonna pay me by the hour plus I can keep all my tips." She gazed out the kitchen window and took a deep breath. "It's the first real job I've had since I married Bill. He wouldn't let me out of the house, even after Kerryanne started school."

"What did you do all day?"

Her eyes met mine. "The house had to be sparkling clean, lunch on the table at exactly noon, and dinner darn well had to be hot and ready when he came home from the quarry at 5:30. Or else." She gazed down at her hands, so tightly clasped that her knuckles turned white.

I patted her arm. "Or else what?"

She stared into the dark brown brew. "Or else he'd start yelling... then he'd push me. After I fell on the floor he'd sometimes kick me in the back, maybe the stomach." Her eyes lifted to meet mine. "Sometimes he'd leave me lying there and go to the bar in town. And when he came back, his dinner had to be hot and ready for him to eat the second he walked in the door. And I had to serve it to him with a big smile on my face."

"My God," I said under my breath. "You couldn't leave, go to a friend's house, call the police?"

"I didn't have any friends. He wouldn't even let me go next door to have a cup of coffee. He once told me if I ever left and took Kerryanne he'd hire an attorney and prove I kidnapped our daughter." She shrugged. "I know it sounds impossible, that after all those years I couldn't have saved up enough money and run as far away as I could and hide somewhere, but—"

"I'm not judging you, Julia. I can't imagine being in such a horrible situation. I'm sure you did the best you could."

"It wasn't always bad. Sometimes months would go by and if I did everything right, if I didn't slip up, he'd be so kind and loving." She took another sip of coffee. "But if I messed up, if dinner was late by even five minutes or there was a hair in the bathroom sink..." Her bottom lip quivered and a tear slid down her cheek.

I refilled her mug. "I'm not a psychologist, but what happened wasn't your fault. You can't change people. Your husband sounds as if he has some mental problems. You did nothing wrong. No one deserves to be beaten, Julia."

She swiped at her tears with a napkin. "I had no one to turn to, no friends or relatives to help me out. It was like one of those Lifetime movies. I'm such a fool."

I lightly squeezed her hand. "You're not a fool. He's the fool. He sounds like a very sick man, feeling better about himself by beating a defenseless woman, threatening to take her child, forcing her to be his slave for years."

She looked at me with eyes full of sadness, like a kicked puppy. My heart ached for all she'd had to endure for years.

"What if he finds me? He'll kill me. Or he'll hurt Kerryanne to get to me. My leaving will push him over the edge."

"Now that you're settled in, maybe it's time to see the mayor, find out what you can do legally."

She nodded. "As soon as I have some money saved." Her mouth set in a tight line. "I have to do this on my own. And I have to pay your grandmother for living here, too."

"I understand. And I'm not pressuring you. I'm just trying to help."

The edges of her lips quirked up in a tiny smile. "You and your grandmother have been like angels from Heaven. I thank God every night for you two coming into my life. And you've done enough, taking me and my daughter into your home, feeding us, giving Kerryanne a job."

"It's our pleasure." I stood up and patted her on the back. "I have to go to the clinic. There's a new litter of puppies I need to check on."

* * * *

Kerryanne and Kathy had lunch at Billy's diner on Tuesday. They invited me, but I wanted to remain with the puppies and peruse the patient charts. Christmas was fast approaching, and the clinic would be open fewer days in December because of the holiday vacation. I didn't want to get behind in my notations.

A loud knock on the front door interrupted my much-needed quiet time. Kathy always locked the office and hung a sign indicating when we would re-open after lunch. However, I could tell whoever was pounding incessantly on the door was not going to give up. The banging grew louder and it sounded as though the door frame would crack.

I rushed down the hallway toward the front of the office, and I could see a figure through the clouded glass. I swung the door open before it came off its hinges.

An older woman burst through the doorway carrying a medium-size black and white English Sheepdog. "My dog's been hit by a car!"

It was obvious the dog had sustained a trauma to the head. Blood dripped from his nose onto the linoleum floor, his left eye was swollen shut, and he wasn't moving or whimpering.

"Follow me." I gestured toward the back of the office, opened the door leading to the hallway and raced into the operating room. I could hear the woman following me, her breath coming in deep gasps as she struggled to carry her pet while running behind me. She placed him on the operating table and attempted to explain what had happened.

"He ran out the front door... into the street... the car didn't even stop... just ran over Baker like he wasn't even there."

I snapped on a pair of sterile gloves and began a quick examination of the dog's head. "Was he thrown far by the impact or did the car run over him?"

"Thrown. About ten or so feet. The driver didn't even stop. The bastard. I yelled but he just sped off down the street." Her voice cracked and she placed her hand on the dog's hind leg and rubbed up and down. "Is he gonna be alright, doctor? Can you fix him?"

The dog's heartbeat sounded thready and I surmised he had internal injuries as well as a severe concussion. He would need a head x-ray before surgery. I didn't recognize the dog or the woman but they could have visited here before I started working at the clinic.

"He's going to need surgery, Miss..."

"Parker. Susan Parker. I'm visiting my daughter around the corner and she told me you were the closest vet. Can you help him?"

I laid my hands on the side of the dog's abdomen, took a deep breath and looked into her watery blue eyes. Tears dripped off her chin and her entire body trembled.

"Miss Parker, this will be very expensive. And Baker may not make it through surgery. He looks pretty bad and has probably sustained some internal injuries. I won't know until I see what he looks like inside." I paused and tried to temper my words with sympathy and understanding. At the same time, I felt compelled to explain the entire picture, which included costs and her financial obligation. "I'm not sure I can save him and I'm willing to try, but it will be upwards of two thousand dollars. And that doesn't include post-operative care and drugs." I paused. "Do you have pet insurance?"

She shook her head from side to side, never breaking her stare. "You're telling me you're gonna just let him die cause I don't have the money to pay for his surgery?" Her lip twitched up in what looked like a sneer as tears slid down her weathered brown cheeks onto her dog's back.

"Miss Parker, I..."

"I lost my job. I don't have medical insurance for myself. I sure as hell don't have medical insurance for Baker here. I can hardly afford dog food." Her gaze shifted to Baker's head and she leaned over, placing her lips next to his ear. "I'm here, Baker," she said, her voice muffled against his furry ear. "I love you, baby."

She straightened her posture and stood facing me across the abyss I'd created between what I could do for her beloved friend and what she couldn't do for him, i.e. pay for the medical care necessary to save his life.

"So that's it, huh?" Her voice raised to shouting level.

My heart wobbled. I'd experienced my share of cases in which the owner was unable to pay for their pet's treatment. But most of the pet owners at Middleton Veterinary Clinic were financially well-off and money hadn't been a factor.

"Miss Parker, I understand you don't have thousands of dollars lying around to pay for your dog's—"

"I don't have a savings at all, doctor," she spit out. "I'm living on my daughter's couch, for God's sake. But you're a doctor. I thought there was some saying, one of those promises you guys had to live by. First do no wrong or something like that."

"First do no harm. And that's for human physicians, Miss—"

"You can't just let my dog die."

I closed my eyes for a second. When I opened them, all I could see were the wrinkles of defeat in her face, a heavy veil of sad-filled years and lost hope in the future.

At that moment I heard Kerryanne and Kathy return from lunch. "I'll be right back, Miss Parker."

I met Kerryanne and Kathy in the waiting room just as they closed the front door.

"Kerryanne, can you take care of the front desk while Kathy and I are in the operating room?"

"Of course."

"Kathy, there's a Miss Parker in the O.R. with her dog, Baker. Would you please take her to the waiting room so we can do cranial and abdominal x-rays. Then I'll scrub for surgery."

"Certainly, doctor." She instantly turned into efficient assistant mode. "What are we dealing with here?"

"Concussion, possible internal injuries."

I raced into the small room attached to the O.R. while Kathy dealt with Miss Parker. After Kathy helped me take the radiographs, I scrubbed and snapped on a pair of sterile gloves then walked backward through the swinging door into the operating room where she was prepping Baker for surgery.

Two hours later, I threw my gloves into the waste basket with a gigantic sigh. "That's one lucky dog."

"And you're a magnificent surgeon, Dr. Bradford."

"Thanks, Kathy. Couldn't have done it without you."

"Between you and me, doctor, I've never helped with such an extensive surgery before. Most of the time the animals don't make it after being hit by a car." She paused. "This is going to cost Miss Parker an arm and a leg. Excuse the pun."

I chuckled under my breath. "It's called pro bono."

"Isn't that when lawyers work for free?"

"Yep."

"But... can't she pay anything? I mean, like, a payment plan or something?"

"She doesn't have a job and she's living on her daughter's couch. She can hardly afford to feed herself."

"So you did this surgery outta the goodness of your heart?"

I reached my hand around the back of my neck and massaged the muscles at the base of my scalp. "Alright, alright, I'm a pushover. What can I say?" I ripped off my surgical mask. "I'll tell Miss Parker that Baker looks like he's going to make it."

Kathy and I used a sling to bring Baker to a cage in the back of the clinic. After she arranged a blanket behind him and situated a bowl of water to the side of the cage, I headed to the waiting room.

Susan Parker huddled in the corner of the couch, her face cradled in her hands. She brought her head up slowly as if pushing through quicksand, her mouth turned down in a scowl. Her hands gripped the edge of the couch and she pushed herself out of her seat and stood up, looking at me with bloodshot eyes.

"Baker's going to be just fine, Miss Parker. The surgery went exceptionally well. He has a concussion and will have to stay here for at least a week but he's a strong guy."

Tears leaked over the rim of her eyes and she choked on a sob then whispered, "Thank you, thank you, thank you."

"You're more than welcome." I turned to leave.

"Doctor!"

I turned around to face her. "What about the money I owe ya?"

Her voice was clouded with upset and what sounded like fear. Perhaps she thought I'd hold Baker hostage until she paid her bill.

"Don't worry about the bill."

She just looked and me, unsmiling.

I grasped both her hands in mine and made eye contact. "I'm happy your dog friend has you to love him. Take good care of him, okay? Make sure he doesn't sneak out again."

Her lips wobbled in a smile and she reached out to give me a tentative hug. I gave her a solid squeeze before walking back to my office. I closed the door, plopping down in my desk chair, let out a whoosh of air, leaned my head back and closed my eyes.

"Jessee?"

I recognized Kerryanne's voice and opened my eyes. She and Kathy were standing at the side of my desk.

"Must have fallen asleep." My mouth felt dry as cotton.

"It's time to go home, don'tcha think?" Kerryanne said.

I sat up straight and blinked several times. "How's Julia doing at her new job?"

Kerryanne's smile couldn't have been wider. "She served us lunch." She looked so proud. "Mom loves working there. Being around people is something she's dreamed about for most of her married life." Her eyes glistened.

"And I think she and I will be good friends," Kathy added. "We really hit it off. I may have found a pal to hang out with. Dan gets tired of tagging along on all of my shopping sprees to Des Moines. As soon as Julia gets on her feet, she and I plan to take a trip into the city on a Saturday and have some girl fun."

I smiled inside and out. Seeing Julia happy was a wish fulfilled for Kerryanne. Now neither of them would have to live under the cruel thumb of Bill Otten, a mean alcoholic as well as a dangerous man. That combination was potentially lethal, and I was glad they were nowhere near him any longer.

Kathy's grin widened. "You saved the day."

"More like he saved the dog." Kerryanne chuckled. "Baker would have died if you hadn't performed surgery. Kathy told me he was close to death."

I stood and put one arm around her shoulders and the other around Kathy's, and walked toward the door. "Thank you, ladies, but it's my job."

"Doesn't make it any less important," Kerryanne insisted.

"Saving an animal's life is no small feat, Doctor Bradford," Kathy chimed in.

We broke apart and filed through my office door to the hallway. "Let's go home. It's really been a lo-ong day."

CHAPTER THIRTY-ONE

On Christmas Eve I picked up Laura and drove to Antonio's on Main Street to have dinner before our trip into Des Moines to see the opening of the artist She's work at the Persoll Gallery. It was in the upper twenties outside, and we both wrapped in neck scarves and wool coats for the few seconds it took us to walk from the truck to the pizzeria.

We found a window table and waited for the waitress to bring us menus. Laura shrugged off her long coat and pulled at the fingertips of her gloves to remove them. She rubbed her hands together next to the candle in the middle of the table.

"I'm so excited to be going to the Persoll, Jess. I'd never been there before my mom's showing last month, and here I am going again."

I smiled and took her hands in mine to warm them. "And you need to come by the clinic soon to see your portrait hanging in my office. When times get tough it always cheers me up."

She intertwined her fingers with mine. "It's been a rough year for you."

I shook my head. "No. I mean, being a vet can be hard sometimes. People love their pets but when they don't have the money to take care of them when they get really sick, it sometimes comes down to a financial decision. And that's always a difficult one to make."

She nodded. "I know what you mean. The veterinarians in this area who deal with large animals can't live on a hope and a prayer. They have to get paid to be able to afford food and a house just like the rest of us. I've seen many owners get outraged when the vet tells them how much it'll cost to save their horse from dying of colic or something equally tragic."

"I bet," I said. "For some odd reason people have it in their heads we'll work for free because we love animals, that we won't let them die no matter what. They fail to see it's their responsibility to take care of their pet, not ours. We'll do everything in our power to keep their pets alive, but the owners have to do their part, too."

She rubbed the back of my hand with her thumb. "Don't feel guilty. I know exactly what you're up against. A couple of horses have been euthanized at my barn because the owners just didn't have the extra money to pay for surgery. In my opinion, if they have enough money to put their horse in training then they should have money saved for medical expenses or carry insurance on their horses."

I glanced out the window, thinking about Baker.

"Hey." She squeezed my hand. "What's wrong?"

Giving my head a shake, I turned my gaze back to her and chuckled. "I'm so full of it, as they say. All talk and no action."

She dipped her eyebrows. "What're you talking about?"

Leaning back in my chair, I flicked my eyes upward. "A woman brought her dog in today. He'd been hit by a car. She didn't have the money to pay for surgery." I leaned my elbows on the table but avoided looking straight at her.

"It's hard when an animal's life is sacrificed for lack of money, Jess."

I fiddled with the salt shaker. "I performed the surgery pro bono." I glanced up at her.

Her lips formed a perfect "O" then she laughed low and sexy. "You always wanted to be a lawyer, right?"

I shook my head and burst out laughing. "Not."

At that moment the waiter brought our pizza to the table, and we each pulled a slice off the tray.

I took a huge bite. "This would rival any pizza I've had in California. Who would have thought you could find real Italian pizza in the middle of Iowa."

She tried to smile around a mouthful of dough and cheese. "That's not the only thing we have here in Madison County. We should take a drive in the spring to visit the covered bridges."

"The bridges of Madison County, eh? I can break out the Mustang when the weather changes, and we can go on a day trip."

"Did you see the movie?"

I nodded.

"The Roseman Bridge was featured in the film as well as the Holliwell Bridge. Both of them were renovated in the early 1990's, and I haven't seen them since I was a girl."

After a salad and several slices of pizza we were both full and decided to head to Des Moines for the seven o'clock opening. It wasn't snowing or raining, though the temperature hovered in the mid-twenties. We parked behind the gallery and joined the crowd milling around on the steps leading up to the entrance.

"Your parents are coming, right?"

"They won't arrive until later. Daddy had a dinner that was scheduled months ago with a bunch of stuffy bankers. Mom wasn't looking forward to it, but their life together is all about compromise with her being an artist and Daddy working in a profession that's very rigid and controlled." We stopped to get a glass of champagne. "But, hey, it works for them. They've been together since high school."

We strolled through the doorway leading to the inner gallery and continued along the right side. Immediately a sense of deja vu hit me like a bucket of ice water. Goosebumps crawled up my arms and chest, and I shivered.

Every canvas was a mix of bright pastel oil colors, all beach scenes, each painting signed in the bottom right corner with what looked like a small white "S" with black dots for eyes, like a snake.

I pointed toward the corner of one of the paintings. "That's She's signature."

"Uh-huh."

"Has Colleen seen photos of this She person?"

Laura shook her head. "No, but Mom's dying to meet her. Why?"

"Just curious."

Laura took my arm and turned me toward her. "You have this odd look on your face. And you're shaking. What's the matter?"

I cradled her face in my hands and looked in her eyes. "Nothing's wrong, Laura. It's just that these paintings are so—"

"They remind you of your wife's art."

"Well, yeah. It's sorta weird."

"Weird as in..." She paused and her eyes grew wide. "Do you think the S-curve of the snake stands for Serena?"

"I don't know. What would be the odds of that happening?" I took her hand and continued toward the curve at the far end of the room where a woman stood with her back to us.

Five or six people surrounded her, all listening intently as she talked and gestured toward a large painting on the rear wall. Her auburn hair reached her shoulders, and she wore a long lilac skirt with a dark purple shawl draped across her shoulders that had a white "S" embroidered across the back. Her feet were bare.

"That must be her." Laura stopped near the last painting on the right wall.

My gaze was riveted on the artist's bare feet. She was wearing a toe ring.

I turned toward Laura. "Do you want to meet her?"

"I wouldn't know what to say." She shrugged. "My mother would be able to have a discussion with her about art or something, but me?"

The small crowd hovering around the artist turned toward the right wall as the woman in purple pointed at a canvas hanging in the middle of our side of the gallery.

In that instant I caught a glimpse of her face beneath the auburn bangs.

Serena.

CHAPTER THIRTY-TWO

"Oh... my... God," I said under my breath.

A second later Serena turned back to her audience and continued gesturing toward other paintings around the room. Apparently, she hadn't noticed me.

"Ow, my hand," Laura cried, tugging on my arm.

I looked down and realized I was squeezing her fingers like a vise. I quickly let go. "Oh, geez, I'm sorry." I rubbed her hand with both of mine.

"What happened to you? I was saying your name over and over and it was like you couldn't hear me."

"That's Serena," I whispered.

"Who is? What? Do you mean She is really Serena?" Her eyebrows rose so high they were hidden beneath the black veil of her bangs.

"I'm not hallucinating." I watched the artist with the auburn hair walk away from her fans and hurry to the other side of the gallery toward the foyer. "I have to talk to her." I tugged on Laura's hand and she let me lead her past the crowd of guests to the gallery doors.

"I can't believe this," Laura said as she trailed behind me to the front of the gallery. "Are you sure?"

I glanced back at her for an instant. "Positive." I weaved in and out of the crowd in a sprint toward the front doors. I caught a glimpse of purple near one of the gallery doors on the right side. "Serena," I shouted, panicked. I was not going to let her escape a second time.

Everyone in this section of the gallery turned in my direction. Some of the women covered their mouths with their hands, shaking their heads. Their glaring eyes pierced my vision as I searched every single person headed toward the gallery doors.

We reached the foyer, and I shot a glance left then right,

searching for the woman with the auburn hair and purple outfit. I noticed a gentleman wearing a jacket with the Persoll Gallery emblem embroidered on the breast pocket and grabbed his arm. "Do you know where I can find She? Which way did she go?"

He pulled his arm out of my too-firm grasp. "No, sir, I don't know where Ms. She has gone. She wasn't scheduled to stay at the opening for the full three hours. I imagine she's left for the evening."

I stood still, going over and over in my mind the artist's face when she turned in my direction. It was Serena. I was sure of it.

"What are you going to do?" Laura said.

I shook my head and scanned the crowd once again. If Serena was in the foyer I'd recognize her in an instant with that purple outfit and the shawl emblazoned with an "S" on the back.

"She's gone." My heart was beating so hard I could hear it thrumming in my ears. "Dammit! She must have seen me. Why else would she have skipped out so quickly?" I paused, trying to figure out what to do next. "Maybe the owner of the gallery can tell me how to get in touch with her."

I gazed down into Laura's face and saw the mask of sadness that had replaced the happy expression she'd worn when we arrived at the gallery only moments ago. I wrapped my arms around her and hugged her as tightly as I dared. "I'm sorry. This is such a shock. Is your hand all right?"

She nodded but I could see imminent tears in her eyes. "I'm not trying to hurt you. But it was Serena. I need to find Sofia. I have to find her."

She rose up on tiptoe and gave me a kiss. "Of course you do. And I'll help you." She paused and cleared her throat. "Let's find the owner. I think his name's Anthony Persoll. My mom's spoken to him before. He has an office on the second floor."

I perused both sides of the foyer and noticed a flight of stairs to one side leading up to the next floor. Laura and I rushed up the stairs. Various closed doors lined one side of the hallway.

"This must be it," I told her, noting the brass letters designating "Director" on one of the doors.

"What do you plan to say to him?" she said.

I grabbed her hand, looked into her eyes. "Go along with whatever I say, okay?"

She nodded. "I'm game."

I knocked and heard a loud voice beckon us to come in. An older gentleman with a full head of silver hair sat behind a massive gleaming wood desk in front of a bay window overlooking downtown Des Moines. He leaned forward in his chair. "What can I do for you?"

I coughed to allow myself time to think. I needed a phone number or an address for Serena.

"My name is Craig Smith and I live in Earlham." I turned toward Laura. "And this is my wife, Susan." I gave Laura's hand a light squeeze and stared her directly in the eyes. "We're interested in commissioning the artist She to do a painting. Privately, that is."

Mr. Persoll leaned back and squinted. "I see, Mr. and Mrs. Smith. I'll have to talk to, uh, the artist first before I give out any personal information. You do understand, I'm sure. We honor our artists' privacy." He paused. "Followers can be, uh, fanatical, if you will."

I nodded. "Of course. I can give you my telephone number and perhaps you'd be so kind as to pass it on to She. Hopefully I'll hear from her soon."

He handed me a tablet with a pen. I printed my fake name and the telephone number of Nana's house. I didn't want Serena to phone and hear Kathy say the words "Bradford Veterinary Clinic" when she answered the phone.

"Thank you, Mr. Persoll. I appreciate your help. If you could inform She that we're anxiously awaiting her phone call." I smiled, and Laura and I walked out of his office and down the stairs to the foyer.

"Your hands are still shaking, Jessee."

I closed my eyes for a second and pinched the bridge of my nose. "I'm sorry this is happening right now."

"Don't be sorry. This is the day you've been waiting for for months. I don't blame you for being excited. You've found your wife. And hopefully your child, too."

"Serena has obviously created a completely new identity for herself, otherwise the FBI would have found her."

She put her arms around my waist and hugged me. I dipped my head and gave her a long, deep kiss. "I love you, Laura. That's not going to change."

"And I love you, Jessee Bradford."

Once again, that eerie feeling invaded my gut when she said my full name, that queer sensation that had been telling me Serena was alive.

Now I knew all along I'd been right.

CHAPTER THIRTY-THREE

We left the gallery and, though the temperature had risen and it wasn't as chilly, it had started to rain. Sheets and sheets of water slid from the sky like curtains. Those desperate enough to drive in this downpour crawled along at fifteen miles per hour.

We didn't say much during the return trip home, except for frequent comments on the treacherous roadway and awful winter weather in Iowa. My mind was a whirlwind of jumbled thoughts and guesses as to what I should do next. Laura must have been uncomfortable as well, wondering what my next move might be. It was all up to me now, and I had to make a decision, fast.

What if Serena didn't call me back? Should I wait for her to get in touch with me or call Agent Caruso tonight, on Christmas Eve, and enlist the help of the FBI to expedite matters? Serena was alive. Why was she in Iowa? Was she just passing through one of the many galleries where her work was on exhibition? And where was Sofia?

I couldn't stop the endless questions, and there was no space in my mind for anything but thoughts of what the future might hold. What would I say when, or if, Serena called me? She obviously kidnapped our daughter and hid from me for almost a year. When charges were brought against her for kidnapping Sofia, would she go to jail for a very long time or would her father pull strings to get her out sooner?

It took us almost two hours to arrive in Earlham. When I pulled up in front of Laura's house and shut off the engine, her hand clutched my forearm.

"Not tonight, Jessee, okay?"

I turned toward her and noticed her lip quivering. A tear escaped down her cheek. I placed a finger under her chin and turned her head in my direction.

"This doesn't mean the end of us, Laura."

Her eyes looked off to the side, not meeting mine. "I know what it means." She finally shifted her gaze in my direction. "I'm going to lose the only man I've ever loved besides Jeff. But this time it's not the war that's taking him away. It's another woman."

I leaned over the console and wrapped my arms around her, holding her tightly as her body shook with sobs. Of course I felt relieved Serena was alive. But since she obviously left me and took our child with her, my relationship with my wife was over. I couldn't forgive her for committing such a cruel act. And I could not imagine any extenuating circumstances that would change my mind.

"It'll take some time to wade through all of this but my feelings for you aren't going to change." I pulled away and looked at her tear-streaked face. "I told you I thought Serena left me. Now I've got to find out why. And I have to find Sofia. You know that, honey." I wiped the tears from her face with my fingers.

"You never know," she said. "Perhaps there's some perfectly logical reason why she's been missing. A form of amnesia, a kidnapper holding Sofia hostage unless Serena does what she's told. I don't know. And right now neither do you."

I let out a deep breath and clenched my jaw. "For your sake, and because of everything you've been through since Jeff died, maybe it would be easier for you if we don't see each other until I work this out. I never wanted to cause you more heartbreak. You've had enough to last you a lifetime."

Her eyes searched mine, her pupils dilated then shrank back to their normal size then dilated again. I couldn't imagine the trauma this situation was putting her through.

"I feel as if my heart's been stepped on. I can't breathe," she said.

I searched her eyes. "Don't give up on us. I'll call you as soon as I've worked this out, okay?"

She nodded. I kissed her, jumped out and ran to her side of the truck. I walked with her to the front door and took the key from her shaking hands and opened it.

"Please don't write us off. Serena left me of her own free will. I know it. Hopefully I'll find the answers soon."

She nodded again but didn't answer me as she shut the door. I stood on the porch and waited to hear the click of the dead bolt then walked back to the truck and headed for home.

I wanted to climb into bed and wake up to find this had never happened, that I was back in Des Moines, sharing a dessert and coffee with Laura after having a wonderful time at the gallery.

And if wishes were roses I'd have twelve dozen bouquets waiting for me when I got back to the farm.

Tomorrow was Christmas and it sure didn't look like it would be very merry.

* * * *

It was late when I arrived home. I found Agent Caruso's cell phone number and phoned him immediately. He told me someone would be by the house the next day to put a wiretap on the phone. If Serena called and I could keep her on the line long enough, the FBI could trace the call.

After we hung up, sleep was an elusive hope. I tossed and turned until four. Hauling my weary body out of bed, I showered, threw on sweatpants and a Lakers t-shirt, and headed downstairs to brew some extra strong coffee and sit in the kitchen to think. I was taking my first sip when Nana entered, her hair in pink sponge curlers with her bathrobe wrapped around her.

"Merry Christmas, Nana."

"Merry Christmas to you, too. What in the blazes are you doing up already?"

I grabbed another mug as she sat down across from me. "I saw Serena at the Persoll Gallery last night."

She gasped, and her eyes grew wide as she covered her mouth with both hands. "Are you sure? Did you talk to her? Is Sofia—"

"Wait, wait, Nana." I held my hand up like a stop sign. "Turns out that Serena is the artist Laura and I went to see, but she goes by the name She. When I saw her face I thought I was—"

"Dreamin'?"

"More like having a nightmare. I mean, where has she been and why did she leave me?"

She patted my hand. "So you didn't have a chance to talk to her."

"I swear she must have seen me or heard me call her name because we ran after her and she just vanished into thin air. Then Laura and I spoke with Mr. Persoll himself and he said he'd get a message to Serena that a Craig Smith—that would be me—wanted to commission her to do a painting. I gave him our number here, to give to Serena."

She nodded, looking pensive. "So if a woman calls askin' for a Craig Smith I'll hand the phone to you."

"If she calls."

"Did you notify the police or the FBI?"

"I called Agent Caruso the minute I got home last night. Someone will be by today to install a wiretap on the phone so if Serena calls they'll be able to trace it." Silence enveloped the kitchen like a blanket. "I don't know what to say to her."

"What do you want to know?" she asked in a low voice.

My heart lodged in my throat and I tried to swallow around the words. "Why she left and took my only child from me."

"Then say that. I've never known you to be shy or at a loss for words. When do you think she'll call?"

I shook my head. "I don't know. What if she doesn't?"

She stood up and opened cupboards, taking out plates and silverware. "You need to eat a good breakfast. Your mind needs fuel to function properly."

I smiled. Nana was the perfect grandmother, always concerned about my health in times of crisis. "Sounds perfect."

After breakfast I helped her with the chores and we finished by six. I felt restless, but didn't feel like opening gifts, putting on a smile, celebrating Christmas. Lurking in the back of my mind was the nagging hope the phone would ring but I didn't know when or if that would even happen.

I'd felt so helpless since Serena and Sofia went missing. There hadn't been much I could do to aid the authorities in their quest to find them and realized now that my plea on the television for their captor to bring them back had been for nothing. They hadn't been kidnapped! My ego felt bruised at the humiliation of it all. My wife had been so unhappy in my presence that she resorted to stealing my child and fleeing while I was at work.

However I didn't have to feel nor act like the sorry husband.

Now that I knew for a fact that Serena was alive I could damn well do my best to find out something, anything, about where she'd been for the past eleven months.

I ran upstairs and grabbed my laptop, sat my butt in the chair in the kitchen, and went online. There had to be information somewhere concerning the artist She. And I was determined to find it. My search revealed nothing more interesting than a short, completely false biography, along with her past and future appearances at various galleries, mostly in the Midwest.

* * * *

Laura and I had planned on spending Christmas together and now, well, now I'd promised not to call her until I worked through this situation with Serena. But I already missed her, and I'd bought her a Christmas gift. Perhaps I was being selfish, but I decided to call her, just to say Merry Christmas. It felt almost cruel not to, given how close we were.

She picked up after one ring. "Hello, Jessee."

"I know we agreed I wouldn't call until I worked through this thing with Serena but—"

"You haven't talked to her, have you?"

"Please believe me, Laura. I want more than anything to talk with Serena and find my daughter, but she hasn't called. I've searched online and everything leads to a very well-orchestrated trail to nowhere, a false biography and gallery appearances in the Midwest. I called Agent Caruso last night and someone's coming today to put a wiretap on our phone."

Silence blared through the phone line. "Why'd you call me?"

I paused, thinking how best to say what was in my heart. "I miss you. It's Christmas, and I have a gift for you."

"And I have a present for you."

"Maybe we could exchange gifts?" You could cut through the stillness. "Sorry. This was a bad idea and selfish of me."

"No, I want to see you, too. My parents invited me over for dinner so perhaps I could drop by your house before that."

I sighed with relief. "Anytime is fine. I look forward to it."

"Me, too," she whispered.

I didn't want her to hang up the phone. My heart ached with missing her, more than I realized. "You still there?"

"Yes."

"I love you, Laura."

"I love you. I'll see you later."

I hung up the phone and stared out the kitchen window. Who would have thought I'd be sitting in my grandmother's kitchen on Christmas day after talking on the phone with my girlfriend about my wife's sudden reappearance? I cradled my head in my hands and took a deep breath.

People talk about needing closure. Well, I wanted it so badly it was like heroin to an addict. I could feel the crack running down the middle of my heart, widening like a fissure. One side filled with what was becoming a form of hatred for my wife, the other half brimming with love for Laura. I couldn't handle the constant tug on one side then the other. It was impossible for my heart to become whole again with each side vying for attention and space. My heart was like a puzzle with pieces whose edges no longer fit together. My emotions would remain forever torn until the two sides became one.

And the only way to mend it was to find Serena and discover why she deserted me. Once I had the answers, I could let go of the hatred for her and my heart could heal.

CHAPTER THIRTY-FOUR

The kitchen bustled with Nana, Julia, and Kerryanne preparing the turkey and side dishes. They shooed me out of the kitchen, telling me I wasn't needed, that I should relax in the other room. But no one had any idea how lonely I felt right now, sitting on the couch in front of the Christmas tree, watching the tiny rainbow-colored lights blinking on and off. A wooden Nativity scene my grampa carved many years ago stood under the lower boughs of the tree, the tiny manger empty until Nana would place the baby Jesus there.

It started to snow. My first white Christmas in Iowa, yet my insides were like a turbulent, swirling cauldron. Serena was alive and healthy. And I was sure my daughter was, too.

The fact I would have to wait one more minute to discover why Serena deserted me meant more time I'd have to be away from Laura. And I hated Serena for causing this pain for Laura, an innocent pawn in whatever sick game Serena was playing.

I couldn't help but wonder what I'd be doing next Christmas. Would Laura and Sofia and I be exchanging gifts at her house before joining her parents for dinner in Des Moines? If only crystal balls were real, right now I'd give anything to be able to tell my future.

Ever since discovering Serena was alive, my shoulders were tense, my neck ached. I paced from one side of the front room to the other, finally stepping through the doorway into the kitchen. Nana was just putting the pies in the oven. Kerryanne was washing dishes, Julia was drying them. The three of them turned toward me and smiled.

"We're just finishin' up," Nana said. "Ready for Santa later?"

I shook my head and gave her a half-smile. "I don't know if Santa got me anything this year."

Nana walked over to where I stood and gave me a hug. "What's wrong, besides the fact you've been waitin' for Serena to call and the phone's barely rung?"

I hugged her back and looked at Kerryanne and Julia, who stood at the kitchen sink, watching me. "Sorry I'm such a dud. Of all the days to feel out of sorts, right?"

"You don't have to apologize," Kerryanne said.

"She'll phone soon," Julia added.

My life was an open book. Living under the same roof with three women, it was impossible not to share what was happening in all of our lives. I understood that and didn't resent it. However, right now my life was in limbo and I didn't want to talk about it on Christmas.

I gave Nana a kiss on the cheek. "Can I help? I could set the table or—"

Nana gave me a quick hug and gently patted my arm. "Everything's already done."

"Laura's dropping by today so we can exchange gifts."

"Is she havin' supper with her parents?" Nana asked.

"Yes, she is. When's dinner?"

Nana glanced over at Julia. "Around three o'clock, wouldn't you say?"

Julia looked at her daughter. "Kerryanne's finishing up the green bean casserole and then we'll be done. All we have to do is wait for the turkey. I'd say around two or two-thirty."

I returned to the front room and sat down on the couch when I heard a car's tires on the gravel. Looking out the window, I saw Laura had arrived. I opened the front door and stepped out onto the porch.

"Merry Christmas," I said.

The long black curtain of her hair swayed from side to side as she walked up the stairs. She gave me a hug then looked into my eyes. "Merry Christmas, Jessee."

I dipped my head and gave her a chaste kiss. Her body curved into mine and she deepened the kiss. When I pulled back and looked down at her, her eyes appeared misty under the thin veil of her bangs. "Are you angry that I called you?"

She shook her head and glanced over my shoulder. "I just want all this to be over. When I thought I wouldn't be seeing you for days or weeks or maybe ever, I already missed you. More than I thought I would."

"I'm sorry this is happening to us. I never wanted to hurt you."

She laid her head on my chest. "Don't apologize. When I agreed to go out with you... slept with you... I knew you were still married, that your wife could turn up at any time."

Weaving my fingers through her hair, I cradled her head in my palm. "Maybe I should never have let it happen. You and me."

She leaned away from me and pressed a finger against my lips. "Shh. Don't." She paused and smiled. "Let's go inside. It's cold out here."

We walked into the foyer where I helped her off with her coat and hung it up on the hat tree. We sat on the couch in front of the blazing fire, settling back into the pillows.

"Is everyone fixing dinner?" she asked, glancing toward the kitchen.

I nodded. "They're almost done. We'll eat around three o'clock. What about you?"

"I'll head over to my parents' place after I give you your gift. The weather's beautiful today so the drive should be an easy one."

Nana popped her head out of the kitchen doorway and smiled. "Merry Christmas, Laura."

"And Merry Christmas to you, Rose. My mom and dad wanted me to tell you Happy Holidays."

Nana untied her apron and glanced at the Christmas tree. "Tell your parents Merry Christmas too. I'm goin' to change clothes. You have a lovely holiday." She turned and walked up the stairs.

I could hear Julia and Kerryanne talking in the kitchen. Then they walked through the kitchen door, waved to Laura and yelled, "Merry Christmas" as they scurried up the stairs.

We turned toward each other, our faces inches apart. Our eyes locked and a tug of emotion drew me into her gaze. She leaned in and our lips met in a slow, easy kiss.

"I love you," I whispered as I wrapped my arms around her and pulled her toward me. She laid her head on my chest and I nestled my chin on top of her head, breathing in her scent of lemon and cloves.

A loud bang on the front door interrupted our warm embrace, and we both jumped at the unexpected noise. Laura sat up and glanced toward the foyer. "What was that?"

I stood up and laid my hand on her shoulder. "Stay here. I'll find out who it is." I peeked around the edge of the Christmas tree through the side curtains. A stocky, greasy-haired man stood on the porch, one fist on his hip, the other moving toward the door handle as though he was going to turn the knob.

I rushed over and yanked it open, startling him. He pulled back his hand as if he'd been shocked, and shoved it into the front pocket of his pants.

He scowled. "Where... is... Julia?" he shouted.

Drunk, I thought, the whites of his eyes streaked with red lines. His breath smelled so strong of whiskey I turned my head to the side to get a breath of fresh air.

"Are you Bill?" My mind whirled in different directions. Where was Julia? Hadn't I seen her rush upstairs a few minutes ago? Was Nana with her? Where was Kerryanne?

His left hand grabbed the handle of the screen door as the other pulled a gun out from under his stained t-shirt.

I put both my hands up in front of me, palms out, and backed up as he pulled open the screen door and walked toward me. "Hold on, Bill. There's no need for that. Put down the gun, please."

He grasped my right arm, turned me around and pushed me toward the front room. He followed me for a few steps. "Siddown and shuddup," he yelled, shoving me in the direction of the couch.

I lowered myself onto the cushion and glanced at Laura, her eyes wide with fear.

"What do we have here?" He pointed the barrel of the gun in Laura's direction. He licked his lips and smiled, his yellow teeth glaring against the reddish color of his face.

I placed my arm protectively around Laura's shoulders and squeezed her reassuringly. "Bill, will you please put down the gun. We aren't your enemies."

He took a few steps toward me. Before I realized what he was doing, he slammed the gun down into the side of my face.

I heard Laura scream at the same time as a wave of stars danced in front of my eyes and a sheet of black clouded my vision.

CHAPTER THIRTY-FIVE

Pleading words echoed at the perimeter of my consciousness. "Please, I'm begging you. Don't, Bill. I'll do anything you say. Leave them outta this."

Trickles of blood dripped into the corners of my mouth, rusty and sweet-tasting. I struggled to touch the side of my face but my wrists were bound together behind my back. Slumped in a dining chair, my head bent so low my chin touched my chest.

I tried to open my eyes but the left one had swollen half-shut. That side of my face felt as if I'd been beaten with a block of concrete. My head throbbed, a pounding rhythm equal to the quickened pace of my heart.

I groaned, blinked my right eye. The first thing that registered was the blood spatters decorating my white button-down shirt. I lifted my head and focused my one eye. Sitting next to me on the couch were Laura, Nana and Kerryanne, huddled next to each other, hands behind their backs, eyes blazing with terror, teardrops streaking down their cheeks.

Their gazes focused over my left shoulder. I turned my head in that direction and pain shot up my neck to my temple. Julia's husband was standing in the foyer, one arm wrapped around Julia's neck, forcing her to face the ceiling. His other arm stuck straight out, gun gripped in his hand, pointed at Laura, Nana, and Kerryanne.

"Let her go, Bill." My words came out sounding as if my mouth was stuffed with a rag.

"Shut the hell up," he shouted, waving the barrel of the gun. His hand shook wildly up and down and sideways, eyes shifting from me to Laura to Nana to Kerryanne.

"Bill, please. Let's get outta here," Julia croaked, her neck encased in the crook of Bill's beefy arm. "You and me, honey... just the two of us. Let's go home. To Little Rock. Right now. Come on, baby, let's leave this place. We'll go anywhere ya want. Just you and me."

"Shuddup! Shut the hell up, bitch!" He suddenly let her go and she dropped to the floor. He crooked his leg backward and kicked her in the side once, then again. She tried to crawl away from him and he kicked her in the back. She screamed, stretched her arms out above her head, and crawled in my direction, away from his feet.

"Leave her alone, you sonofabitch," I shouted at the top of my lungs.

He turned his head in my direction, eyes glazed over. Spittle dripped from his lips. He grimaced and leaned against the wall.

"I need a drink," he mumbled. He looked right through me, seemingly unaware I was sitting in the chair in front of him. Gripping his stomach with the hand not holding the gun, he grunted.

I motioned with my head, pain shooting into my left ear like a hot poker. "There's liquor in the kitchen." Perhaps he'd leave the room for just a few moments, and I could untie my hands.

He stumbled toward the kitchen, and I immediately began fiddling with the rope wrapped around my wrists. I glanced over at Laura. "I've almost got it. I'll take care of Julia. You work on Nana and Kerryanne."

Laura nodded then wrenched her hands from side to side, twisting her arms in an effort to undo the knots around her wrists. The knots on mine loosened. If Bill stayed out of the room for just a few more seconds I'd be able to free my hands and reach Julia.

She lay face-down on the floor a few feet from the bottom of my chair's legs, her breathing labored, blood dripping from her nose. She struggled to sit up and looked up at me, tears inching down her cheeks as her eyes shifted from me over to the kitchen where her husband was opening and slamming cupboard doors in his search for alcohol.

"Julia, can you untie me?" I whispered.

She moved her knees underneath her, placed both hands on the floor, and pushed herself up to a half-standing position. She shook her head from side to side as she stood upright, swaying.

Just then there was a knock at the front door. The next few moments passed in slow motion.

Julia turned around and lunged toward the front door, fumbling with the door knob. At the same time her husband rounded the corner, gun leveled at Julia's back.

"Julia," I yelled.

She turned at the exact moment Bill fired the gun. I heard a sharp crack, saw a hole blast open on the left side of the front door.

A child's cries echoed through the silence.

CHAPTER THIRTY-SIX

Bill dropped the revolver on the floor and bolted through the kitchen. I heard the side door open then his heavy footsteps sprinting away from the house.

Julia turned around to face the front door, twisted the door knob, and yanked it open. The screen door dangled on its frame and Julia pushed it open. It fell off, clattering onto the side of the porch.

I untied the last knot and stood up, took one step, fell to my knees then pushed myself up and ran toward the front door. Julia knelt over a body. The lower half was covered in a purple skirt where bare feet stuck out, a gold ring surrounding one of the toes. I rushed to Julia's side and looked down. Serena's face was turned in my direction, her eyes open, the front of her shirt soaked in blood.

"Call 911," I yelled. I knelt next to Serena, tore off my shirt, rolled it into a ball, and pressed it over the chest wound.

I could hear Julia's voice on the phone, a jumble of words, along with the background murmurings of the others. Serena's lips moved but I couldn't distinguish what she was saying. Bending my ear toward her mouth,

I was immediately assaulted with her signature lavender scent.

A distant memory of Serena and me on the beach the first day we met swept through my mind. I squinched my eyes closed for just a second to erase that mental picture.

When I opened them, I noticed Sofia sitting on the top step of the porch, thumb stuck in her mouth, her sobs muffled by the blanket she held next to her face.

My heart contracted into a tight glob in my chest. Nana's dress flowed by me and she scooped Sofia into her arms, my baby's tiny fingers clutching the collar of Nana's dress. She laid her head on Nana's shoulder and her eyes fluttered closed as her crying ebbed to a small hitch in her throat.

I sat back on my heels and looked up at the two of them, making sure my hand remained firmly pressed against Serena's chest. "That's my daughter you're holding," I whispered.

The edges of Nana's lips quirked up in a small smile. "I thought so. I'll take her inside... away from all this."

I glanced down at Serena's face. Her eyes flickered open. I leaned closer so she could see me. "Serena, it's me, Jessee. Hold on. The ambulance is on the way."

The wail of a siren streaked through the silence.

Serena's eyes closed and I placed two fingers on the underside of her jaw. Her pulse was faint but she was alive, although I didn't know for how much longer. The splotch of blood in the middle of her chest had expanded, spreading out from under the wadded-up ball of my shirt.

The crunch of gravel in the driveway blasted through the quiet as the ambulance screeched to a halt at the side of the house. I backed away as one of the paramedics knelt beside Serena's body and took a peek under the bright red wad of cloth on Serena's chest. He placed both hands flat against my blood-soaked shirt, exerting pressure against the wound. "What happened?"

"She was shot. It was a handgun. I'm not sure what caliber. Is she going to live?"

Another medic joined him and my question was ignored as they inserted an IV into Serena's arm and a third medic angled a flattened gurney close to Serena's side. The three of them lifted her onto the white-sheeted gurney, pulled it to a standing position and carried it down the stairs to the open doors at the back of the ambulance.

I ran down the stairs just as they were closing the rear doors. "I'm her husband. I'm going with her."

Kerryanne handed me my jacket just as the paramedic gestured me inside. I jumped in and sat across from where Serena lay on the gurney.

As the ambulance pulled away from the house I glanced out the small back window. Laura stood on the porch, cradling Sofia in her arms, feeding her a cookie. Laura raised her arm and waved.

She looked as sad as I felt.

* * * *

The muffled wail of the siren was the only audible sound in the back of the ambulance. After placing an oxygen mask over Serena's mouth and nose, the paramedic wrapped a blood pressure cuff around her arm. Underneath the mask, the color of her face resembled that of a grey porpoise, her breathing uneven and raspy.

After starting her on IV fluids, the paramedic removed my shirt from her chest wound and replaced it with a sterile dressing, placing it firmly over the wound. He handed me a frozen compress for my face, which I held against my left cheek and eye. The vision in my left eye had cleared, but it was still swollen. That was the least of my worries at the moment.

We reached Mercy Hospital in Des Moines in what seemed like minutes though my awareness of the passage of time was inconsistent with reality. My mind was a jumble of visions clouding every thought: the gun in Bill's hand as it discharged the bullet, the cracking sound as it sliced through the front door on its way into Serena's chest, the clomping of that maniac's feet as he sprinted out the door, the look in my baby's eyes as she watched her mother's blood seeping through her blouse, and Laura's hand waving to me as I sat in the back of the ambulance.

The rear doors flew open almost before the ambulance came to a stop. I jumped out and shuffled backward, eyes riveted on Serena's lifeless form. Two people dressed in blue scrubs ran through the Emergency Room doors and pulled out the gurney, flipped down the legs, and wheeled Serena through the doors.

I followed behind until we reached the end of a long hallway. Two massive silver doors glistened in front of us, "Staff Only" written across them in oversized red letters.

A young woman stepped in front of me and pressed her hand on my forearm. "Why don't you come with me and I'll have someone take a look at your face."

"No, I'll be alright. The medic gave me a frozen compress and I can see out of my eye now. I'll be okay."

She pursed her lips and nodded. "Why don't you go to the second floor visitors' lounge then. After they finish in the operating room, someone will come out and give you an update on your wife's condition."

I thanked her, wishing I didn't feel so alone, wanting to turn to

Laura for comfort, knowing I couldn't ask her for it right here, right now. I retraced my steps down the hallway where a nurse directed me to the waiting room on the second floor. They were taking Serena into surgery and, if she survived, I'd be in the lounge next to the recovery room where they'd inform me of her status.

I slumped into an easy chair situated in front of a bay window overlooking the center of Des Moines. My phone vibrated in my pocket, and I realized I hadn't called anyone since I scrambled into the back of the ambulance. The caller ID read "Laura" and I flipped it open.

"How is she?"

"I'm at Mercy Hospital. She's in surgery. I don't know anything yet."

"I'm sorry about Serena. Julia and Kerryanne both feel so guilty about what happened. I finally made Julia lie down. She couldn't stop crying. And Kerryanne blames herself for bringing Julia here in the first place. Lord, what a mess."

I leaned my head in my hand then winced at the pain. What must I look like? I stood up and walked down the hall, searching for the nearest bathroom.

"No good deed goes unpunished, right?" I pushed the door open to the men's restroom.

"You don't live your life like that, Jess. You'd take Kerryanne and Julia into your home again if you had the choice."

I glanced in the mirror above the sink and grimaced at my reflection. The left side of my face was purplish-red and a trickle of blood had dried below my ear.

"What about the police?" I asked.

"They arrived shortly after the ambulance left. We all gave our statements. Rose explained the situation to them about Serena and Sofia. They said they'd keep in touch. I think one of them was on the way to the hospital to talk to you."

"Could you tell Nana she can reach me on my cell? I'll wait here till Serena comes out of surgery." I grabbed a paper towel and soaked it in cold water, wiped the blood from the side of my face. "If she makes it." I threw the towel in the garbage can as I exited the bathroom.

"I'll be here, waiting for you." Her voice sounded small and quiet.

"I love you, Laura. But you understand, don't you? I have to see this through."

"I know. I didn't call to discuss our relationship. I just wanted to make sure you were okay. See how Serena's doing."

"How's Sofia? I didn't even get a chance to hold her." My throat constricted, but I held the tears in check, needing to be strong for whatever happened next.

"She's the sweetest little thing. You said she's a year and a half old, but she already has a great vocabulary. We explained we're her friends and her daddy will be home as soon as you talk to her mommy."

I closed my eyes, never dreaming I'd be having this discussion with my girlfriend. And would she still be my girlfriend tomorrow? "Thank you. It means more to me than I can explain, you taking care of my little girl, being there for Nana."

She sighed. "You'd do the same for me," she whispered. "What goes 'round, comes 'round... karma and all that."

"Talk to you soon," I said, ending the call.

To one side of the waiting room stood a tiny Christmas tree on top of a square table, its lights twinkling on and off. I forgot it was Christmas day. Here I was sitting alone in a hospital, waiting to hear whether my wife would live or die.

I tucked myself into a chair in the corner of the room and closed my eyes. There was nothing I could do right now to help Serena, but I sent up a heartfelt prayer to Heaven that she'd make it through surgery, not only so I could find out why she'd been gone for months, but to tell her I didn't wish her dead. I'm not a vindictive person and I didn't want her physically disabled because of unlucky circumstances.

I must have dozed off because the next thing I remember someone was calling my name.

CHAPTER THIRTY-SEVEN

I opened my eyes and turned my head in the direction of the voice. A middle-aged man dressed in a dark blue suit stood next to me.

"Are you Dr. Jessee Bradford?"

I nodded.

"Detective Thompson. Des Moines P.D. Can I talk to you for a few minutes?"

I gestured toward a chair across from me. He sat down and leaned forward then opened a small notebook.

"I understand from your grandmother, Rose Bradford, that Serena Middleton is your wife." He looked down at his notebook and flipped back a few pages. "The FBI's been searching for her and your daughter for almost a year?" He glanced up, eyebrows raised.

"That's right. I haven't heard from her since she disappeared back in January. Agent Caruso from the Los Angeles FBI is in charge of the case. As a matter of fact, I should call him—"

"I already have. He should be here any minute now to talk to Ms. Middleton."

"What about my daughter Sofia?"

"We sent pictures to Agent Caruso of both Ms. Middleton and your daughter Sofia to verify their identities. He explained you have a custody order and advised me to let her stay with you and your family. Of course we don't know the full story but from what the agent told us, Ms. Middleton will be remanded to the Santa Barbara police until she stands trial for parental kidnapping, evading the FBI, use of false identification. For starters."

"And Bill Otten, the man who shot Serena?"

"The police found him stumbling around on the side of the road. He could barely walk. Drunker than a skunk. He's being held in the Des Moines city jail. We've been in touch with the police in Little Rock where he lives." He closed his notebook and stood up.

I pushed myself out of the chair and we shook hands. "Thank you for your time, Dr. Bradford. I'm sure Agent Caruso will be in touch soon. I'm glad your daughter's back."

I smiled and sat back down, more weary than I could have imagined possible. Everything was happening so fast, from the nightmare with Bill Otten to Serena's surgery, now talking with Detective Thompson, and Agent Caruso's impending arrival.

I leaned my head back and let my mind wander over the scenes of the last several hours then jerked awake when I felt a tap on my shoulder. A young man with a hospital mask hanging around his neck knelt beside me.

"Dr. Bradford, your wife is out of surgery."

I blinked several times and sat up straight. "She's alive?"

He nodded then stood up.

I pushed myself out of the chair to stand next to him. "Can I see her? Will she be okay?"

He patted my shoulder and smiled. "It could have been much worse. Fortunately the bullet went straight through her chest and out her back. Didn't nick any vital organs. After some time in the hospital she'll be on the road to a full recovery." He shook his head. "Honest to God, I've seen a lot of shootings in my day but this one was a miracle. She's one lucky lady." He glanced at the side of my face. "Better get that taken care of. Are you dizzy or nauseous?"

"No. I'm fine, doctor. Just a bit swollen. Thank you for everything."

I shook his hand, then followed him down the hall to the recovery room. Serena was still groggy from the anesthesia but when I held her hand and squeezed it lightly she opened her eyes.

"Where have you been for eleven months, Serena?"

"I'm sorry." She closed her eyes.

I squeezed her hand, and she opened her eyes once more.

"Why'd you leave?"

She shook her head slowly from side to side and her eyes fluttered shut once more.

It was too soon after surgery to engage her in conversation so I walked over to the nurse's station and asked when she'd be moved to a regular room. The nurse told me it would be at least another hour or more so I decided to go to the cafeteria for something to eat. I hadn't eaten since breakfast. It looked like my holiday dinner would be cafeteria food a la Mercy Hospital.

I took the elevator to the top floor to the cafeteria, grabbed a tray and stood in line behind several men and women dressed in hospital garb, some in blue scrubs, others in green. When I reached the end of the serving line, my plate was filled with turkey, dressing, mashed potatoes, cranberry sauce, and a slice of pumpkin pie for dessert. I poured myself a cup of coffee and took the tray to an unoccupied table near the window and sat down.

"Merry Christmas to me," I mumbled, dipping my fork into the middle of the potatoes and gravy. I was starving, and the meal was actually quite tasty. I was sipping a decent brew of dark coffee when my cell phone vibrated. I flipped it open.

"Jessee, this is Nana. How're you doin', hon?"

It warmed my heart to hear her voice, and all of a sudden I felt incredibly lonely, sitting by myself in a hospital cafeteria eating Christmas dinner.

"I'm sorry I didn't call sooner, but I fell asleep in the waiting room. When the doctor woke me up I went in to see Serena."

"She made it through surgery then." She sighed. "My prayers were answered."

"That's nice of you. I tried to talk to her, but she was too groggy from the anesthesia. I'm in the cafeteria having a cheery Christmas dinner with all my friends."

She laughed. "Well, good for you."

"I was kidding. This isn't how I pictured spending Christmas."

"We're waitin' for you to come home no matter what time you get back. We'll just pretend tomorrow's Christmas day and open gifts then. When do you think you'll be back?"

"I'm heading up to see her as soon as I finish eating. I should be home in a few hours. How's your granddaughter?"

"Oh, good Lordy." I could almost see the smile on her face. "She's so precious. We just put her down for the night. Kerryanne got the crib from the attic and cleaned it all up. Sofia's in your bedroom with the door open so we can hear her if she cries. Tonight may be a rough one. Poor little thing."

I smiled to myself, knowing the three of them would take excellent care of my daughter. "Did Laura leave already?"

"No, no... she's still here, waitin' for you to return."

My heart gripped. I missed being with her and regretted that our first Christmas together had to turn out this way.

"I've gotta go. I'll be home as soon as I can."

I took a few more bites of pumpkin pie, bussed my tray and took the elevator to the first floor and asked the receptionist Serena's room number. When I stepped off the elevator on the third floor I took a deep breath and squared my shoulders, tried to ready myself for the encounter I'd dreamed of for eleven months and ten days.

CHAPTER THIRTY-EIGHT

Serena looked small and fragile lying in the hospital bed, her chest wrapped round and round with white gauze like a mummy, her thin arms at her sides, lying outside the bedcovers. Her eyes were closed, but when I approached the side rail, she turned her head in my direction.

"How're you feeling?"

"Thought I was going to die, so this is a much better alternative." She gave me a weak smile. "What happened back there? One minute I was knocking on your door, the next minute someone fires a gun at me. Was it you? Did you try to kill me?"

I shook my head, disgusted with her ridiculous question. "Long story short, my grandmother took in a woman whose husband had been abusing her. He showed up with a gun and fired a shot at his wife, missed, and the bullet went through the front door and struck you in the chest."

"Guess I was lucky, huh?"

I didn't answer her.

"I know I have a lot of explaining to do, Jessee. I just want you to hear me out before you say anything."

I nodded, waiting for the answers to all the questions that had been living in my head since January.

She took a deep breath, grimaced, then leveled her gaze over my shoulder. "I was unhappy. I felt trapped. I wasn't ready to be a wife. You were never home. I talked to my father on the phone more often than you ever knew. He told me he'd help me. He…"

"Your parents were behind this?" I gritted my teeth and waited. I already knew what was coming.

She lifted a hand, palm facing outward. "Just Daddy. Let me get this out."

I pursed my lips and promised myself I'd remain silent until she finished. But at the mention of her father, that he'd somehow been involved in this, my heart pummeled against the walls of my chest and I clenched the bedrail with both hands.

"All he ever wanted was for me to be happy. I deserved to be happy. Daddy said if I divorced you, you'd get half the money he worked so hard to give me, my inheritance he strived for his entire life. I felt so guilty. I didn't want to disappoint him. He'd done so much for me.

"He told me I should take some time away from you, get my head straight, decide what I wanted. He said something about proving you'd forced me to combine our assets, and that you talked me out of signing a pre-nup, but that it would take time for him to pull it off. Said he'd take care of everything. All I had to do was get in a car that would pick me up at the house, bring nothing but the clothes I was wearing and Sofia in my arms, and he'd take care of the rest. He moved me to Kansas. I had a new identity, new house, everything. He took care of the finances.

"So I got my freedom to figure out what I wanted. Daddy had a plan so I wouldn't lose all the money he'd given me. And you weren't straddled with a woman who couldn't be a real wife."

It took everything inside me to control my voice. "So it was all about the money?"

"Money means everything to Daddy. You know that."

My mind swirled with questions. "There was never any private investigator searching for you and Sofia, was there?"

She shook her head.

"And after all these months, did you decide what you wanted to do with your life?"

"Yeah."

She paused. I waited.

Seconds passed until I finally spoke. "So?"

"I love my freedom."

Then she looked in my eyes. And she hadn't shed one tear, not one, for what she'd done. She didn't sound remorseful, didn't ask my forgiveness, nothing.

"You-love-your-freedom," I repeated in a monotone.

She said nothing, just nodded, a faraway look in her eyes, as if I wasn't there. Looked straight through me, as if I didn't exist.

"And Sofia? How does she fit in with your need to have your so-called freedom?"

"I thought it was just being married that was making me crazy." She turned her head away and faced the wall. Seconds later, she looked back in my direction and this time there were tears running down her cheeks. "I can't take care of a child. I can barely handle my own life and I sure can't make decisions for a kid."

"So that's it, huh?"

She grimaced and I didn't know if it was because of the physical pain or guilt over abandoning her only child. I doubted it was the latter.

"Jessee, you'll get married again, have more kids, be happy living the life you've always dreamed of. But you can't have that life with me. It could never work out for us, ever."

"I can accept that. But you took my child." I drew in a deep breath to calm my seething nerves. "For God's sake, how could you desert me like that? Allow me to think you and Sofia had been kidnapped, maybe even murdered? How could you be so intentionally cruel?"

She looked at the ceiling, sighed, then glanced back at me. "You're strong and resilient and smart, all those things I could never be. I knew you could handle the fallout from this, that you'd get on with your life. And I was right, wasn't I? You're living with your grandmother. When I saw you at the gallery you were with a beautiful woman. It's all good, Jess. In the long run we both get what we want. I get my freedom. You'll have the future you always dreamed of. Just not with me."

My pulse quickened. My face was on fire. This was unbelievable. "And you thought you could just take my daughter from me and there wouldn't be any consequences for your behavior?"

"When I saw you at the gallery I knew you were close to finding me. I dreaded moving again, getting a new identity. I was ready to come back. I'd pretty much come to a decision in the last month anyway. So I went to your house to explain why I did what I did, hoping you'd understand."

"You know, Serena..." I pursed my lips and tried to get my emotions under control. I wanted to kill her, I was so mad. How could anyone with a heart do this? "If it's at all possible, I hope they put you behind bars for the next twenty years. What you did was reprehensible and cruel. I'll get the best attorney I can find so you get the maximum penalty the law allows."

I turned and walked out of the room, my heart tripping madly, my chest heaving under the weight of anger and hurt, my hands shaking so badly I grasped them together to stop the uncontrollable twitching. My body felt weak from the emotional trauma of the last several hours.

Half-way down the corridor I leaned against the wall to catch my breath. I closed my eyes just for a second and savored the feel of the cool wall against my face. When I heard a man and woman talking, I took a deep breath and walked toward the elevator around the corner.

And ran smack into David and Barbara Middleton. Chalk it up to mental exhaustion, frustration, or just plain anger at what Serena just told me, but when I saw her father's face I grabbed him by the lapels of his expensive suit, and slammed him up against the wall. "Why'd you do it?"

He struggled to wrench himself from my grasp, but age won out. My fists held tight to his jacket and he remained plastered against the wall.

I pulled him toward me then shoved him back again and felt the deep exhalation of breath as his head smacked against the wall. His eyes wobbled around in their sockets then focused on me.

"Did you hate me so much you had to hide my wife and child from me, you son of a bitch?" Spittle flew from my lips and spattered his face.

I felt a sharp tug on the back of my shirt.

Barbara Middleton's voice broke through my livid reverie. "What are you talking about? Please don't hurt him."

I let go of Serena's father and he slid down to the floor, gasping for breath.

Mrs. Middleton knelt on the linoleum floor and cradled her husband's head to her chest. She glanced up at me. "Why did you say that? About hiding your wife and child?"

I swiped at my mouth with the back of my forearm and looked down at her. I never realized I was capable of hating someone as much as I hated David Middleton. At that moment I wished him dead for all the misery he caused me.

"I feel sorry for you, Mrs. Middleton. Married to such a despicable human being."

Her eyebrows dipped down and she shook her head. It was obvious she hadn't a clue what I was talking about.

I gestured toward her husband, still sitting on the floor, legs splayed out. "Ask him." I turned and walked toward the exit sign at the end of the hall.

I made it to the parking lot in front of the hospital before breaking down completely. How could Serena and her father have been so cruel? I'd loved her with all my heart and soul and she knew that. I didn't deserve the treatment they leveled on me and my life for nearly a year. And I certainly didn't deserve my child taken away from me. I wanted to wrap my hands around her father's throat and squeeze the life out of him.

I walked down the street, headed in no particular direction and walked and walked until I was so cold my face and hands were numb. I fumbled for my cell phone and tried to press the tiny buttons with my frozen fingertip. Laura answered.

"Could you pick me up in front of Mercy Hospital?"

"I'll be right there."

CHAPTER THIRTY-NINE

I stood in the lobby of Mercy Hospital, staring out the window, waiting for Laura to arrive. Thirty minutes later she pulled up in the curved front driveway and I rushed out.

"Thank you." I shut the car door and slumped into the deep cushioned seat.

She reached over and gave me a hug.

I wrapped my arms around her, pulling her in close to my chest. She felt warm and smelled of cinnamon and sugar cookies. "I'm so sorry you were involved in this nightmare. Leave it to the California homeboy to ruin your perfect Iowa Christmas."

She pulled back and studied my face. "I don't blame you for any of this."

"Mind driving me home?"

"Not at all. You look exhausted."

"I'm dead on my feet. And I'd like to explain what happened."

She silently nodded then pulled out into the street, headed for the freeway.

"Serena's father helped her run away."

She glanced in my direction, brows furrowed. "Why?"

"She didn't want to be married. Said she needed to be free. Her father didn't want me getting half of her money if she divorced me so he helped her disappear so she could figure out what she wanted to do with her life. That gave him time to devise a plan to keep me from getting anything."

I took in a deep breath, my emotions still clinging very close to the surface. "In his mind, it was all about the money. And Serena didn't want to disappoint her daddy, so she did what he suggested and just took off." I grasped Laura's hand and held it tightly. "After all these months she's come to the realization she doesn't want to be married and she doesn't want to be a mother anymore, either."

Her head twitched in my direction, a severe frown on her face. "You're not serious."

"Completely serious." I paused. "I love you, Laura. Can we go to breakfast tomorrow morning, just the two of us?"

She nodded. "Uh... sure. I wasn't able to give you your Christmas gift today."

"I know. But I need to get some sleep. I'm physically and mentally wrung out. Why don't I pick you up at nine o'clock tomorrow morning?"

"Sounds good. And Jessee?"

"Hmm?" My eyes fluttered closed and I wasn't sure whether I even answered her.

"I'm so glad you have your daughter back, safe and sound."

At least that's what I think she said. I was dreaming about the three of us, Laura, Sofia, and me, sitting around the kitchen table in Laura's house having breakfast, sharing the Sunday newspaper and comics, eating French toast with tons of syrup.

I could almost taste the melted butter when I noticed the car had stopped. I opened my eyes. We were parked at the side of Nana's house.

"I'm not coming in. You need to get some sleep."

"Nine tomorrow morning, then." I kissed her deeply and passionately for the first time in what felt like forever. "I love you so much."

She smiled, and I dragged my weary body out of the car and up the front steps. Home. More today than ever before, the word resonated with truth.

I was too tired to tell the whole story to Nana, Julia, and Kerryanne. They politely suggested I go to bed, that we'd continue our Christmas celebration tomorrow. I explained Laura and I were having breakfast together the next morning so she and I could talk. I didn't need to elaborate. Nana understood. She hugged me, wished me sweet dreams and I headed upstairs.

Once inside my room I noticed the bedside light turned low and the crib at the foot of my bed. I'd become so accustomed to being alone that seeing the tiny bump under the covers that was my daughter gave me a jolt— physically, mentally, and emotionally.

Bending over the side of the crib, I drew back the top edge of the blanket. Sofia was sucking her thumb just as she'd done eleven months ago when I last saw her. Watching her like this tugged at my heart, vivid memories of the three of us as a family sneaking into my mind.

I mentally gave my brain a firm shake and straightened the comforter over her back then tucked it in at the bottom and sides. Her tiny lips moved around the base of her thumb and she moaned. Was she dreaming about her mommy lying on the front porch, blood seeping through her blouse? I hoped not. Would she awaken in the middle of the night, crying for Serena? I pulled off my jeans and flopped into bed, completely exhausted from the day's trials. The Christmas from Hell.

I made myself a promise before sleep overtook me. I'd make next December twenty fifth the best Christmas ever.

* * * *

Sofia woke me up several times during the night, whimpering. I rubbed her back, whispered to her as I'd done during the first nine months of her life. Each time, she fell back to sleep after a few moments. I supposed she was exhausted from all that had happened.

In the morning, after a long, hot shower, I returned to my bedroom and had just finished dressing when I noticed Sofia standing up in her crib, thumb in her mouth, wide-eyed and teary.

"Hey, Pumpkin." I smiled. "Remember me?" I pointed at my chest. "I'm your Daddy. Wanna go downstairs and have breakfast? Nana's probably already down there making French toast. You used to eat French toast with lots of syrup. Would you like that?"

I couldn't have asked for a more avid listener. Her eyes followed every gesture I made with my hands but she stared at my face as if I were Michael Myers, the psycho murderer from the movie Halloween. I reached over the side of the crib and picked her up. She hadn't started crying yet, and I considered that a giant hurdle we managed to overcome.

While carrying her downstairs, clean diaper in hand, I sang a song that had been one her favorites, "Hush Little Baby, Don't Say A Word". She looked pleasantly mesmerized by my personal rendition of the tune.

When we entered the kitchen Nana was flipping golden brown pieces of French toast on the griddle. She turned toward us and stuck out her arms. "Come to Nana?"

Sofia leaned away from me, and I let Nana take her. I smiled. Within a few hours Sofia looked as if she already felt comfortable here, lessening my fears that the transition she'd face living in Iowa would be a difficult one. It appeared she would adapt well, but I held my optimism in check. It hadn't even been twenty-four hours yet. I was still bracing for the "Mommy" scream that I was afraid was inevitable.

"Nana, I want to apologize for not asking you if you'd look after Sofia while I go to breakfast with Laura this morning. Yesterday was such a nightmare I wasn't thinking straight and—"

Nana interrupted me. "Don't worry about it. I'm lookin' forward to gettin' to know this little one." A wide grin spread across her face.

"Laura and I need to talk. I should be home in a couple of hours. If you need me just call my cell phone."

She patted my arm. "Stop worryin'. We'll be just fine."

She nuzzled the baby's neck, making Sofia giggle.

My mind reeled back to other times. "I used to do that."

"And you'll have the rest of her childhood to look forward to." Nana paused, her mouth set in a straight line. "Do you have any idea what'll happen to Sere—?"

I shook my head. "Detective Thompson spoke with me last night at the hospital. He told me she'll likely be sent to Santa Barbara. Hopefully she'll do a lot of jail time for kidnapping my daughter and evading the FBI and Lord knows what else her father and she cooked up to change her identity."

Nana's face scrunched up and she shook her head. "Why did she do it?"

I let out a deep sigh and rubbed my temples then explained the story all over again, reliving my encounter in the hospital with my wife.

Nana put her hand on my shoulder and let it rest there for a few seconds. "I'm so, so sorry. To think this all revolved around the almighty dollar."

"She doesn't want me or Sofia. She wants her freedom. You know, anyone who would do something like this has some serious problems. I'm glad Sofia won't be living with her any longer."

She nodded, sympathy written all over her face.

I shook my head to clear out the mental meanderings. "But, anyway, I'll deal with the legal stuff later. Right now I have a beautiful young lady waiting for me to take her to breakfast."

Nana's eyes lit up and she smiled. "Have a good time." She patted Sofia on the bottom and kissed her cheek.

"We'll open our Christmas presents when I get home?" I said.

"We'll be waitin' for ya'."

I picked up Laura, and we drove to Winterset, scene of the famous movie Bridges of Madison County. There was a cafe well known for its homemade pastries, private and away from Earlham.

After parking in the lot behind the restaurant I turned to Laura. "This place holds special significance for my grandparents. It's where they met back in 1945. Nana was a waitress. She served Grampa his first scone. They came back here every year on their anniversary."

She laid her hand on my forearm. "That's so sweet. Makes me want to cry."

I leaned over and gave her a quick kiss. "No crying today. We're celebrating the fact none of us was killed yesterday."

We walked around to the front of the restaurant. The foyer was filled with people waiting to be seated, but I'd made a reservation earlier that morning and we were led to our table right away.

Laura looked from left to right as we followed the waiter. "This place is amazing. I can't believe I've never eaten here before."

I glanced around at the interior of the restaurant. The tables were set discreetly apart, each covered with a white linen tablecloth. Laura tapped my hand and motioned her head upward.

Hanging from the ceiling were antique wooden kitchen chairs, wicker baskets, even an old-fashioned, hand-cranked washing machine. Windows lined the back and side walls and overlooked the backyard, a mixture of flowers and shrubbery interspersed with rock pathways and a fountain highlighting the center of the garden.

"In Rose and Harper's honor, I guess I should have a scone," she announced after looking through the menu.

"I will too."

We placed our orders, and the waitress poured two coffees and scooted away.

I stared across the table at her. "You look beautiful. New dress?"

She glanced down at her sparkly green, scoop-necked dress.

"Yes, it is. Thank you for noticing. You look handsome as well."

"Yesterday wasn't exactly how I pictured spending our first Christmas together." I reached across the table and took her hand. "I have your Christmas gift. I hope you'll like it."

"I'm sure I'll love it... whatever it is." She gave my hand a squeeze. "And I have your gift right here." She reached for her purse on the chair next to her and pulled out a small flat box wrapped in bright red paper.

I'd tucked her gift in my jacket pocket and brought it out, placing it on the china plate in front of her. "You first."

She smiled and unwrapped the shiny green Christmas paper that covered the tiny blue velvet box. Her brows furrowed and she looked up at me and tilted her head, then flipped open the box. She gasped, and stared down at the diamond solitaire ring.

"Will you marry me, Laura?"

Her bottom lip quivered and a single tear escaped down her cheek. Several seconds passed, and she still hadn't given me an answer.

"Is that a no?" My heart lurched half-way up my throat.

Her eyes looked up into mine and she nodded.

"Oh." I felt more disappointed and hurt than embarrassed at the major faux pas I just committed.

"I'm surprised you asked me, Jess."

The rhythm of my heart ramped up several beats. "Why would you be surprised? I love you. And as soon as everything is settled in court I want to marry you."

She dabbed under her eyes with the cloth napkin. "But Serena's alive. Maybe with counseling you two could—"

"Never gonna happen. What she did was heartless and uncaring. I can never forgive her for that. And she doesn't want to be married to me. I told you that. And I accept her decision." Our eyes met and I held her gaze. "You still haven't answered the question. Will you marry me, Laura Driscoll?"

She tried to smile through the rush of tears flowing down her cheeks. Happy or sad?

"Are you sure about this, Jess?"

"I've never been more sure of anything in my entire life." I stood up, knelt down beside her chair, and took her hands in mine.

"Oh, Jessee." She shook her head from side to side. "You don't have to do this." She closed her eyes and kept shaking her head.

I squeezed her hands, forcing her to look at me. "Laura Driscoll, will you do me the enormous favor of marrying me? I promise to spend the rest of my life trying my best to make you the happiest woman in the world."

A torrent of tears gushed down her cheeks, and the corners of her mouth curved into a smile. "Yes. Yes, I'll marry you, Jessee Bradford."

I leaned forward and our lips met in a chaste kiss. "If everything works out, how do you feel about being an instant mommy?"

She chuckled and swiped at her tears again. "I can't believe this is happening." Her lips slipped into a huge grin. "I'd be honored to be Sofia's stepmother."

I returned to my chair and reached across the table, took hold of her left hand, and started to place the ring on her finger, then suddenly stopped. "It was my mother's wedding ring. But if you'd like to pick out another I'll take you into Des Moines and you can select anything you want."

She stretched her arm further toward me. "Not in a million years."

I slipped the ring on her finger.

She moved her hand from side to side. "This is the most beautiful ring in the world." She glanced across the table at me, eyes glistening. "And it's more special because it was your mom's."

"You've just given me the best Christmas present ever." I leaned over and kissed her lightly.

"I love you so much." She looked down at the gift she'd given me. "Open it."

I picked up the box and shook it a few times, grinned at her then tore off the paper wrapping and pulled out a four by six-inch photograph of a Friesian horse. "Forgive me if I don't understand the inner meaning."

Laura pointed at the picture and smiled. "My mom used that photograph of Decimus to paint a portrait for your office... or wherever you want to hang it. She just finished it but I haven't had a chance to pick it up."

"I didn't know she did animal portraits."

"She doesn't. But she made an exception for you."

"I'm sure it's beautiful. I love your mother's paintings. But who's Decimus?"

She tapped her chin with her finger, looking to the side of me.

"What is it, Laura?"

"There's a story that goes with the portrait and I hope you'll accept it."

I raised my eyebrows. "Accept what?"

"Consider this your entry into the equestrian world."

I scratched the side of my head and frowned. "What's this all about?"

Our waitress arrived with a basket of scones straight from the oven, refreshed our coffee cups, made sure we had cream and sugar then left us alone.

Laura sat up straight and arranged the napkin on her lap. "I have a very good friend who owns Decimus. He's at my barn now, and he looks exactly like Maximus. My friend Terry just gave birth to triplets, and she doesn't have time to ride now or in the foreseeable future." She spooned a dollop of whipped butter onto her plate then looked up at me. "She can't bear to sell him. She's had him since he was a foal. So she gave him to me with the understanding that if she ever has a few hours free to take a trail ride, she'll just come by the barn and jump on."

"This story must be heading in an interesting direction."

She held up one hand like a stop sign. "She said her riding days are over, what with taking care of the three kids and all. I told her about my plan." She paused.

"And that plan would be...?"

"To find someone to ride Decimus. You know, to keep him in shape. And I was thinking that someone could be you. We could ride together whenever we want to. Decimus would pretty much be your horse."

I sat back in my chair and blinked several times. "Wow! This is unexpected." I thought about our future together and how riding on trails would be an excellent way to spend quality time with each other. It would also help me get past my uncomfortable feelings around equines. "So Decimus is good on the trail and in the arena? Not like Carmel?"

"He is, as they say, da bomb. I promise you'll love his demeanor. He's well-mannered, kind, easy to ride." She paused, and the look on her face turned serious. "Bad gift idea?"

I shook my head. "No, not at all. If Decimus is as you describe, I can't wait for us go out on the trail together."

She grinned, looking oh-so-satisfied with herself. "This way my friend will still own Decimus but she'd rarely ride him. It saves her from having to sell him and lessens her guilt of giving up riding altogether."

I leaned over the table. Her face met mine half-way across. I engaged her mouth in a deep, sensuous kiss. When we broke apart her eyes remained closed.

"Thank you for the gift, Laura."

Her eyes fluttered open and she smiled. "It was worth the kiss."

Taking her hand in mine, I glanced down at my mother's wedding ring encompassing her finger. "We can pick up the painting of my new horse when we visit your parents to make our announcement."

CHAPTER FORTY

We finished our breakfast and drove back to Nana's. I wanted to announce our engagement to my family, and Laura wanted to phone her parents to set up a time when we could have dinner with them, announce our upcoming marriage, and pick up my Christmas gift from Colleen.

When I pulled up to the house a car neither of us recognized was parked at the curb. As we walked to the front door it opened, and Nana met us on the porch.

"Agent Caruso's inside. He wants to speak with you, Jessee."

"O-kay." I drew out the word slowly.

We walked into the foyer. Nana and Laura veered off into the kitchen and I entered the front room.

Agent Caruso extended his hand. "Hello, Jessee."

We shook hands and I sat down across from him and leaned forward, elbows on my knees. "Merry Christmas. How can I help you?"

"I wanted to come by before I left town." He leaned back on the couch, one foot on top of his other knee. "It seems to me you've had a wild Christmas. Our guys were on their way to your house to install the wiretap when it all happened. Mrs. Otten was almost killed, your wife was shot, and you got your daughter back. That's a lot to happen in one day."

I nodded. "Yes, it is. Have you spoken with Serena yet?"

"I have. As soon as she can be moved from the hospital, I'll fly back here and accompany her to California, where she'll await trial."

"How much time will she have to serve?"

"Depends." He shrugged. "I'm sure her father will have the best attorney possible."

"And her father?"

"I have confidence our computer guys will be able to trace the transactions Mr. Middleton orchestrated in order to keep his daughter hidden beneath our radar. Most people leave clues they're never aware of. Happens all the time. If he's found to be an accessory, he could do time as well."

"What about spousal emotional abuse? You know, keeping my child from me for months?"

"Oh, she'll serve time all right. As to how much time? That'll be up to a judge and jury, I suppose. But if I were you, I'd hire the best attorney you can find if you want her to serve the maximum sentence. For right now, try to get on with your life."

I leaned back and thought about what he just said.

"She doesn't want anything to do with me or our daughter. Can you believe that?" His eyebrows flicked upward and he shook his head. "You know what? It's like a burden's been lifted and I can breathe again. But I'm so angry at Serena's father. My revenge will be knowing how furious he'll be when I get fifty percent of all the money he worked so hard for."

"He meddled where he shouldn't have been sticking his nose... his daughter's marriage."

I nodded, still plagued by the knowledge that Mr. Middleton hated me so much he was willing to risk his own, as well as his daughter's, future over money. "I agree. He should never have interfered in our personal lives. Then again, Serena's an adult. She didn't have to go along with him on any of this. So, will I have to testify in court?"

"I'm not sure that'll be necessary. Depending on her statement and what our guys find out about her father, your testimony may be totally unnecessary. And your divorce should be a slam-dunk. Perhaps the attorneys can work it out and you won't even have to see your wife. You'll have to wait and see."

I shook my head. "This whole conversation... actually, the past couple of days, have been surreal." I stood up, and he followed me to the foyer. "Thank you for everything, Agent. I'm glad Serena and Sofia are alive, of course, but I can't believe to what ends her father was willing to go to keep me from sharing his daughter's money. I would gladly have left the marriage with the shirt on my back and a few dollars for the bus."

He gave my hand a firm shake, looked me in the eyes. "Money is the root of all evil. I know it's cliché, but I've found in my experience that it's true. You're young, Doctor, with a lot of years ahead of you. Good luck in your future." He turned and walked to his car.

I watched as he made a U-turn and drove down the driveway to the street. I continued to stare at the back of his car until it was a mere speck in the distance.

"Is everything okay?"

I felt Laura's hand on my back and glanced at her, standing at my side. "Everything's just fine. Agent Caruso said he'll take Serena back to Santa Barbara when she's well enough to travel. She'll be arraigned on various charges."

"Was that all he wanted?"

"Pretty much. I'll have to talk to Mayor Morrison about my divorce. This changes things."

She looked up at me and frowned. "Changes things how?"

I pulled her around in front of me and looked down into her golden eyes. "It shouldn't take that much time to finalize my divorce and California is a fifty-fifty state. Serena's worth millions."

She stood on tip-toe and kissed me thoroughly. When we finally broke apart I could hardly catch my breath.

"I don't care about your money. I'm in love with you."

"I never wanted to be rich. Serena and I lived a fairly modest life because her father invested most of the money he'd given her. But now?" I paused. "I could expand the clinic, make it a twenty-four hour emergency animal hospital so people wouldn't have to travel all the way to Des Moines. You could build a bigger stables and..." I stopped, captured her gaze. "After we have our first child you could hire an assistant to help train the horses."

She leaned back and her eyebrows shot up under her bangs. "Our first child? I didn't know you wanted to have another child."

"I want to have children with you, Laura. Fill our home with lots of sisters and brothers for Sofia to play with. You told me once that you and Jeff planned on having a family."

"I've always wanted to have children. And I want to have a baby with you, too."

"Money will only make our lives easier, but it doesn't have to change the way we live entirely."

She laid her head on my chest and wrapped her arms around my waist. "I'm glad we agree because I don't want to become a different person. My goal in life was never to be rich. Money couldn't bring Jeff back, and it couldn't make Serena happy, either."

I ran my hands up and down her back, pressing her warm body nearer to mine. "You're right. Money doesn't solve man's, or woman's, problems. But I believe love does." I brought my mouth down over hers again for a deep, engaging kiss. "You've changed my life, Laura. And it's going to change even more after we're married."

Our eyes met and held for a few seconds before she grinned, looking like the cat that ate the mouse. "Another child, huh?"

"Don't you want to have a baby soon?"

"Everything's happening so fast. Can we get married first? We don't even know how long it will be before your divorce is final."

I grabbed her hand and tugged. "You're right. Let's talk about this later. I believe we have an announcement to make."

We walked from the foyer into the front room where Nana, Kerryanne and Julia sat on the couch, waiting for us. Laura and I plopped down on the rug next to the Christmas tree across from them.

Julia looked as if she were going to cry, eyes glassy with unshed tears. "I know you don't want to hear this but I have to tell you how sorry I am about yesterday."

Kerryanne nodded. "Me, too. And you don't have to worry about my dad coming around 'cause he'll be in jail for a long time."

Julia shut her eyes for a moment and sighed. "For a very long time, I hope."

They both stared at me, unsmiling.

"Both of you, please stop." I glanced at Julia then Kerryanne. "I accept your apologies but they're unnecessary. When all is said and done, everything turned out well. You two are free of Bill Otten, and I have my daughter back." I looked around the room.

Nana smiled. "Sofia's takin' a nap, Jess."

I nodded. "I'm still not used to having her around. I haven't spent any time with her yet."

Nana scolded me with kindness. "You were at the hospital most of Christmas day. And today you had breakfast with Laura. It hasn't even been twenty-four hours that she's been back."

"I know. And thanks for taking care of her. I had something I had to do today."

Laura laid her left hand on the table in front of the couch and tapped the wooden surface with her fingertips.

All three women looked at Laura then at me, their faces etched in frowns.

I watched Nana's eyes as she focused on the table where Laura increased the sound of her tapping fingers. Nana's hands flew up and covered her mouth. "That's your mother's weddin' ring."

Laura's face lit up with a wide grin. "Jessee asked me to marry him at breakfast this morning."

I grinned. "And she said yes."

All three women gushed over the ring and the questions began: where did we want to have the wedding ceremony, where were we going on our honeymoon.

"Hey, hey." I put my palm up to stop them. "Laura and I have been engaged for," I glanced at the grandfather clock, "maybe an hour. So can we please wait to discuss the particulars at another time?"

Everyone laughed.

And so the day progressed.

* * * *

Sofia had a great time, enjoying the attention of four women and her father. At times she'd stop and make what I called her boo-boo lip, probably noticing Serena wasn't around. Nana went shopping and purchased a slew of toys and stuffed animals, hoping to distract Sofia whenever she looked sad and teary-eyed.

My daughter found herself in the middle of a whirlwind of opening presents. Then we ate our Christmas dinner, and ended with Nana's apple pie, covered with candles that Sofia blew out.

I drove Laura to her house later that evening. After parking the car, I walked her to the front door where she greeted Brewster first then looked up at me. "Can you stay?"

I bent down and kissed her. "Honey, I can't. I haven't spent much time with Sofia and—"

"Oh, my God, I'm sorry, of course." She twirled her finger near her temple. "I don't know what I was thinking."

"Hey, this is new for me as well."

She nodded. "You have a lot of help. Will Rose be taking care of Sofia while you're at the clinic?"

"I don't know." I shrugged. "We haven't had a chance to talk about it. I don't want to be a burden, and at Nana's age, a baby might be too much to handle."

"Or just what she needs to keep active."

"You have a point."

"I'll help in any way I can, Jess."

"Thanks for offering. I'll talk to all the ladies living at the house. We should be able to work something out. You have your own work."

She tilted her head and smiled. "But it would be good practice, don't you think?"

I took her in my arms and wrapped my hands around the back of her waist. "Another point well taken."

"You think about it."

We lingered awhile at her front door, kissing, until I realized we were both shivering and pulled back. "I should go. We'll talk tomorrow."

"And I'll set up a date to get together with my parents."

"I'm assuming they'll be happy for us?"

"Absolutely."

CHAPTER FORTY-ONE

I had two more days off before I had to go back to the clinic. I used that time to get reacquainted with my daughter. She manifested no outrageous signs of distress at having her mother disappear, but I continued to sit on the edge of my seat, waiting for the eventual outburst. Perhaps there would be none. I could only hope.

Laura was busy training a new horse. She said she'd try to get in touch with her parents so we could visit them and make our formal announcement. Late Saturday afternoon the phone rang, and I glanced at the caller ID. It was Laura.

"Did you talk to your mom and dad?"

A few beats of silence greeted my question before I heard her voice, strained and unnatural. "Could you come over as soon as possible?"

I did a mental tally of who was home to take care of Sofia and knew Kerryanne or Julia would be more than happy to stay with her. "Yeah. Is there something wrong? You sound upset."

"We can discuss it when you get here."

I told her I'd be right over, then snagged Kerryanne, who was in the TV room. She assured me Sofia would be in good hands. I explained I'd be back shortly.

In less than five minutes I arrived at Laura's house. The sound of her voice on the phone worried me. Before I had a chance to knock, she opened the door, looking tired, eyes bloodshot, cheeks streaked with mascara.

She stepped back as I walked through the doorway and when I leaned over to kiss her she turned and walked toward the front room. I shut the door behind me and followed her.

"What's going on?" I sat on the couch next to her, keeping a discreet distance. She'd never pulled away from me before.

She turned her face toward me, tears streaming down her cheeks. "Someone, I don't even recall his name, phoned me and said..." She shook her head then covered her face with both hands and sobbed.

Reaching out to her, I pulled her into my embrace and rocked her back and forth. "Shh. What's going on, honey? Are your parents okay?"

She pushed herself a few inches away from me, swiping at her tears. "Jeff's alive."

My mouth opened and I stared at her, blinking. "I thought Jeff was killed in Iraq."

She stared at her hands folded in her lap. "They told me he was blown to pieces when he stepped on the IED. All they found were his tags." She looked up at me through her dark bangs. "They said there was no actual body."

"But... where has he been for two years?" I was having a difficult time digesting this bombshell. This was unreal.

"The man wouldn't tell me. He said he wasn't authorized to give out any further information, that someone else would phone me later today."

I grasped her hand and felt the poke of my mother's wedding ring against my finger. She didn't pull away. "I don't know what to say, Laura."

Her head shot up. "I don't know what to say either. Of course I never wanted him to die but... I love you. We were going to get married."

Her words struck me like a slap in the face but I took her into my arms and held her. "Your husband's alive."

"I'm so confused. I don't know what to think, what to do, what to say to you. I—"

I drew away a few inches and our eyes met. "You don't have to say or do anything. Jeff is your husband." My heart constricted and my chest felt as if someone was sitting on top of me. I didn't know if I could keep my emotions under control much longer before I broke down. I didn't want to make her feel any more guilty than she already did.

I moved away from her and stood up. "I have to go." I took a few steps toward the front door, hoping she'd beg me not to leave her, knowing in my heart she had to let me go. I drove back to the farm with my heart in my throat, wishing I could cough it up and throw it away so I wouldn't feel so devastated.

For the second time in less than a year I'd lost the woman I loved.

CHAPTER FORTY-TWO

When I arrived home Nana, Julia, and Kerryanne were sitting around the kitchen table. Sofia sat in an old high chair that must have belonged to my father when he was a tyke. They glanced at me when I reached the kitchen door.

Opening my mouth to speak, I realized I didn't know what to tell them. How do you explain your heart has been smashed to pieces—again—and you want to just get in the car and drive as far as you can to escape your life? But I had a child who needed me. I wasn't going anywhere. This was our home now.

"Jessee." Nana's voice rang out how worried she was. "What's wrong?" She got up from her chair and for some reason, didn't walk toward me. It was as if she knew what I had to say would be hard enough without having to deal with her sympathy.

"Laura's husband is alive."

Her eyes widened and her jaw dropped open. I could hear the intake of breath from either Kerryanne or Julia or both.

I'd explained everything with those four words.

I turned away and went upstairs. When I reached the second floor, I could hear their hushed conversation and knew they'd leave me alone. I shut my bedroom door, lay on top of the comforter and wept.

I didn't awaken until dawn's light eeked its way past the curtains and covered my face with its wintery rays. Sofia wasn't in her crib. I suspected Nana must have taken her downstairs for breakfast. It was Sunday, and she always fixed a special morning meal before chore time.

I showered and shaved, then dressed in old jeans and a sweatshirt before going downstairs.

Nana was fixing pancakes, and the scent of hot maple syrup wafted through the kitchen. She turned and motioned toward the table. "Three pancakes comin' up. Sit down and pour yourself some coffee. I'll join you in a second."

I gave Sofia a kiss on the cheek. She was using her fingers to pick up tiny pieces of pancake, syrup dribbling down her chin. She smiled up at me, two front teeth poking out of her upper gums.

"Dada." That one distinct word was like music to my ears.

My eyes filled with tears, and I swiped at them with my sleeve. I crouched down to her level. "Yes. Dada. And I love you, Sofia." She grinned and I kissed her gooey cheek. I felt Nana's hand on my shoulder and stood up.

She placed a plate of pancakes on the table and motioned for me to sit, then dropped down in a chair across from me. "I'm sorry about what's happenin' to you and Laura. I know you must be hurtin'."

I nodded, grasped the fork, and dug into the stack of pancakes, trying to keep my mind occupied on anything but the visions clouding my mind since last night: Laura and Jeff sitting together on the couch in front of the fire, Laura and Jeff making love in her upstairs bedroom, Laura and Jeff laughing over breakfast.

I swallowed the one bite of pancake I managed to get into my mouth, then dropped the fork and stood up.

Nana reached across the table, laying her hand on my wrist. "You'll make it through this."

"Could you watch Sofia? I have to clear my head, take a drive. I don't know what else to do."

"Of course. Take your cell phone. Call if you need anythin'."

I grabbed the keys, ran out the side door and jumped in the truck. Driving way over the speed limit on Chestnut Avenue, I headed nowhere in particular, running away from everyone, escaping nothing, followed relentlessly by thoughts of my nonexistent future with Laura—what would never be mine, what would forever be Jeff's.

A truck filled with hay bales turned in front of me, ignoring the stop sign posted at the corner. I didn't have enough time to react, and when I did, the brakes couldn't stop Grampa's truck in time. I twisted the steering wheel to miss hitting the other truck broadside. The sound of the two vehicles colliding reached my ears at the same time the airbag burst into my chest and face.

* * * *

A beeping sound slid into my consciousness like a dripping water faucet.

I was alive.

I struggled to open my eyes, tried to turn my head in the direction of the sound, and felt fingers intertwined with mine. Someone stood beside me, the silhouette blurred and indistinct. Man or woman? I couldn't tell.

"Jessee?"

It was Laura.

"Hnnn?" My mouth wasn't cooperating with my mind. I was trying to say "what" but that wasn't what escaped my lips.

"Jessee, you wake up and look at me. Please, Jessee, wake up."

I wasn't sure whether I was really awake or not. Perhaps I was in a place between Heaven and Hell. But that would be Limbo and I assumed Limbo wouldn't have a hospital. So, what was going on? Maybe I was dreaming and she wasn't really here at all.

My throat felt so dry, swallowing was useless. I had no saliva in my mouth. I tried to move my lips, make some noise. A hand slid under the back of my head and pushed it upward. I could feel a straw touching my lips.

"Take a sip."

I took several sips, dripping water down my chin which she wiped away with a tissue.

I opened and shut my eyes, and she shimmered into focus. "What're you doing here?" Words were coming out a bit easier, but to my ears I wasn't speaking normally. I was exhausted, beyond tired, and couldn't come fully awake.

"You scared me to death. And everyone else."

"How's Jeff?"

"It wasn't Jeff. They made a mistake. A horrible mistake."

She kissed my lips, and something wet dripped onto my cheek. She was crying.

"Of course I wanted Jeff to be alive. And I was sad about losing you. Then... oh God, Jessee, then that man called back and apologized, said someone mixed up the files. After he said "I'm sorry" for the hundredth time, I hung up and called you. Rose answered the phone, and she was so upset. The police had just left and told her you'd been in an accident. I rushed here as soon as I hung up the phone."

My eyes felt so heavy, I could hardly keep them open. Had I heard her correctly? Jeff wasn't alive? I couldn't focus, my mind like a video in reverse: Laura's face when she told me Jeff was alive, Sofia calling me "dada", my foot slamming the brake pedal as I swerved away from the other truck.

"Mistake?" I was trying my best to keep my mind focused on what Laura just told me.

"Yes, a mistake." She cradled my face between her two hands and kissed me softly on the lips. Her features shimmered again, her voice fading in and out.

I reached for her hand, and she grasped mine. My fingertips met with the nub of the diamond. She hadn't taken it off. I knew this was for real.

"Will you marry me?" I whispered, concentrating on her blurred features.

She bent nearer, and another tear dropped onto my cheek. "Yes, I'll marry you, Jessee Bradford." She kissed my lips and it felt as if angel wings had brushed across my mouth.

THE END

ABOUT THE AUTHOR

Born and raised in the San Francisco Bay Area, Patricia attended St. Mary's College, studied her junior year at the University of Madrid, received a B.A. in Spanish at UC Santa Barbara then went on to get a Master's degree in Education at Oregon State University. She lives with her husband and two children in Alameda, across the bay from San Francisco, along with three chocolate labs-Jack, UJE, and Remy. Her Friesian horse Maximus lives in the Oakland hills in a stall with a million dollar view.